Blood sprayed over the table

Hot droplets of the blood splashed Ryan's face as Doyle flailed his spurting stump. The baron grabbed it with his remaining hand and staggered toward the door, howling like a tornado.

J.B. slammed the lid of the ammo box shut on its precious contents and stuck the container under his arm.

The agonized yelling of their baron finally penetrated the yammer of blasters and the roar of bloodlust in the sec men's ears. They might have failed to protect the man they were hired to guard, but as Ryan drew his SIG-Sauer, he realized they intended to make up for the damage as best they could by killing Doyle's attackers.

Dozens of blasters swung their way....

Other titles in the Deathlands saga:

Nightmare Passage

Freedom Lost

Way of the Wolf

Dark Emblem

Crucible of Time

Starfall

Encounter:
   Collector's Edition

Gemini Rising

Gaia's Demise

Dark Reckoning

Shadow World

Pandora's Redoubt

Rat King

Zero City

Savage Armada

Judas Strike

Shadow Fortress

Sunchild

Breakthrough

Salvation Road

Amazon Gate

Destiny's Truth

Skydark Spawn

Damnation Road Show

Devil Riders

Bloodfire

Hellbenders

Separation

Death Hunt

Shaking Earth

Black Harvest

Vengeance Trail

Ritual Chill

Atlantis Reprise

Labyrinth

Strontium Swamp

Shatter Zone

Perdition Valley

Cannibal Moon

Sky Raider

Remember Tomorrow

Sunspot

Desert Kings

Apocalypse Unborn

Thunder Road

Plague Lords
   (Empire of Xibalba Book I)

Dark Resurrection
   (Empire of Xibalba Book II)

Eden's Twilight

Desolation Crossing

Alpha Wave

Time Castaways

Prophecy

Blood Harvest

Arcadian's Asylum

Baptism of Rage

Doom Helix

Moonfeast

Downrigger Drift

Playfair's Axiom

Tainted Cascade

Perception Fault

Prodigal's Return

Lost Gates

Haven's Blight

Hell Road Warriors

Palaces of Light

Wretched Earth

Crimson Waters

No Man's Land

JAMES AXLER

DEATH LANDS®

Nemesis

A GOLD EAGLE BOOK FROM

WORLDWIDE®

TORONTO • NEW YORK • LONDON
AMSTERDAM • PARIS • SYDNEY • HAMBURG
STOCKHOLM • ATHENS • TOKYO • MILAN
MADRID • WARSAW • BUDAPEST • AUCKLAND

Recycling programs
for this product may
not exist in your area.

First edition January 2013

ISBN-13: 978-0-373-62618-2

NEMESIS

Printed in U.S.A.

If I had a formula for bypassing trouble, I would not pass it round. Trouble creates a capacity to handle it. I don't embrace trouble; that's as bad as treating it as an enemy. But I do say meet it as a friend, for you'll see a lot of it and had better be on speaking terms with it.

—Oliver Wendell Holmes

THE DEATHLANDS SAGA

This world is their legacy, a world born in the violent nuclear spasm of 2001 that was the bitter outcome of a struggle for global dominance.

There is no real escape from this shockscape where life always hangs in the balance, vulnerable to newly demonic nature, barbarism, lawlessness.

But they are the warrior survivalists, and they endure—in the way of the lion, the hawk and the tiger, true to nature's heart despite its ruination.

Ryan Cawdor: The privileged son of an East Coast baron. Acquainted with betrayal from a tender age, he is a master of the hard realities.

Krysty Wroth: Harmony ville's own Titian-haired beauty, a woman with the strength of tempered steel. Her premonitions and Gaia powers have been fostered by her Mother Sonja.

J. B. Dix, the Armorer: Weapons master and Ryan's close ally, he, too, honed his skills traversing the Deathlands with the legendary Trader.

Doctor Theophilus Tanner: Torn from his family and a gentler life in 1896, Doc has been thrown into a future he couldn't have imagined.

Dr. Mildred Wyeth: Her father was killed by the Ku Klux Klan, but her fate is not much lighter. Restored from predark cryogenic suspension, she brings twentieth-century healing skills to a nightmare.

Jak Lauren: A true child of the wastelands, reared on adversity, loss and danger, the albino teenager is a fierce fighter and loyal friend.

Dean Cawdor: Ryan's young son by Sharona accepts the only world he knows, and yet he is the seedling bearing the promise of tomorrow.

In a world where all was lost, they are humanity's last hope....

Prologue

"It's the greatest thing," the drunk said. "The greatest thing ever. You gotta believe me, pal. I saw it with my own two eyes."

Maybe it was because Bass Croom was drunk, too, or maybe it was because his youthful eyes were dazzled by the bright colored lights, powered by an alcohol-fueled generator, strung over the crowded gaudy's bar. Maybe it was the way an older, seasoned guy had attached himself to a young man out on his own for the first time and begun speaking to him and him alone in this dark corner of a lively room.

But Bass did believe.

"It's *treasure,* man," his companion said. "Everything a man could ask for and more—a storehouse of riches. Tools, meds, weps, ammo. Tucked away all by its lonesome in a corner of a valley like a little green slice of Heaven."

"Ain't no such thing as Heaven," Bass said, souring slightly.

The Asian man smiled at him. "Ah, my young friend. You wouldn't say that if you saw this place!"

Bass grunted.

He emptied his shot glass in one convulsive swallow. This time he managed not to spatter any of the contents on his tongue. From painful experience he knew the Towse Lightning he'd bought with his last crumpled scrap of jack burned like liquid fire. It was bad enough going down his throat.

He brought the glass back onto the tabletop, an ancient cable spool gouged with knife marks and stained by every fluid spilled across it during its term of service, including obvious blood, with a decisive crack. The glass was stoutly made, anyway, and didn't shatter. Not that he cared.

Any more than he cared how grime-smeared and filthy both the glass and half-empty bottle were. At least their cruddiness obscured the bits of random stuff floating in the colorless liquid they contained.

The rotgut the Mine Shaft served contained a shitload of alcohol. That was all Bass Croom cared about. It would serve to get him drunk.

Maybe drunk enough to forget.

His table partner was staring at him intently. "You should believe, my friend," he said. "A man needs something to believe in."

"I believe," Bass said, "I need another drink," which he proceeded to pour himself.

The gaudy was crowded with bodies and the noises they emitted. His nose had quickly adjusted to the odors, of stale sweat, man-grease and raw alcohol, as well as many fouler things which tended to accumulate on the dirt floor.

At least it was cool inside, as opposed to either the midwinter snowstorm howling outside or the humid hothouse most gaudies were, cool here in the dark corner where Bass sat with his uninvited guest.

The Mine Shaft was literally that, so the story went, built in the entrance to an old hard-rock mine. Supposedly, also, obstreperous customers—or merely those who drank more than they could pay for—tended to disappear down a vertical shaft in some back room.

"I saw it with my own eyes," the Asian man went on.

"Saw it myself, the greenest valley left on Earth. And nestled deep within that beautiful land, a stockpile out of dreams. Out of dreams, man. Enough to start a whole new civilization like the one the predark people had."

"You mean the one that blew itself to Hell and left us this shithole of a world?"

Smiling, the stranger shook his head. "You don't get it, man. We know the mistakes the predark people made. We can do it better."

"So why didn't you?"

Even drunk as he was, Bass was surprised by his own vehemence. He wasn't by nature aggressive or confrontational. It had served him well in a world where for many if not most violence was a first option.

But the Asian man never blinked. From his breath, the slurring of his speech, and the drooping at the edges of his eyes, Bass guessed the man was drunker than he was, even.

"Ah, man." He shook his head. "I couldn't. Had to go. No time. Had people counting on me. And then, well, the winds blow, man. They blow hard. Good and bad. They blew me two-thirds of the way across the continent, in time. And I've spent better'n ten years working to the point I could get back there and get to building."

He grinned and hoisted a glass half full of browning liquid the barkeep called whiskey. Bass reckoned it was the same shit he had, colored with tobacco spit.

"Ten years working toward today. Got my wife and child meeting me in just an hour or so. Brave girl, Lisa. All knocked up again and everything—even if early days— and she's set to make the trek cross-country now."

"Huh," Bass said.

The man's expression grew serious. He leaned toward Bass across the much abused tabletop.

"You should join me, man," he said.

"Huh?" This time Bass reared back like a startled horse.

"Join me. Come with me and my family. We could use the extra blaster. Extra hands, to build us a new world. A better world!"

Bass found his thoughts, steeped in booze and bitterness—both eating at the lining of his stomach—going back over the events of the day.

I was on top of the world when I rolled into town this morning, he thought sullenly. And now the whole fucking ball of shit is sitting on top of me.

He'd spent the past five years, ever since his dad died in a cave-in near the Nashville rubble, combing through the burned-out corpses of cities in the South and Midwest for the pick of the scavvy.

Then he'd headed for the little ville called Choad well up in the Zarks. It wasn't far from the cache where he'd stashed his treasures after arduously gleaning them for years, just a two-day trip through the mountains. He'd heard it was a prosperous ville, and reckoned he could score big there. Taking his profits for a grubstake he'd go into trading big-time.

It had all gone south so suddenly.

Just that morning Bass Croom had been on top of the world. He'd led his quartet of heavy-laden pack mules boldly up to the gate into the walled ville—and was relieved of all his hard-won scavvy at gunpoint by Baron Doyle's laughing sec men, down to his trusty Savage .270 longblaster he'd inherited from his daddy. They had taken his mules, too.

They had talked about tariffs and imposts and license fees, but their own leveled blasters did the real talking. And when Bass had dared to ask to talk to a higher-up—the ville sec boss, a man named Tug or so he had heard—his reward was a steel-shod rifle butt across the chops. His cheekbone still smarted from the blow hours later.

When they had stripped him of everything but his hat, clothes and boots, and emptied his pockets, they'd told him no vagrant was allowed to enter the ville. He had to be on his way; they wouldn't let him in, and if they caught him skulking around the steel cattle gate with the razor-tape tangles on top, they'd shoot him like a mutie coyote.

He had been brave or foolish enough to stand up on his two still-shaky legs and ask if they were going to turn him into the outlands with nothing. So they'd tossed him a canteen of water and a handful of jack, then slammed the gates and leveled their blasters at him.

So Bass had stumbled away, utterly defeated, utterly ruined.

Now he sat here, now totally flat broke, listening to some fool go on about the roll of jack and gold coins weighing down his pocket, and how that would suffice to carry him and his family clear across the continent to where this likely mythical Promised Land awaited.

"I still carry the map on me," the drunk said, patting himself on the breastbone. "Here in a special waterproof packet, right over my heart."

He was about to ramble on, but just then looming shadows surrounded their table.

A hard hand closed on Bass's jacket collar and hauled him to his feet.

"What's going on?" he demanded in surprise.

"You, thinking you can rip us off," said a burly young man with lanky dark hair framing a meat-slab face. Bass didn't remember seeing him before, but judging by the filth-smeared and encrusted apron he wore, he had to be one of their kitchen workers.

"What are you talking abou— Uh!"

His question ended in a burst of air exploded from his lungs as a second man buried a ham-hock fist in his gut.

"Ordered a whole new bottle of the house's best," said a voice Bass vaguely recognized as the gaudy's manager, Dill. He was a long, lanky man with long, lanky brown hair and tattoos snaking up his wiry arms. "Then asked for credit."

He spoke that last in tones more of disbelief than anger.

"Here, wait!" Bass heard his companion say. "He hasn't drunk any. Anyway, I can pay—"

"Back off," a third man snarled. Bass raised a head as heavy as the world to blink blearily at a figure a good head shorter than his own six-three, but wider across the shoulders. A shiny brown bald head sprouted a fringe of wiry white hair, and a black beard striped down the sides like a reverse skunk's ass completed the image of the gaudy's owner, Dug.

He pointed a hickory ax handle at Bass's companion. The man sat back holding his hands up, palms out in surrender.

"We gonna show him the back room, boss?" asked the side of beef dude who'd braced him first. He sounded way too eager.

"Shut the fuck up, Mikey Bob," Dug said. "That's for them as don't take a hint the first time. What the fuck you think we are, stickies?"

Bass tried to winch his aching body straight. He wasn't half as drunk as he'd been a few moments before, and nowhere near as drunk as he wished he was.

"But—" he began.

Another pile-driver fist to the gut made him double over again. Puke that stung with stomach acid as harsher hooch filled his mouth and burned his nostrils.

Then something hard hit him in the back of the head. Sparks shot through his skull.

When they went out, they took him with them.

BEFORE ANYTHING else Bass Croom was aware of a massive ache, then he was aware of freezing through and through.

He stirred, moaning at the rebellion that set off in his belly, and the pounding at his temples from the inside out. He felt hard edges against his ribs and gut.

Bass found his hands and felt the irregular surface he was lying on. It proved to be a mass of rock or maybe brick chunks and dirt.

He pried one eye open, then the other. A wavering red-orange light lit a scene of outdoor desolation: bare rock, trampled earth, a few scrubby bushes that hadn't been anything to brag about before winter stripped them to bare spavined twigs. Harsh rocks rimmed the empty area, with blackness beyond. A few structures of flimsy board scraps and crudely thrown-together stone slouched around the edges of his vision.

He realized it was just the regular view outside the Mine Shaft's entrance.

Snow fell in tiny, dry white grains on his right hand, which was the one he first saw. He felt each speck sting like a biting insect.

Sensory-impression scraps jumbled into his mind: pain. Fear. A dimly lit room with stone walls almost as cold as the hearts of the burly men surrounding him. The smell of spilled booze and puke.

So they didn't dump me down the shaft in the back room, he thought. And no longer doubted its reality. Just dumped my sorry busted ass on the rubble pile outside their door.

I suppose I should be fucking grateful.

But he didn't feel grateful. He felt hot past nuke red. He had been abused by every single person he'd come across that day. His dreams had been stolen, his labor and risk of years pissed on. Then he'd been beaten up and tossed out like a whore's used moontime rag.

He heard a sound.

Somebody was singing, slurring, stumbling over the words "Oh my darling, oh my darling, oh my...darling Clem-en-tine...."

He raised his head farther. His neck bones creaked like rusty gears loaded with grit. His eyes, unable to focus right and further blurred by the little dry snow turds clinging to the lashes, saw a figure stumbling into the shadows between shacks off to his left. It was the Asian guy who'd been talking his ear off all evening about his pocketful of jack and dreams of a Promised Land.

He *dared* to boast about that shit to a man who had none of those things.

Some unknown time before Bass's vision had been blacked out by a bat to the back of the head. Now his vision was covered in red.

Numb now to everything but utter rage, Bass rose. He felt the hardness of the chunk of rock clutched in his right hand.

Never after would he remember seeing anything but a sort of glowing red curtain. But he could never forget the feel of repeated impacts, grunts of effort—his—of pain—somebody else's, the repeated impacts that dug hard points of icy busted stone into his palm and sent shocks shivering up his arm, the hot wet that splashed his face and stubble of beard.

Then he was on all fours, swaybacked and panting like a horse run to the point of dropping dead from exhaustion, his tongue hanging out as he tried to fill his burning lungs with air that cut like blades. Right in front of him a human figure lay sprawled on its back with arms outflung.

From the fleece-lined collar of the heavy jacket up there was nothing even vaguely reminiscent of a man, except for a few odd wet prominences that shone shocking red in the light of the wind-whipped torches outside the gaudy door.

Terror too stark for words flooded Bass, as did remorse.

But spilled blood didn't go back in the body, his old granny who'd raised him always said. Stern old bitch she was, too.

And as usual, Gran had been right.

Without forming conscious intent Bass found his hands, the fingers like frozen sausages, fumbling open the thick woolen jacket. They delved into the pockets of shirt and pants beneath, coming out with a wad of jack and then a fistful of dully gleaming gold and silver coins that was everything the man had boasted about.

Seized by a wild impulse as inexplicable as his early onset of rage, Bass tore open the shirt. There was a packet of some kind of skin or leather, shiny with oil, hung by a rawhide thong around the chill's neck. It resisted his attempts to break it; he had to haul it upward and then out, dripping with clotted red and black gunk, to free it.

The prize. The way to the Promised Land, to which the man had dedicated his whole life.

For which he'd lost it.

Bass felt eyes upon him.

They'd always told him, the old coldheart-fighting hands and convoy scouts, that a man properly in tune with his senses could feel another person looking at him. He had always doubted that.

Now he knew with sudden fear he'd been wrong about that, too.

He looked up. Despite the pain it sent surging through

his skull and crackling down his neck to radiate throughout his rib cage, Bass turned his head frantically this way and that. If somebody's come out of the gaudy… Well, he doubted that swag-bellied old bastard Dug gave two smears of stickie shit for what happened to the stranger. But murdering a recent patron right outside the Mine Shaft door could be bad for business.

Boss didn't doubt that if he got caught, he'd shortly find himself introduced to the fabled back room and the forever fall into blackness that promised.

But the door was resolutely shut against the sounds of bad music, allowing only murmurs to escape.

He looked around again. Between a couple of storage sheds he made a darker shadow in shadow. He had the impression of a bulky jacket, slim legs and eyes: dark, wide, feminine.

He jumped up and ran. He didn't know where. Just away into the darkness, which he knew already he'd never truly escape.

Part I:

The Ville

Chapter One

"You like this?" Krysty Wroth asked. She held a strand of brightly colored clay beads to her throat.

Mildred Wyeth eyed the tall, statuesque redhead critically. "Gilding the lily, Krysty," she said. "How do these look on me?"

The twentieth-century freezie physician was a head shorter than her friend, dark-skinned and full-figured, with her hair done in plaited beads, and light brown eyes. She dangled a bright green polished-malachite earring by her right lobe.

"They suit your coloring," Krysty said. Her emerald-green eyes danced, and both women tittered like little girls.

Ryan Cawdor turned away. The women's byplay, with the old vendor in her many layers of woolen shawls, was half for show. But, he sensed, perhaps no more than half.

Oh, well. Both women stood steady as stone when the bullets started flying, especially Krysty. There was no one other than his best friend, J. B. Dix, who stood by his elbow gazing blandly through his wire-rimmed specs at the crowd inside the Doylesville trade center, Ryan would rather have at his back than his life mate.

He switched his attention to scoping the center in general. Its cavernous interior was already packed with buyers and sellers from all over the southern Zarks.

Doylesville had prospered under the decades of enlightened rule by Baron Murv Doyle. While the ville had expanded steadily over the years, so Ryan heard tell, every expansion was marked by a corresponding expansion of the razor-tape tangle perimeter that sealed it off from the rest of the world. The trade center still lay more than a hundred yards outside the recently advanced gates.

"Used to call this place Choad," J.B. said, taking off his glasses and polishing them with a handkerchief. "We came by here once, when I rolled with Trader. Back before your time."

"They've gone up-market between then and now," Ryan said.

"Baron's a cocky son of a bitch," J.B. said, putting the glasses back on his nose. He was a runt of a man, utterly nondescript from his battered fedora, past his scuffed brown leather jacket, to the even more thoroughly scuffed toes of his work boots. He said little and what he said was always to the point.

He looked completely harmless and liked it that way. So did Ryan. It made enemies underestimate him.

"Lets people in here without even disarming them," J.B. said. He wore his full pack with his Smith & Wesson M-4000 shotgun and his Uzi strapped openly to the outside. Ryan himself carried his Steyr Scout longblaster slung over his shoulder next to his backpack.

"Indeed," said Dr. Theophilus Tanner. A tall man in a long black Victorian frock coat, with long silver white hair and pale blue eyes, he looked seventy, and those hard years. In fact he was in his late thirties, in terms of years actually lived through. "Especially inasmuch as they say subjects inside the wire are allowed to possess no arms more threatening than a cleaver or butcher knife in home or shop, nor carry any but a pocketknife."

"Now *that* actually suits you," Ryan heard Mildred say.

He glanced over to see Krysty holding a choker of bright yellow metal disks against her ivory throat.

"I make my pieces myself," the proprietor said with pride in her cracked voice. "Make 'em out of found scraps—old wire, buttons, busted machine parts. That choker I made from clapped-out cartridge cases I beat into disks."

"And are you paid directly for the sale of your wares, my good woman?" Doc asked. Ryan acknowledged that the man had a strange way of talking, but not for a man who was born a century and a half before World War III blew up the planet in 2001, or so Ryan gathered. He had a courtly way about him, though, that women in particular responded to. So they tended to overlook his peculiarities of speech.

His words, though, clearly made the old vendor uncomfortable. She looked around surreptitiously, then, with a meaningful nod at a sec man who stood a dozen feet away holding a pump-action riot gun by a pistol, she said, "The baron takes care of all us vendors."

"Indeed," Doc said.

"Triple-good care," J.B. said even more softly than usual. "Must have a dozen sec men posted around the place, all armed for a fight."

"That's why he doesn't sweat letting us customers and traders carry our weapons," Ryan said. "It'd cut into his trade, and from what I hear he reckons if he has to make an example out of somebody every so often, then he does."

"The baron enjoys a less than savory reputation," Doc murmured. "I do not relish doing business with him."

"We brought him what he agreed to pay a pretty price for," J.B. said.

"So much the more reason for my discomfort."

"Can hurry up?" a voice asked from behind. "Heavy."

It was the last member of the companions' trade delegation: a young man with dead-white skin and hair and shocking blood-colored eyes, whose slight frame was bent under the weight of a hard-used green metal ammo box.

That had been Krysty's idea, to make him carry the wares. Jak Lauren was loyal to a fault to his comrades, especially their tall, one-eyed leader. But inside he was still the wild youth who'd grown up waging guerrilla warfare against invaders in his home Gulf Coast swamps. What Mildred referred to as his impulse control was still not everything it could be. Krysty had calculated toting the massive box would tend to keep him out of trouble.

"And speaking of the devil," Doc said, nodding toward the end of the center farthest from the entrance, "here we behold Baron Doyle himself, emerging at his leisure from his annex to tend to serious business."

He looked at Ryan. "Are you sure this is wise?"

"No," Ryan said. "That's why we've got insurance."

IT STILL SURPRISED Ricky Morales that the wooden stair around the corner of the big trade center was left unguarded, but Jak had spent a whole day watching the place from the surrounding hills and confirmed it was true.

When they had first met, the young albino had treated Ricky—only a handful of years younger at sixteen—as a rival and unwelcome. But then Ricky had demonstrated his worth, saving the lives of his companions—and Jak himself—during the course of guiding the party around the mountains of his home island of Puerto Rico. By the time it came to jump out of the place outlanders called Monster Island, by means of the magical secret mat-trans network by which Ryan and his friends traveled the Deathlands, they had accepted the boy as one of them.

Jak and he were fast friends now. It was inevitable, he

supposed. They were by far the closest together in age. Everyone else in the group seemed old to him, although none had lost much vigor. Not even Doc, who looked to be a hundred to Ricky's young eyes.

A pair of guards stood at the main entrance to the center, sure enough, giving the hard eye to the crowd queued outside hugging themselves and stamping their feet against what seemed to Ricky to be an unendurable cold. One of them had a Mini-14 longblaster, the other a remade machine pistol, all right angles and perforated barrel with a folding metal stock, that Ricky recognized as a 9 mm Karl Gustav M/45.

Ricky knew a lot about weapons. To the despair of his pacifistic and respectable parents, he had always been far more at home in his uncle's metal shop than helping them and his adored older sister, Yami, stocking shelves and sweeping floors in the shop they ran in his home ville of Nuestra Señora. Eventually José and María Elena Morales had given in to the inevitable and acquiesced to his becoming apprentice to his Uncle Benito, the town mechanic—and weaponsmith.

In the end, when El Guapo's coldheart army came to punish Nuestra Señora for refusing to submit to the rule of its self-proclaimed general, neither passivity nor spirited resistance had sufficed to save either Ricky's parents or his uncle. He felt again the agony of seeing his parents brutally murdered by El Guapo's shark-toothed sec boss Tiburón, and his beautiful sister kidnapped.

He had seen both evil ones paid back with interest, but he hadn't been able to rescue his sister, whom he'd learned had been sold into slavery. He had been unable to trace her further; but the desire to one day find her trail, find her and liberate her was never far from his conscious mind.

With a well-rehearsed effort of will he pushed those

memories back into his subconscious. He had a task to perform. His new friends—his new family—relied upon him.

With a last quick look around—trying not to look as suspicious as humanly possible—Ricky moved up the rickety wood steps as fast he could. They creaked alarmingly, but since well-armed sec men tramped up and down them many times a day, he doubted his own lesser weight would challenge their load-bearing capabilities. Not even with the burden strapped to his back.

As for the noises, the cold, impatient mob awaiting entry to the trade center was more than enough to cover those. Still, each little wood squeal was like a fear-dagger to his heart.

The door, as Jak reported, was locked with a dead bolt. Among the many marvelous arts his new mentor, J. B. Dix, was teaching him was the skill of picking locks. The Armorer disdained the use of lockpick guns as for those who needed to substitute predark tech for skill. Regardless of which, he'd provided one to Ricky, with training and assurance it would serve to get him in. Ricky had talent, as he did for anything to do with machines, but his skill wasn't yet great. And J.B. was no man to let scruples get in the way of survival.

Ricky was especially fearful of being spotted breaking into the second-story door. He somehow managed not to hunch over the lock like a total burglar on the little wood platform at the top of the stairs.

Nor did it turn out he needed to. It took a quick poke of the predark gun and the lock clunked open. He could hardly have gotten in more quickly and slickly had he had the key.

Inside was empty. There was usually a sec man watching the floor from the little wood booth built out over the concrete floor of the converted industrial building. But he usually got there a bit late, apparently confident the baron, who entered always from the building's other end, wouldn't find out.

Fortunately the door locked on the inside with a twist-knob, not a key. Ricky locked it behind him. He hoped the guard took his time.

Unslinging his precious burden—the legacy of his beloved uncle, who had made it with his own capable hands, and Ricky's less capable but avid help—Ricky moved to the chair waiting below the window looking out over the center's interior.

"So, GENTLEMEN," the man said, smiling through a gray-dusted ginger beard, "ladies. What treasures did you bring me today?"

"Same as we agreed on, Baron," Ryan said in a level voice.

Baron Murv Doyle of Doylesville was a big man, made bulkier by the wolfskin coat he wore with the silver and black fur on the outside. Rumor had it he added to his natural mass, abundant in fat and muscle both, with a Kevlar bullet-resistant vest worn under his shirt. Ryan was inclined to believe it simply because of his willingness to expose his person in spite of his doubtful reputation. A tall black Astrakhan hat added half a foot to an already impressive six-four or- five frame.

Ryan guessed the outfit was calculated as much for psychological effect as it was for warmth. As, for that matter, was the chill inside the trade center. And the massive presence of sec men with blasters in hand. Everything was designed to keep those who had come to do business with the baron and his minions as uncomfortable and off balance as possible.

That didn't work as far as Ryan was concerned, or, so

he reckoned, his companions. They'd been cold before, and they'd faced bigger, more threatening presences than Murv Doyle without letting themselves get intimidated.

Ryan nodded over his shoulder. With a relieved grunt Jak placed his burden on the heavy hardwood table in front of Doyle. The grim-looking sec men flanking the baron started forward, then relaxed. Their boss, Tug, who stood right behind the baron's left shoulder, remained still, his grin fixed through his own ash-blond beard, his gray shark eyes glittering like the ball bearings they resembled. The sec chief looked to be about the same height as his boss, if you subtracted the tall woolly hat. His own hair was close-cropped and retreating back onto a narrow skull. The ring in his left earlobe glinted like steel as if to add to his impression of having iron in more than just his blood.

"Here," Ryan said. "We promised to trade twenty prime grens. Ten frag, five concussion and five tear gas."

"Where'd you get them?" Tug asked.

J.B. produced a brief chuckle. "Somewhere you wouldn't want to go," he said.

Tug glared at the Armorer, who failed to quail. The little, unassuming man in the battered fedora, scuffed leather jacket and wire-rimmed specs didn't look at all intimidating. He didn't try to. He was also as tough a customer as Ryan had ever encountered in his years spent knocking around the Deathlands.

Instead, J.B. took a dried apple from his jacket pocket. He examined it without favor and bit into it.

Ignoring the byplay, the baron opened the box and reached inside. Black-gloved fingers picked up first a spherical frag, then a cylindrical concussion gren. He held the latter up to examine it in the morning light drifting through the wire mesh over the windows.

"These work?" he asked.

Ryan laughed. "Only one way to find out."

That wasn't true, strictly speaking. Master armorer and weaponsmith that he was, J.B. and his equally gadget-crazed sixteen-year-old protégé Ricky Morales had taken each and every gren apart and inspected it to ensure that the charges and initiation mechanisms were intact, not time-degraded enough to be duds or worse, more danger-ous to the user than to the intended targets. All checked out.

Of course that wasn't guarantee they'd go off as ad-vertised, but it was the best possible method short of ac-tually lighting them off. Which of course wouldn't leave much to trade.

At Ryan's remark Tug shifted his stance to ferociously glare at him. Ryan ignored him as effortlessly as J.B. had. Looking mean was part of his job—as a sec boss in gen-eral, and apparently, here specifically during the baron's daily appearance at his trade center to oversee the serious transactions. Such as this one.

That didn't mean Tug was all show and no go. Ryan understood that perfectly well. A person didn't last over twenty years as a baron's sec boss without being hard enough to back the hard eyes with harder hands. That was a given. Especially considering the rep Doyle and his heavy hitter enjoyed in the Zark region.

Doyle looked at Tug, who cocked an eyebrow. Doyle tossed him the gren.

One of the sec men actually flinched. Ryan set his jaw. It was a triple-stupe reaction as well as a yellow one. If the grens were touchy enough to go off just by being thrown around—even dropped on the stained concrete floor—they likely wouldn't have survived the hazards of retriev-ing them from the redoubt and transporting them here.

Ryan was proud that of his crew only Jak snickered.

That didn't much bother him. Jak was Jak; you didn't look to him for sophistication in dealing with other people.

Tug frowned at the small, round bomb. There were things you could tell by exterior inspection of the things, mostly obvious signs of corrosion. In the hidden redoubt where Ryan and his friends had uncovered the treasure they'd been properly sealed away so they were as fresh as new the day they were made—at least as far as anything short of using them could reveal.

Tug looked back at his boss and nodded.

J.B. cleared his throat. Ryan didn't turn his head. Though he couldn't consciously hear anything extra over the general hubbub in the trade center, he could feel extra presences closing in behind. He didn't need to look around to know they were more Doylesville sec men, hemming in Ryan and the others.

No surprise. It wasn't the outcome he'd hoped for, but…

Baron Doyle took the gren from Tug and laid it carefully among the others in the open green metal box.

"You have delivered the goods, just as you promised, and that's a fact," he said, then grinned. "So I'm sorry to announce there's been a slight change of plans. I'm placing you all under arrest for transporting and possessing illegal ordnance in the sovereign barony of Doylesville. And I'll just be confiscating these dangerous contraband goods."

Chapter Two

"Bastard," Mildred Wyeth hissed.

"And then some," Baron Doyle agreed. "But then, we hold the whip hand here, don't we?"

Behind him Ryan heard a sec man yip a curse. He guessed the man had made the mistake of laying a hard arm on Jak's shoulder and discovered the hard way that the shiny metal bits sewn onto the camou jacket were razor sharp and meant to discourage just that kind of familiarity.

"Baron," J.B. said, "you're making a mistake."

Doyle laughed. "Then we'll certainly find that out during the forthcoming investigation," he said, "carried out by our own elite investigators under the direction of my good friend Tug. We'll soon get to the bottom of this matter, and you can trust me on that."

He put back his big-hatted head and laughed at his own cleverness and at his latest victims' futile display of anger.

Too bad, Ryan thought, he didn't know it was all for show.

RICKY SAT on the chair in the sec-booth overlooking the trade center floor. He had already slid back the window to clear his field of fire. He held his stubby-barreled DeLisle carbine ready across his lap, out of sight from below.

When the sec men made their move on his friends, he went to an even higher level of alert than he had been, which was quivering eager. Now, though, an odd calm settled on him.

Ryan had clenched both fists by his sides. Ricky had good eyes and had no difficulty seeing that from about forty yards away, nor did he have any trouble seeing it when Ryan suddenly stuck out his right thumb without moving the hand from beside his jeans-clad leg.

With practiced smoothness Ricky raised the carbine to his shoulder, thumbing off the safety as he did. Pulling the longblaster into a tight shooting configuration, with his left elbow properly placed directly below the foregrip, he got a flash picture over the open sights. As he did so, he gulped down a big breath.

He let it out to steady himself, caught it, squeezed.

The weapon bucked. The steel buttplate hit his shoulder, well padded by the puffy jacket he wore against the cold he hated.

The DeLisle made but the slightest whisper of sound. Far louder was Ricky's reflex throwing of the bolt to eject the short, fat empty shell and slam in a new round as he rode the recoil and brought the longblaster back online.

His target went straight down. Immediately Ricky sighted the man who stood to the chill's right. That sec man turned his head to gawk at his inexplicably collapsed buddy lying in a black leather heap on the floor.

Ricky put a bullet in the second man's left earhole. He fell as limply as the first.

Then the door lock clattered behind Ricky.

FROM THE WAY Baron Doyle was suddenly frozen in the act of drawing his hand back from the ammo box and the direction of his stare, more frowning concern than wide-eyed amazement—Ryan formed a quick flash picture in his mind.

He knew what was supposed to happen, too. That helped. But he knew well that what was supposed to happen didn't always. He was already in motion when he heard the unmistakable crunching impact of a bullet entering a man's head.

Ryan's own head snapped around and he gazed over his left shoulder. A red-bearded guard with a shaved head was frowning down at the floor to his right, where Ryan guessed lay the huddled heap that a moment ago had been a brother sec man. Rank-and-file sec men weren't usually recruited for their quick wits and discernation. A good sec boss had those things, and he wasn't eager to see them expressed in his subordinates, unless it was one he was grooming as a successor.

This one didn't seem to be on what Mildred would've termed the fast track to promotion. His eyebrows were creeping up his head as he grasped the fact that his buddy was dead, just about the time Ryan's left boot heel slammed into his breastbone right over his heart and launched him backward.

Ryan felt a crunch, just before the man went flying backward into the mob of shoppers, knocking over a table full of metal parts that clattered to the floor. He might have stove in the man's ribs, maybe even into the heart directly below. Then again, he'd known a man's heart to be stopped by a powerful blow right over it.

It didn't matter to him now. He followed through into a counterclockwise turn to face the other sec man who remained on his feet out of the six who had hemmed them in from behind. The man was grabbing Mildred's beaded plaits from behind. Big mistake…

Worse, Sec Chief Tug had grabbed Krysty around the waist from behind and jammed a short-barreled revolver beneath her ear.

Ryan caught a quick impression of the crowded floor, of pale and dark brown faces turned their way in blank surprise. The very large number of weapons that the hefty sec crew posted around the trade center were lifting in the direction of the companions.

And from high up at the rear of the vast and echoing floor came the sound of a handblaster shot.

RICKY MORALES GOT the bolt of his DeLisle carbine thrown about halfway home when it locked up tight. Though he still wasn't all that seasoned a shooter, Ricky already knew his way around weapons malfunks. Even as his heart threatened to stop dead in his chest he realized what had happened. In his excitement he had short-shucked the empty, failing to yank the bolt back to its full extent and properly eject the spent casing before ramming home a fresh round off the top of the 10-round magazine. As short as the .45 ACP cartridges were, he'd never anticipated he could even do that.

But he had, and somehow instead of panicking he reacted.

A wiry sec man with a shock of dust-colored hair sticking up above shaved sides to his head gaped at him from the open door. As the wind reached inside to stab its icy claws into Ricky's marrow, he grabbed for the sling of the longblaster hung over his narrow black-leather-clad back.

Clinging to the momentarily useless DeLisle with his left hand, Ricky was already fumbling his Webley handblaster from under his coat with his right. The man came up with an M-1 carbine.

As the barrel came level with Ricky's face, the burly handblaster bucked in his hand. He hadn't been aware of pulling the trigger.

The muzzle-flash underlit a look of shocked surprise in yellow.

Ricky wasn't sure he'd actually hit the sec man. So making an effort to squeeze the trigger instead of just yanking at it, he went ahead and cranked through the rest of the six rounds in the blaster's chambers.

By somewhere around number three the sec man vanished completely from Ricky's sight. But the youth was in full-on shooting mode, and kept cranking out the big booming blasts until the hammer clicked on empty.

Only then in the ringing silence did he notice how deafeningly loud the shots were in the enclosed booth.

Without even popping open the top-break action to swap the empties for a fresh magazine of cartridges, Ricky jammed the blaster back in its holster. Somehow he managed not to drop it or spend more than a minor eternity getting it to fit back in. Then he grabbed the DeLisle with both hands, banged the buttplate hard on the windowsill and yanked the bolt hard for all he was worth.

Sometimes when a person jammed up a cartridge on a failure-to-eject, it stayed well and truly stuck. But this time the reflex tap-rack-bang drill his Uncle Benito had taught him worked its magic. The dented empty shell flew off to bounce tinkling on the floor. A loaded round slid butter-smooth into the waiting chamber.

Ricky raised the blaster to his shoulder. He knew his companions needed him more than ever.

HEADS TURNED at the sudden bellow of blasterfire from an utterly unexpected direction: high up at the back of the Doylesville trade center. Blasters turned with them.

A flash of fast red motion drew Ryan's eye back around to what was now his left. He was in time to see Krysty, who was almost as tall as Tug, smash her head straight back into his nose. He grunted, and his grip around her weakened.

More importantly, when his attention had strayed up to the sec booth, his handblaster had slipped away from Krysty's ear. Not that that made a load of difference; all of Ryan's people knew what a bad idea actually touching someone with a blaster's muzzle was. It let the victim know exactly where the weapon was pointed and made it dead easy to get out of the way of the bullets. If one had the presence of mind.

In danger, Krysty had the speed and chill purpose of a catamount. She twisted in her captor's grip, grabbing his gun wrist with her left hand and pushing it toward the rounded ceiling.

Her right hand shoved her own snub-nosed Smith & Wesson 640 revolver into the pit of the Doylesville sec boss's stomach, where she promptly blasted all five rounds through his gut.

That was the one time it helped—or didn't hurt—to touch someone with a blaster: when you were blasting.

The sec boss fell to the floor puking blood that strangled his own screams of intolerable agony. Turning back to the table, Ryan saw that Mildred had also evaded her captor—and saw him falling, trailing a stream of blood and what was maybe a busted-off tooth, courtesy of a stroke from the steel-shod butt of J.B.'s shotgun.

The two goons backing Baron Doyle had been dealt with. Doc had the slim steel blade that had been concealed in his swordstick thrust through the throat of the man to Doyle's left. The one on the right brought up a lever-action Winchester, and a terrifying roar slammed out from beside Ryan. It felt as if a spray of fine grit hit the left side of his cheek; he felt some patter off his eye patch. The side blast of Jak's .357 Magnum Colt Python was almost as damn deadly as what came out. But not quite; the sec man with the longblaster went over backward with a little hole in his front and a doubtless much larger one in his back.

The small army of sec men dotted around the giant room were for the moment fixing their attention on the booth where Ricky had just emptied his own big handblaster, presumably into one of their buddies. The place echoed to a barrage of shots that almost drowned out the panicked screaming of dozens of terrified customers.

Ryan paid no mind. Baron Doyle, his face chill-white behind his beard, was grabbing for the open box of grens.

"No, you don't," Ryan said. His big panga flashed from the sheath strapped under one arm.

Its heavy blade slammed into the tabletop and sunk in half an inch—and that was after chopping through the flesh and bones just above the baron's thick wrist.

Blood sprayed over the table. Hot droplets splashed Ryan's face as Doyle flailed his spurting stump. The baron grabbed at it with his remaining hand and staggered back toward the door through which he'd entered the center, howling like a tornado.

J.B. appeared next to the table, slamming the ammo box lid shut on the precious contents and sticking it under his arm.

The agonized yells of their baron began to penetrate the dim awarenesses of his sec man squad even through the yammer of their blasters and the roar of their own blood lust in their ears. They may have conspicuously failed to protect the man they were hired to guard, but as Ryan drew his SIG-Sauer handblaster he realized they were now looking to make up for the damage as best they could by killing his attackers.

Dozens of blasters swung their way.

Chapter Three

Curled up on the floor of the sec booth, in a half-fetal curl around the longblaster he clutched like a child would his teddy bear, Ricky said a prayer only he could hear over the terrible voices of all the blasters.

They were shooting at him and punching right through the relatively thin walls and even floor of the booth.

Some of the hard cases who had hung out in his uncle's shop, to shoot the shit with Benito, had tried to impress upon Ricky the difference between cover and concealment. As quick-witted as he was, Ricky found that distinction somehow hard to grasp.

Not even the months he'd run with Ryan and the others had taught him quite the difference. But now he got it.

Lying there on the floor with shot-out window glass falling on and around him like giant razor-edged snowflakes, the pissed-off sec men couldn't see him at all. That was concealment.

But the wood walls and floor offered almost no protection against their vengeful bullets. He could feel them punching through the planks all around him. He felt a couple yank at his coat like spiteful fingers.

The flimsy booth wasn't providing any cover.

I'm dead. That phrase hammered in his brain louder even than his frantic, futile prayers and the blasterfire. It could only be a few heartbeats before some sec man struck an ace on the line. And Ricky Morales's luck and brief life would run out at the same time.

And then…it stopped.

For a moment Ricky still lay screaming and quivering. Then somehow he got control of himself enough to notice that nobody was shooting at him anymore.

He flinched as more shots cracked out. But even in his terror he recognized they came from farther away, even though still within the center.

My friends! I've left them in danger by acting like a little baby, he thought.

Cursing himself with a fluency that would've appalled his poor dead parents, he jumped up still clutching his DeLisle to his chest.

Not even considering what a fine target he'd make for any sec men still aiming their blasters his way, Ricky flung himself back to the now vacant window. His friends counted on him to give them fire support. He only prayed that he hadn't let them down.

GRINNING LIKE A PALE DEMON, Jak stepped into Ryan's field of view. In one white hand he held something that looked like a can, painted drab tan.

"Now?" he asked.

Ryan looked at all the sec men preparing to blast him and his friends. The only thing holding their fingers off their triggers was concern for hitting their baron, whose thrashing and screaming couldn't be steadying their nerves. Sooner or later one would either remember to aim or they'd just cut loose regardless.

But the plan the master strategist Ryan Cawdor and his sly companion J. B. Dix had concocted in the event their little deal with the devil of Doylesville turned out as it had accounted for that, too.

Ryan wasn't a soft man. His companions all knew that. Sometimes even they thought he acted too harsh, too stone-hearted. But he did what it took to keep them, and him, alive and struggling with their dream of eventual sanctuary and safety, which none of them could even clearly envision.

But he didn't chill without need, nor was he cruel. At least, never for cruelty's own sake.

Naturally they hadn't intended to give over all the best grens they found to the baron, presuming he kept his deal, but of course he hadn't. There were a few in the trove they had discovered that held little market value.

But that didn't mean they weren't valuable.

Ryan nodded. Grinning still wider, Jak yanked the pin from the cylindrical gren and lobbed the bomb under-handed into the middle of the concrete floor. It bounced off a table stacked with piles of cloth and garments, some scavvy, some recently put together.

The shoppers had begun to pick themselves off the floor where they dropped when the shooting started. Now those near the gren began to yelp in shrill terror.

But Ryan wasn't going to blow up random customers of the Doylesville trade center not without a good purpose, at least. And anyway the blast radius of a gren was too limited, and the confines of the center way too big, for a frag to take down more than a single sec man. They were too spread out even to hope to bring down two. And even that wouldn't trim the odds against the group surviving enough to count.

But instead of exploding, the gren suddenly erupted in a giant cloud of dense white smoke.

Cries of "Gas!" pealed out even as the smoke spread across the floor, hiding most of the shoppers from Ryan's sight. It may have been that some of the first voices to yell the word belonged to his own friends, namely J.B. and Mildred.

Of course it wasn't. It was just a smoke gren, doing what a smoke gren was meant to do—foul the bad guys' line of sight, allowing the good guys to shift elsewhere in a hurry with a much reduced chance of stopping any stray large metal particulates moving at high speed.

The last sec man in view at least knew that was no toxic-gas bomb. He swung his pump-action shotgun toward Ryan, who already had his P-226 leveled and ready.

He gave the sec man a double tap, aimed at his chest. Ryan shot left-handed freehand almost as well as he shot with his right hand properly braced in shooting stance. The sec man fell. His shotgun blasted its loads toward the steel rafters. Ryan heard the zing of a couple of buckshot pellets ricocheting.

"Out the back!" he shouted.

He and his friends ran for the baron's personal entrance in the rear. They raced right past the man, who hadn't managed to bleed out yet, which was good. As long as he was still hollering, his bodyguards would be reluctant to start blazing away at random through the smoke screen that was slowly filling the entire hall.

As Ryan drew alongside Doyle, the baron's head jerked sideways. His eyes bulged unnaturally far from their sockets. Blood shot out one temple.

Doyle's screams cut off. Ryan knew at once—by a .45-caliber bullet, not moving fast enough to exit Murv Doyle's skull on the far side—the sniper was a well-aimed by an equally well-meaning Ricky Morales.

"Fireblast!" Ryan cursed. But there was no helping it now.

Somebody had the door open. He was the last man through, coming right behind Krysty.

He couldn't help noticing that the rear door of the trade center opened into a small but luxuriously appointed office, with a potbellied stove merrily giving out the heat from one corner that the baron cunningly denied his customers out in the center itself. He even had scavvied oak veneer paneling the walls around his big desk, which was piled high with papers and ledgers.

There would be excellent plunder here, Ryan knew, but without another thought he followed his friends without slowing around the desk and out the open back door into the frigid embrace of a Zark spring morning.

WITHOUT A RUSTLE of branches Jak Lauren stepped into the small clearing.

"No follow," he said in his abbreviated speech.

"Well," J.B. said, tipping his hat back up on his forehead and gazing down the narrow forested valley they had just climbed. "That went well."

Mildred scowled at him. J.B. was capable of dry and cutting wit, but the man sounded as if he meant it.

"Are you a few rounds short of a full mag, John?" she demanded. "That went just about as far sideways as a deal could possibly go!"

"We're alive, Millie," J.B. said mildly—and unrepentantly. He gave her a placid smile and slapped the heavy steel box he held beneath one arm. "Plus we still got these prime grens."

"Indeed," Doc said.

His blue eyes were still shining brightly from his wrinkled face. Sometimes after the heat of battle wore off he lapsed into the vagueness that often beset him, deeper and longer than his usual bouts. But now he still seemed hyped-up. Maybe the several hours they'd spent fleeing at a brisk pace from the scene of their latest adventure still had him worked up enough to stay focused in the here and now, and not wander off along the mists of time that always swirled in his mind.

And never had the trite phrase "mists of time" been so literal. While Mildred had slept the years from her own time away as a frozen near-corpse, Dr. Theophilus Tanner had been snatched from his happy home and trolled away through time by the whitecoats who ran Operation Chronos, the same ultrasecret late-twentieth Century project that created the mat-trans gateway network that enabled the companions to travel instantaneously among redoubts scattered all across North America and indeed the globe.

Doc's time had been the mid-1890s. After using and abusing him as a test subject, the whitecoats had dumped him in the hopeless future of Deathlands.

"Still, we managed to come away intact only through our quick wits and skills," Doc went on, "and the fact that our esteemed leader possesses what my contemporaries would have called the Devil's own luck. Mostly the latter, I fear."

"Any fuck up we can walk away from," Ryan said, still frowning back the way they had come, "is, well, we walked away."

"With all our parts," J.B. added.

Once they got into the woods on the slopes close to the trade center, they had slowed, seeing no sign of pursuit. Clearly the loud and sudden fall of Baron Doyle and his sec chief had caused disorder in the ville.

"Why aren't they chasing us?" Mildred demanded.

"We don't know that they aren't," J.B. said. "They're just not close, is what Jak's saying."

"I don't know what other kind of powerful types were in the ville," Ryan said thoughtfully. He had been born and raised a baron's son—before a brother's treachery robbed him of his family, his inheritance and his left eye.

"I don't reckon Doyle would've allowed too many to get big enough to threaten him," Ryan said. "But he may have had family. One way or another, there'll be a struggle for power. He's got too sweet a deal, the way he's got that ville beat down. Someone'll step in and take control."

"Power vacuum, you mean," Mildred said.

Ryan shrugged. "Not sure there's really such a thing. But here—I guess. Might as well call it that as any other thing."

"What you're saying, lover," Krysty said, "is that whoever does succeed Doyle may not be all that eager to hunt down the people who gave him that power. Or her."

"We have learned how far we can rely on the gratitude of barons," Doc said.

"We can't know," Ryan said. "There are plenty of reasons whoever takes charge might decide to run us down hard and fast."

"So what do we do?" Mildred asked. "Sadly there's no handy-dandy gateway anywhere within a fifty-mile radius."

"I would suggest we relocate as expeditiously as might be," Doc suggested, "both from the immediate environs and from the Ozark region as a whole."

"For once I agree with you," Mildred said. "We ought to get out of here."

"Yeah," Ryan said.

Right about then Mildred realized how little her aching buttocks and trembling legs cared for that notion. You had to go and open your big mouth, she reproached herself. Then she realized there would be plenty of time to rest her tired walking muscles. Once she was dead.

"Where there's a will..." she murmured.

"What's that, Millie?"

"Never mind, J.B."

"One thing before we go," J.B. said, turning to the group in general. "Ricky, that was a pretty sweet shot you put through the baron's head back there."

Ricky had been sitting on the winter-brittle humus floor of the clearing. He had been worn down by the exertion of the rapid, mostly upward hike, under the weight of his blasters and his still mostly full pack of spare 10-round ammo mags. He wasn't yet as trail-toughened as his companions.

But now he jumped to his feet. His olive cheeks flushed pink. Mildred saw him visibly inflate with pride at his mentor's praise.

Too bad he doesn't see the needle coming as clearly as I do, she thought.

She even knew what it would be, little as she cared for it.

"Thing is," J.B. went on, as gentle as ever, "when you got an enemy squalling and carrying-on like, you don't want to chill him, as a general rule. He tends to distract the other side. Demoralize them, remind them the kind of hurt we can lay on them.

"And you don't want to chill an injured, screaming man when he's important. Not to mention when the very fact he's still alive and hollering is mebbe all that's keeping a dozen sec men from cutting loose through that little smoke screen we laid down and cutting us all to pieces. Got that?"

Ricky's utter deflation would've been comical if it wasn't so heartbreaking. And for the fact that for a moment Mildred thought his own tired legs would give out on him completely and she'd have to catch him to keep him from going down and maybe cracking his head on a hidden rock. He sort of fell in on himself, and his black bangs fell to hide his downturned face, which Mildred suspected as beginning to leak water from around the eyes.

Doc stepped up and laid a reassuring hand on Ricky's slumped shoulder.

"Take heart, lad," he said. "You did most noble work on our behalf, prior to that little faux pas. Even the fact you inadvertently wound up drawing the attention of our foes to yourself by firing your revolver helped save our bacon.

"And remember—no one is born knowing all these things. Not even our esteemed leader."

"Yeah," Ryan grunted. "So now you know."

His lone eye blazed like a blue searchlight sweeping over the others. "And now we move."

"Which way, kemo sabe?" Mildred asked.

"South," Ryan said without hesitation.

"Why south, lover?" Krysty asked with a smile.

"Packs are cached that way."

"And one way seems as good as the next," Doc said. "As long as it be away from Doylesville."

"I hear ya," J.B. said.

"Enough jawing," Ryan rasped. "Get walking!"

Chapter Four

"So I hear tell you're fixing to leave fair Menaville."

From the neatly raked gravel-covered walkway, Bastion "Bass" Croom looked up at the dried, spare figure rocking on a chair on the porch of the two-story frame house with the steep slate roof. It wasn't much to look at. Neither was the wrinklie wrapped with a horse blanket over his legs. But he was the most powerful man in this part of the Ouachita Range, here south of the Zarks, and absolute baron of Menaville.

Bass nodded judiciously. "You hear correctly, Baron Billy."

His breath came in puffs. Though spring was clearly on the way, it was still a chilly morning in the wooded Ouachita hills among which Menaville nestled.

Baron Billy Howe looked stern. He was well equipped to do that. He had never been a soft man, nor a very handsome one. But the way age had shrunk his pale, leathery hide made his square chin jut and turned his cheekbones into big high flanges, gave an added authority to the hot blue glare of his eyes.

"And how in the name of glowing night shit is Menaville supposed to get by without the commerce your emporium and trade caravans bring us if you up and leave, Bass?"

Bass smiled through his beard. He was no longer the slim youth he had been years before, age having had the exact opposite effect on him as on the baron. It had left him with a big heavy face and a substantial gut beneath his long black coat. But he was fast enough with his fists or his ParaOrdnance .45 handblaster at need, powerful with the one and lethal-accurate with the other.

He preferred not to use either. He preferred plain talk and fair dealing. Standing by those preferences had made him a very rich man.

They hadn't sufficed to allow him to sleep each night untroubled by bad dreams, though. And now, as he approached the culmination of his own long cherished dream, the nightmares were growing worse.

It was the burden he bore for a sin he could never wash away.

"Just as Menaville and her people have prospered for years under the wise and enlightened rule of their baron," he said, "they will find a way to do so without me."

Baron Billy uttered a dry caw of laughter.

"Horseshit, Bass," he said. "I never liked you worth a pinch of dried owl shit. Nor you me. But I always thought we respected each other. Enough so you wouldn't try to go and soft-soap an old man like that."

Bass laughed. "Habit," he said. "My momma raised me to be polite."

"Mine didn't," the baron said. "She raised me to be a real coldhearted ring-tailed squealer of a son of a bitch. Served me well when I had to scratch and claw my way to the top of the heap in this here ville!"

He scowled ferociously at Bass, with his bushy white brows crunched way down over eyes as bright and merciless as a mountain sky in a bleak winter. Many strong men withered under that baronial glare. Bass didn't.

He'd had worse from the crusty old bastard.

"Well," Baron Billy said, "I reckon neither one of us

did too bad for hisself, walking different ways as we have our whole cussed lives."

"No," Bass said, "we haven't. And I meant what I said before, our differences notwithstanding."

And he had. He couldn't altogether approve of Billy Howe, or any baron, likely. But he knew from bitter experience what a bad baron was like.

Howe wasn't bad. For his breed. He was harsh but never cruel. He could be arbitrary but seldom deliberately unfair. He brooked no opposition, and had been known to crush men on suspicion; but he had also suppressed the coldheart gangs that preyed on the trade caravans and the outlying homesteads. He had stolen little enough and allowed his subjects enough latitude that they had done well, overall.

He even held to a rough code of honor beyond plain self-interest, unlike most barons of Croom's experience, and at least made an effort to keep his word, which being said, Bass reckoned he'd be a triple fool to stake his life on either.

Clutching the arms of his rocker with bare old knobby hands blue-white in the morning cold, the baron leaned forward with a predator's smile.

"And what do you want from me, Big Fish?" he asked. "I know you wouldn't wander into my sight otherwise, unless I ordered you here."

Bass's jaw set briefly, a tic he hoped his beard hid. He hated that nickname, and the one sure way to get a good feel for the temper he usually held in check with an iron hand was to use it in his hearing. Baron Billy wasn't above showing that he held the whip hand.

"As you know well, Baron," Bass said, "these stickie attacks have only gotten worse the past several seasons, in spite of all efforts to stop them."

The baron's already taut face clenched like a fist at

that comment. The "all efforts" to deal with the colony of stickies were those of the Menaville sec boss, Morson, and his men. Baron Billy *hated* to fail, and hated being reminded of it.

If you flourish the whip, Baron, Bass thought, you can't complain when I twist the knife.

Croom wasn't a spiteful man by nature, but neither was he anybody's damn doormat.

The baron's glare didn't transmute to angry words. He was a man capable of seeing the truth when it was plain as a blaster in the face. More, he was that rarity, a man capable of accepting that truth no matter how little he liked the look of it. It made him unusually capable and also dangerous. But seldom, Bass knew, to the person with balls to tell him that truth.

"My own losses of goods, wags and men to the muties have gone up steadily, despite my own ever-increasing security." Having made his point, Bass felt no hesitation admitting his own failure. He made it a practice to take truth when he found it, too. "I'm tired of absorbing those losses, losing good people, as well as throwing good jack after bad trying to hold them down."

"Nonetheless, I'll say it again—you're no poor man, Bass Croom."

"I'm not. I'm also not as young as I used to be. I'm getting tired of waging that particular losing battle, Baron. I mean to retire."

Baron Billy's eyes narrowed to slits that blazed like furnace vents. "And how do you mean to spend that retirement?" he asked.

While there had never been any question who held the ultimate power in Menaville since Billy Howe came into possession of it, there was also no doubt who held the second most power. Bass Croom's honesty, integrity and calm strength of character made him by far the most influential man in the ville, surrounding settlements and homesteads after the baron, long before Bass became the wealthiest man in the Ouachitas. Indeed it was those traits and the consequent influence that made it possible for him to become so rich.

And for all their mutual respect, Bass and Billy had butted heads more often than not over the years. It was no exaggeration to say that Bass was the ville's foremost check on Billy's harshness—and incipient paranoia. As strong as he was, the baron had never had enough power to crush the merchant. And he was wise enough to know not to try.

Also too smart. Aside from the risk, small but unacceptable, that he'd lose such a showdown, the baron saw clearly what a hit Menaville's prosperity—hence his own—would take if Bass Croom was successfully removed from the scene.

"Just as you've heard it said, Baron," Bass said. "I mean to pull up stakes and head West. Find some promising place to settle down."

"Risky."

Bass laughed. He had a deep, rich laugh, and he only laughed when he meant it.

"Life's risky, Baron," he said. "As who knows better than you? Neither of us can stop these rad-blasted muties from picking off my convoys, and no hiding from it. I'd just as soon take a different set of risks."

He shrugged. "Also, truth to tell, I'm feeling a bit of the wandering itch. I made my fortune, such as it is, as much on the road as here in my store in Menaville. But in recent times it's been all the latter and none of the former. I want to roll down some new roads before I find dirt hitting me in the eyes."

And every word of that is true as cold steel, Bass thought. And little as I care for it, I'm lying like a bastard by omission.

He had lived the last two decades driven on by a golden dream, as much as he was haunted by the guilt of the price he'd pay to steal that dream. And that, too, was a part of the cost.

He was *not* going to allow either the death of his nameless companion in the Mine Shaft, or the nightmares that crime had brought Bass since in spite of all his efforts to expiate it, to go to waste. He had that map to the Promised Land, and now he meant to follow it.

Of course Baron Billy couldn't know that, or there was no limit to what he'd hold Bass up for as a price for allowing him to pursue that promise. He might cut himself in for a hefty share. Almost would, in fact.

But as shrewd as he was, Baron Billy couldn't see past the sudden glowing vista of having his greatest rival suddenly removed. And more.

"Your funeral, son," he said, sitting back with a look of triumph plain on his badlands face. "Now the time has come to talk turkey. What's in it for me?"

"BASS," HIS YOUNGER brother, Morty, said as Bass came in the front door of his General Store in the center of Menaville, "we're outta eggs."

Closing the door on the chill, Bass took off his hat and hung it from a peg nearby.

"Why not go buy some?" he asked.

His brother was standing between shelves of dry goods with a canvas apron strapped to the front of his gangly frame and leaning on a push broom. By the looks of the floor, the broom hadn't recently seen much use as anything but an architectural support. Morty was ten years younger than Bass and appeared younger still, with a sort of goofy-kid good looks and a mop of straw-colored hair that just naturally tended to make people like him. Especially women.

"You get mad at me if I leave the store."

"Fair enough," Bass said. "How about sending one of the clerks?"

"They say it's not their job."

Bass laughed. "Their job is to do what we pay them to do."

What I pay them to do, he thought. It wasn't as if Mortaugh Croom had a penny to his name. Ever had, or ever would.

Bass frowned as he shrugged out of his wolfskin coat. No call to go thinking that way, Bass, he told himself sternly. He's a good boy, your baby brother. He just… has problems looking out for himself. Just the way he's made, that's all.

As she lay on her deathbed, their mother had Bass swear to take care of his younger sibling, come what may, and he had done so. He'd always loved Morty.

Morty could make that difficult sometimes, admittedly.

"Where'd you run off to, anyway, Bass?" Morty asked. "You're always running off without telling me."

Bass was unstrapping the shoulder rig that held his blaster under his left armpit, counterbalanced by a case holding two 14-round double-stacked magazines of ammo on the right. He grunted in relief as it came away. He found a shoulder holster uncomfortable at the best of times; in summer heat, or even a room as well heated as his store was by a wood-burning stove in the corner, it made him sweat and chafed something fierce. Baron Billy didn't allow his citizens to carry weapons in the ville—one of the more major areas of disagreement between him and

Bass—and while he thought it was only proper a citizen as leading and important as Bass should enjoy the privilege of bearing arms, he still thought it was a bad example to do so openly.

Bass went behind the counter. He unhitched holster from harness, hung the one from a set of elk antlers mounted on the wall behind him, and slid the handblaster in its holster into a cubby underneath the spot on the counter where the abacus was. Should anyone have entered the store with evil intent and weapons to back it up, an ancient Winchester Model 1897 shotgun, lovingly maintained by Bass's personal sec chief, Dace Cable, hung on brackets behind the wooden counter.

In the nearly two decades Bass had run Menaville's general store it had come out only twice. The first time two chills had been carried out, the second time one. And in going on thirteen years no one had tried again.

The bloodstains could still be seen on the usually swept-clean floorboards, despite frequent attempts to sand them away. Still, even in a settled and respectable ville like Menaville, not many customers tended to be actively squeamish unless they were actively slipping in the fresh stuff, or breathing the reek of congealed blood rotting. Neither of which a man as particular as Bass would ever permit.

"Made my deal with Baron Billy," he said, shifting his weight with a sigh onto the high stool. His feet were more grateful for the break than he was happy with. "The baron's price was steep indeed. But almost to the grain of flour what I reckoned it would be."

Morty made a face. "Yeah. You always do well for yourself. But what about me?"

"Well…" Bass began, somewhat nonplussed. "We're good to go. No worries about Billy making trouble. I'll be happy to get back on the road again, mebbe work some of this flab off the frame that years of easy living has packed onto it."

He finished off slapping the belly that overhung his big belt buckle.

"Do we have to go running clear off across the country?" Morty asked. "We're comfortable here."

"Well, I tell you. I'm fixing to sell the store and what goods we can't take in the wag convoy to Baron Billy. Separate deal from the bribe I'm paying for him to let me walk away free and clear. But I tell you what—I could give you the store. Also free and clear. Then you could live out your days here in comfort as a respected and necessary member of the community."

He shook his head. "Truth to tell, the stickies're only likely to be a minor problem. Stick with basics, buy off the big caravans that come through at wholesale prices, you won't ever have to sweat 'em. And I doubt the stickies're going to get strong enough to make any real problem for the ville. Not in our lifetimes, anyway."

Morty lowered his head and glowered at him suspiciously through lank bangs. "You're just trying to get rid of me, Bastion," he said sullenly. "Go off and leave me behind."

"No, Morty," Bass said, shaking his head firmly. "You know I'd never do that. I love you. You're my brother, and I promised Maw I'd always look out for you. Just reckoned… being the only general storekeeper in a town as big and prosperous as Menaville would set up a man for life even without his having to bust his hump from dawn till dusk."

"You're not leaving me behind," Morty said.

Bass shrugged. "Then you're coming with me to the Northwest."

His sibling looked as if he had more to say on the subject. Before he could, the rear door to the sales floor pushed open. A skinny specimen in a heavily patched hunting jacket poked his head inside the store.

"Mr. Bass," the newcomer said. "Mr. Cable wants to talk to you, if you got a minute."

Bass grabbed his hat and crammed it on his head. "Coming, Dan."

The fact was, he wasn't disappointed to end this little chat with Morty.

DACE CABLE SLAPPED the cab of the big pickup truck.

"All ready to roll," he said. "Gonna be quite the parade there, Chief. A dozen wags. Couple light motorcycles for scouting work. And, uh, two mountain bikes."

The tall athletically built man with the shaved head, the ring in his ear, the trim blond goatee and the devil's grin sounded dubious about the last item.

Bass laughed and clapped his hard shoulder. "Those things'll be worth their weight in meds and more. Believe me. They can go places even the trail bikes can't. And sometimes it's good to be able to move places fast but quiet-like."

"If you say so," Cable said. He sounded doubtful still. But Bass was the boss, and his sec chief knew he was talking from trading convoy experience stretching back before Cable's own birth.

They stood in a huge predark prefab building in the big yard behind Bass's store. The yard occupied a major chunk of what was considered prize real estate in downtown Menaville. But Bass had staked it out when he'd moved here nigh unto two decades earlier. As the ville had grown, it had had to grow around the big yard, no matter how much others might complain and rival merchants might enviously eye all that space. Then again, Menaville was free to grow along its cozy wooded valley. For all his caprice and harsh ways, Baron Billy didn't believe in penning his subjects inside a razor-wire perimeter. Not like that triple bastard to the north.

And after all, the fact that Menaville grew at all, much less as strong and fast as it had, owed at least as much to Bastion Croom as it did to Billy Howe, and Baron Billy knew it.

"This is the pride of the fleet," Cable said, beaming up at the black Dodge Ram that was in fair condition. "That .50-caliber blaster will lay serious hurt on anything short of a tank that tries to mess with us."

Bass smiled. He preferred to settle things in a peaceful manner whenever possible. When it wasn't possible, he preferred to settle things decisively and in a hell of a hurry. It had cost him a mass of jack to buy and equip the vehicles for this convoy. And even more to equip the two blaster wags to escort them through the perils of the Deathlands.

The battered Browning M-2 heavy-barreled .50-caliber machine gun was mounted by a pintle to the top of a steel column, in turn fixed to a pedestal bolted firmly to the bed of the burly pickup truck. It could swivel to dispense its stream of thumb-size slugs in all directions. Those slugs were hard to come by, but enough trade goods could buy about anything.

Behind it, the more modest Toyota mounting a remade M-249 Squad Automatic Weapon seemed tiny and insignificant. While the lesser wag and weapon were more than capable of dealing rapid-fire death at decent range to most things that walked, or crawled, the .50 was Bass's potential ace in almost every hole.

Good thing Morty didn't take up my offer to stay behind and own the store, he thought. We'll need every scrap of jack and gram of trade goods we can muster to make it to the Promised Land, despite the supplies we're lugging along.

He did wonder, a little guiltily, if he had subconsciously manipulated his little brother into going along. Morty could be a handful—he had to admit that to himself—but Bass needed the trade value Billy would give him for the store, even at the rock-bottom price the baron knew he could get away with paying.

I did tell Maw I'd look out for him, Bass told himself.

Cable, who knew his boss had moments of silent introspection and knew to respect them, was engaged in a quiet conversation with one of his ten subordinate sec men. When he saw Bass lift his head and look around, returning visibly to the chilly here and now, he waved off his man and turned back to the merchant.

He led the way back through the structure, past the half dozen panel wags that carried the trade goods wherewith Bass intended to launch his new enterprise—his new life, for him and Morty and their loyal crew—in the Promised Land, including the one that carried most of their personal gear and road supplies—out the back door in the hardscrabble dirt yard proper.

The empty space, surrounded by work and storage sheds within a three-yard-high link fence screen with faded green-metal slats, remained big despite being dominated by the immense wag barn. It also served Menaville as caravan yard for visiting trade convoys. That was one way Billy had justified the way Bass locked up so much valuable land in the ville to the other influential men—because inevitably Bass wasn't the only other man or woman of influence in the town who *wasn't* Baron Billy. Billy liked that fact even less than how he had to accommodate his biggest potential rival in Bass, but he bowed to it. As he did to the need, at least occasionally, to explain himself to them.

It didn't sit well with Bass that Billy had stuck him with the monopoly privilege of serving the ville in that capacity. But of course Bass, too, had made his compromises in the partnership and reminded himself, as he did many times, that a baron could be way worse than Billy Howe.

One wag was parked out back. The impressive number of tarps that protected if from the unkind Ouachitas winter had been pulled off to reveal a battered school bus, more visibly ancient even than most motor wags. Its paint was many colors, but faded to pastel ghosts and grays and dirty white. Someone had refreshed the scrawl "The Magic Bus" on the side. Apparently it had been named for the predark folk song long and long ago. Otherwise Bass hadn't been able to see his way clear to shelling out to repaint it, much as he preferred everything in his control to look as sharp and squared-away as possible.

The costs of this expedition, notwithstanding that it was the main thing he had built and saved for throughout his long and fruitful career, imposed their own stern limits on possibility.

"You sure about this, boss?" Cable asked. "Putting all our eggs in one basket, like. Might not be our best tactic."

"Objection noted," Bass said. He didn't bother trying to stifle a smile at how his sec chief had reminded him in an almost-subtle way that tactics were what Bass paid Cable to know about and handle. Twenty years on hard trade roads had taught Bass Croom more than a thing or two about tactics.

"We should be fine with the off-duty sec and other crew riding in there," he said.

Cable's wide shoulders heaved in a sigh.

"You still look troubled," his boss said, though he knew why.

"Yeah," Cable said with a characteristic dip and turn

of his head. "And you know why. You know what *really* worries me, Chief."

"Yes," Bass said, letting off a sigh of his own. "I do. And it concerns me, too."

"We got a good crew of sec," Cable said. "None better. They can handle themselves in any tight place, and know their way around a blaster.

"But there aren't enough of them. Not for a trip this long nor a convoy a dozen strong. And there's nobody else within a good day's drive of the ville I'd trust across the street. Much less across the entire continent."

"Me neither," Bass agreed.

He laid a big hand on Cable's shoulder.

"But we'll find a way, Dace," he said. "There's *always* a way, and we're just the men to find it!"

Chapter Five

"Stickies from trees," Jak muttered. "How know?"

Even as the horrid muties were dropping from the trees around them on the narrow trail by a stream running through the Ouachitas, Mildred had time to marvel that Jak had actually uttered a preposition. Normally he hoarded words like a miser.

But that doubtless had to do with his distress that his usually infallible scouting had failed to alert his friends to the deadly ambush they'd just sprung.

With a savage buttstroke from his Scout longblaster Ryan knocked a stickie sprawling into some scrub oak by the trail. Mildred had an impression that the dozens of muties hemming them in like hairless mottled-green monkeys were small, none taller than four feet high, but otherwise characteristic of their breed.

She recoiled, grabbing for her ZKR revolver holstered at her hip, as a stickie made a clumsy swipe at her face with its suckered hand. Her skin crawled. She knew the adhesive goo the pads that tipped the spatulate fingers secreted, which gave the monsters their name, could clamp to the skin and tear it clean off the bone. A rope of mucus-thickened yellow saliva trailed from its gaping mouth.

Noise exploded from just behind Mildred's left ear. Hot air slapped the back of her head. The stickie's left eye exploded in a spray of black fluids and gunk. It reeled back squealing.

"Thanks, Krysty!" she shouted without even glancing back, a potential lethal move with an opponent still on its feet in front of her: stickies took a lot of killing. She didn't need to look anyway. A well-trained and experienced shot long before she entered cold-sleep—she had won silver in free shooting for the last ever U.S. Olympic team in 1996—she recognized the sound of her flame-haired friend's piece. Though it fired the same .38 Special round as her own ZKR 551, Krysty's Smith & Wesson 640 made a far louder sound, thanks to its short barrel.

She got the ZKR out. Straightening her right arm, she triggered another shot with the muzzle about two inches from the stickie's face. More black stuff splashed back. The stickie went over backward to fall in the trickle of icy water over rocks and lie thrashing and moaning.

Other shots crashed out around and behind her. Ricky had been bringing up the rear of the single-file procession, right behind J.B., who in turn followed Mildred. He was shooting his big Webley handblaster. She also caught the boom of Doc's stub shotgun barrel slung beneath the main barrel of his replica LeMat revolver, and the crack-of-doom explosion of Jak's Python.

"Gren duel!" she heard Ryan roar. "Everybody down!"

In normal circumstances Mildred was by far the most inclined to question their nominal leader, and give him backchat. Now she flopped straight on her belly on last fall's oak leaves.

The fragmentation grenades cracking around her were like lightning repeatedly blasting the trees nearby. Mildred had her face pressed to the ground and her arms crossed tightly in front of her head, as Ryan had drilled them time and again. She shuddered in violent reaction to noise and terror even before she felt something pluck at her pack like invisible fingers.

A gren duel was a bad idea, except when the alternative was immediate, horrible death. Such as when man- and woman-eating stickies inexplicably started dropping out of bare trees and popping out of the brush on all sides.

Such as now.

The thing was, a gren going off on the ground naturally tended to throw its blast and dangerous fragments away from the ground—up and out in a kind of fan, which was the basic heart of the so-called gren duel. If a person laid on the ground and kept his or her face covered everything should be all right.

Should be. The other thing was, explosions were tricky things, as J.B. liked to say, and gren blasts no more than any other. So *should be* all right was not near the same as saying you *would* be, when the little portable bombs started blowing off a few feet from the top of a person's head.

Though she felt the insides of her thighs trembling, Mildred felt herself still intact. Through the ringing in her ears she heard awful squalling. Worse than stickies usually sounded, which took some doing, and indicated the gren blasts had cut down some of their terrible attackers. More to the point she heard no distinctive human cries of pain, which meant her friends were mostly intact.

Or chilled.

Before her mind could stray far down that path she made out Ryan's voice, his bull-bellow hardly more than a distant mutter over the blast-induced tinnitus. "Throw the rest! Smoke 'em if you got 'em! Now!"

Mildred's lips compressed back from the fear-rictus the horrible noise and shock waves washing over her had stretched her face into. Those grens were their big strike; they were hoping to parlay them into a major score in Menaville, a few klicks down the trail through the winter- bare Ouachita Range.

But she knew corpses had little use for jack, or any other earthly rewards. After the deal with Baron Doyle caught the last train to the coast, along with Baron Doyle, Ryan and J.B. had broken the grens out of their metal box and split them up among everybody, to distribute the load.

Now Mildred fumbled at the buttoned canvas pouch on her belt that held the pair of grens she carried. Though she had worn it around on her hip it had naturally managed to work its way around to the front of her body, so that she had thrown herself right on top of it. In the heat of the moment she hadn't noticed. Now, though, she managed a wince at the thought of the deep bruise it had to have given her.

Unless the weather was freeze-your-fingers-off cold, the group tended not to wear gloves. Mildred had on fingerless gloves, which left her fingers cold and not as flexible as she liked. But then again she wasn't performing surgery. By touch—she didn't dare lift her face or open her eyes, and told herself it was for fear of the next barrage of grens— she got out the two cold, hard metal spheres. Yanking the pins, she threw both bombs in front of her, from each hand, all without lifting her face from the cold ground.

Her left hand brushed something that felt like a sapling with rubber bark. There was only one thing that could be: the leg of a stickie, standing almost over her. She tanked her hand back as if the rubbery mutant skin were white hot.

Her grens went off with a thunderous roar that drowned out the voices of the others. Mildred felt hot breath wash over her. Small particles stung her hands and peppered the arms of her heavy jacket like small shot.

Then something solid landed across both legs, then twitched.

Mildred screamed out loud. She couldn't help it.

She heard Ryan shouting, "Up and get 'em!" Then a

strong hand gripped her left wrist and peeled it away from the top of her skull.

In sheer panic reflex she batted at the hand. "Easy, girl," she heard J.B. grunt. "Gotta get up, now."

At last she raised her head and opened her eyes. Somewhere a few feet away something was flopping like a carp on a bank. She refused to focus on it.

J.B. was straightening his legs from a squat. In effect he dead-lifted Mildred to her feet, then fired his M-4000 scattergun.

As Mildred stood, the object that had landed on her rolled down the backs of her legs. Though they were still under attack, she couldn't help a glance down.

She wished she hadn't. Hard behind her boot heels lay a stickie leg severed right below the knee. The long, splayed toes were still clasping and unclasping like fingers. Yellow goo oozed from the torn-off end.

The M-4000 shotgun roared again. Mildred found her revolver in her hand. Combat reflexes had taken over, with her conscious mind somewhat checked out of the situation.

A freshly decapitated stickie lay on its back right across the body of the one she'd seen flopping near her. It was flopping still, but more weakly, as its lifeblood pulsed out the stump of its leg where Mildred's gren had severed it.

There were plenty of other stickies in view. None was on its feet. They took a mess of killing. These had been killed a mess.

And messily.

"Everybody fit to fight?" Ryan called. His voice was hoarse, as if he'd been breathing forest-fire smoke.

One by one the acknowledgments came back as Mildred looked around to check on her companions. In control of her wits once more, she was now focused on the task she'd trained for: saving lives and healing.

Her friends all claimed to be in good shape. As Ryan barked out orders to J.B., Krysty and Ricky to stand watch against another onslaught of the vicious muties, she gave J.B. a quick onceover.

He grinned at her. His glasses were perched on the narrow bridge of his nose, and his fedora was clamped on his head, albeit it at a bit of an angle.

"I'm fine," he said. "Bastard stickies got the worse end of that debate."

She knew he was as stoic as a terrier. Had that been *his* leg blown off, the good Lord forbid, he'd have been standing on one leg blasting away with his shotgun until he bled out. But his jacket and khaki pants didn't show any holes that she could see. She quickly shed her pack and examined the others.

Jak had blood in his long, tangled white hair. He tried to wave her off, but she glared at him. He held still momentarily until she confirmed he had a nasty-looking but superficial frag wound on his scalp.

"Come back when you're done, young man," she instructed. "I'll get that cleaned up."

Jak grunted, but he nodded. The albino teen was helping Ryan and Doc, the three making sure all the downed stickies stayed down. Meanwhile Mildred gave quick examinations to the rest. She doctored up a few cuts and scrapes, but to her relief nobody was seriously injured.

Indeed the worst casualty was her own pack, whose outer pocket had been ripped wide open by high-speed shrapnel.

"Do you know," Doc called, "these are quite unlike any stickies I have ever seen."

Leaving her torn pack, Mildred straightened. For the first time she really looked at the fallen muties.

"They're an odd color, to start with," Krysty said.

In fact they weren't any one color. Rather their lean bodies and misshapen faces were mottled and streaked in gray, brown and white.

"They've adapted to the environment?" Mildred asked incredulously.

"It stands to reason they might develop protective coloration, living out in these wooded hills for a few generations," Krysty stated.

"By the Three Kennedys!" Doc exclaimed. He had been squatting like a curious stork next to a prone stickie. Now he straightened, waving a handkerchief-wrapped finger that was smudged with brown and light gray. "They have done more than changed the color of their hides. The blighters have camouflaged themselves."

Ryan stepped forward to frown at the handkerchief. "Smeared themselves all over with bird crap and, uh, some kind of animal shit. Mebbe human."

"I wondered why Jak didn't spot them," Krysty said, peering up at the tree branches that stretched like weird fractal claws above the trail from both sides.

"None of us did," J.B. said. "They musta stayed close to the bigger branches. Did a bastard good job at camou, I got to admit."

Mildred shook her head. It was just like J.B. to admire good workmanship. Even in savage muties who moments before had been lusting to tear him apart and feed on his guts.

He paused a moment to drop a reassuring hand on Ricky's shoulder. The boy stood slumped, with his Webley Mk VI revolver in one hand and his DeLisle longblaster in the other. The carbine's muzzle, fattened by the built-in suppressor, was angled well clear of the ground. No degree of shock or after-battle letdown was going to induce Ricky to handle a tool badly, especially not a blaster.

There were reasons why the Puerto Rican orphan and J.B. got on like oil and steel. They were both gadget freaks and gun lovers.

"Remember these things're basically like wild animals, 'cept smarter than most," J.B. told his protégé. "Not like where you come from, where most of them are just folks."

Ricky nodded. He was softhearted, maybe even moreso than Mildred, with her literally otherworldly sensibilities. And while Puerto Rico was known to some as Monster Island because it teemed with dangerous, mutated animals, perhaps a bigger reason was that humanoid muties and norms lived together without any particular friction, as if that was the natural order of things.

Mildred wouldn't have believed it if she hadn't seen it herself. She had conversed with stickie farmers during the group's none-so-restful adventure on Monster Island, and the only problems encountered were posed by their indifferent English and her worse Spanish.

That unparalleled amity didn't mean Monster Island was a peaceful place, though. Muties acted like regular folk, and regular folk regularly chilled each other.

"Back up off yourself, Jak," Ryan said to the albino, who was staring at the fallen muties. "We didn't expect to find camouflaged muties out here in the woods."

He stuck his befouled panga at the ground until he found a soft enough spot to plunge the blade into. When it came out the soil's embrace had cleaned away most of the stickie juices. A crackling handful of scrub oak leaves served to get the heavy, broad blade the rest of the way clean. Ryan examined it, then nodded in satisfaction and stuck it back in its sheath.

"Fact is we were all triple-stupe," he said. "We were heading along the trail and committed the oldest stunt on the book."

J.B. snorted. "Forgot to look up. Me as bad as anybody. Trader would've handed my ass to me for that."

"He would at that," Ryan said. "These fire-blasted stickies came within a heartbeat of doing the job for him."

"L-lucky we had those grens," Ricky said. His depression apparently had given way to a delayed bout of terror, as the reality of what they had just escaped and how narrowly they had escaped it landed on him like a ton of cold pig guts.

"Yeah," Mildred couldn't help saying sourly. "And there went our tickets to easy street."

"Spilled blood won't go back in the body, Mildred," J.B. said mildly. "You know that."

She grunted at his way of saying "no sense crying over spilled milk."

"Anybody got any grens left?" Ryan asked.

"No, Ryan," Doc sang out. The others echoed him.

"Good," he said. "I'd be hotter than nuke red at anybody stupe enough to hold back when our asses were hanging over the edge like that."

He stooped, shouldered his pack and hefted his Scout longblaster.

"Time to march. Daylight's bleeding, and we don't know if there're more stickies where these bastards came from.

"And this time, everybody remember to watch the nuking trees."

Chapter Six

"Boss," a youthful female voice called, "company coming. New bunch of strangers just hit town."

With a sigh Bass Croom straightened from bending over the open engine compartment of Cargo Wag *3, into which he'd just helped Dan Hogue and his grease monkeys lower the just-repaired engine.

"What's up, Shanda?" he asked, grabbing a rag from the top of a rolling tool chest nearby and wiping at the grease that liberally coated both hands.

Shanda Peters was one of his clerks, a short, somewhat stocky young woman who wore an apron over her coveralls and red plaid flannel shirt. She had short sandy hair and an indefatigably cheerful manner, was honest and always worked hard.

If only I could say that about everybody who worked for me... Bass cut the thought off in midstream.

"Why did you think I needed to hear it?"

"Well, Eddie Roybal just came running in with his cheeks all red. Said these seven coldhearts had come into town from the hills and were asking for work. Old Lady Dunham took one look at all the blasters they were toting and sent them straight this way. Eddie overheard and came running here as fast as his eight-year-old legs could carry him."

Bass chuckled. "See that he gets his pick of candies as a reward." As a matter of policy, Bass tried to stay on good terms with the ville's kids. Aside from being plain good business—and in line with his good nature—it sometimes paid dividends. Friendly children provided the merchant his very own intelligence service, right under Baron Billy's pointed nose. And he doubted that either Billy Howe or his own sec boss, Morson, had any clue of its existence, for all that very little escaped the baron's icy-blue gaze.

"Already taken care of, boss."

Bass gave her a big grin and a nod as he headed toward the open door to the back storeroom.

"Good job, Shanda."

"Eddie says Morson's got some of his snitches bird-dogging them," Shanda said as he passed.

"That's their job, I guess," Bass said. "Not like it's any secret what I'm hiring blasters for. Come to think of it, I'd just as soon Billy keep all the eyes he wants on the process. Don't want him getting the notion there's anything underhanded in my intention to hire more heavily armed types. Mebbe especially at this late date."

In the gloom of the storeroom a worried-looking Morty met him.

"We have a problem, Bass," he said. "We just had a whole pack of coldhearts come into the store."

"Reckon their money's as good as anyone else's." Bass didn't bother reminding his little brother that armed strangers came into the store all the time.

If they weren't armed they tended not to make it this far, especially with the triple-damned stickies getting so close and bold these days. If they stayed any length of time, they'd have to give up their blasters.

"But they're probably gonna stuff their pockets with goods and only offer to chill us if we call them on it!"

"Then why aren't you out front keeping an eye on them?"

Morty just shook his head and made an exasperated sound. Bass knew it well: as if he was the biggest stupe ever born for even suggesting such a thing.

Breathing deeply and reminding himself to be patient, he pushed on into the store.

It was a testimony to just how hard a set of hard cases his visitors were, that what might well have been the most beautiful woman he'd ever laid eyes on in his entire life was the second thing he noticed.

The first was the man who stood calmly on the far side of the counter beside the door. He had the pale eye and lean build of a gray Plains wolf in a long black coat. He wore his hair in an unruly black shag and had a patch over his left eye. An old scar ran top to bottom beneath it. He wore a well-filled backpack. The butt of a slung long-blaster stuck up above it on the right side.

The woman beside him was spectacular, flame-haired, emerald-eyed, damned near as tall as the man. Behind her right shoulder stood a shorter, broader black woman with beaded plaits. She looked older than the other but wasn't half bad-looking. Had a nice rack, anyway, Bass noted.

To the tall man's other side stood a like banty cock of a man in a fedora and battered brown leather jacket. He wore round steel-rimmed specs and a mild expression, which fooled Bass Croom not at all—nor likely would've if it hadn't been for the shotgun butt sticking up above his own right shoulder, or the Uzi strapped to the left side of his pack.

A bit behind him a gangly wrinklie with a long frock coat stood blinking, and leaning on an ebony cane. A couple kids—young men, anyway—wandered the aisle behind, gaping at the goods on the shelves. One of them was an albino, with ruby eyes and long white hair hanging to the shoulders of his camouflage jacket with jagged-looking bits of glass and metal glittering on it. He was just a wisp, looking as if a good puff would blow him off his feet.

Standing at his side was a Mex-looking kid, only a little taller than the albino and if anything younger, with a round olive face, black bangs and lively dark eyes.

"Gentlemen," Bass said. "Ladies."

"You Sebastian Croom?" the one-eyed man asked.

"Bastion Croom. Yes. How may I help you folks?"

"My name's Ryan Cawdor." He introduced the rest by name, which Bass filed away. He was good at names, especially when they went with such a memorable set of faces.

"We hear you're hiring," Ryan finished. "We're looking for work."

Bass cocked a brow. This Cawdor hadn't bothered saying we're new in town, suggesting he gave the merchant credit for being bright enough to know that himself, and had a distaste for wasting words. Bass liked talking plenty, and listening, too. Still, verbal frugality was a trait he could respect in others.

"What sort of work you looking for?" Bass asked.

The little guy took off his glasses and polished them with a hankie from his pocket. "We look like store clerks, Mr. Croom?"

Croom laughed. "No, Mr. Dix. That you do not."

He laid both his palms down on the cool glass top of the counter. "Happens I'm hiring blasters, which I gather you know already."

"Were those your people trying to shadow us?" Ryan asked.

"No. Baron Billy's…sec assets, let's say."

"Snitches," the black woman, Mildred, said. Bass found no reason to differ.

"Good," J.B. said "Clumsy bunch. Not looking forward to the prospect of having to count on them in a tight place."

"Small chance of that," Bass said. "What I'm looking for is trade convoy sec. I'm pulling up stakes and leaving this ville."

"Headed where?" Ryan asked.

"Cific Northwest."

"Ambitious," Ryan replied.

"You seem none too taken aback at the prospect of riding sec for a convoy across two-thirds of the whole North American continent."

The redhead showed him a smile as dazzling and melting as he expected it would be. "We've made a few trips like that ourselves," she said. "Both ways."

"Huh. Well, good. Got any convoy security experience?"

"More than a little," Ryan said. "J.B. and I rolled with the man called Trader, back in the day. And we've rode sec on convoys since."

"Seriously? A genuine Deathlands legend! Dealt with him myself, twice. Long ago. He got the better of both deals, but I can't say unfairly so. Haven't heard a peep about him for years."

"He doesn't roll any more," Ryan said.

He seemed to have said what he intended to on the subject. Bass respected that, too.

"Bass," Morty said from behind him, "you haven't sent them away yet?"

DESPITE HIS CUSTOMARY iron self-control, Ryan felt his jaw and brows set a notch tighter. The little pissant with the lank dirty-blond hair and the apron who'd given them the stink-eye when they came in had reappeared. And from the familiar way in which he whined at the master merchant, he had some connection to their prospective boss beyond that of another employee.

The man himself didn't stop his big face from fisting briefly in annoyance behind his salt-and-pepper beard and brows, but he pulled his features mostly out of the expression as he turned.

"Morty," he said, "come meet my new friends here. I think I might very well hire them to fill out our sec complement."

"They look unreliable," Morty said. "Like coldhearts."

"And that," Bass said, "is exactly why I mean to hire them!"

He laughed. It was a hearty laugh, which sounded unaffected. Ryan approved. While he wasn't a man to give free vent to his feelings, he thought to read it as a sign of strength in the trader. Croom clearly didn't fear to show his emotions to others.

At least, not unless it served him to hide them. Ryan hadn't ridden with Trader—*the* Trader—nearly as long as his friend J.B. had. But more than long enough to know that nobody enjoyed the kind of success Bass Croom showed all around him, in the well-kept, well-stocked store and the size of the fenced lot behind, without being skilled at playing things close to his powerful chest.

The gut hanging below that chest suggested the merchant didn't miss many meals, which itself told a passel in the Deathlands.

Ryan wasn't the kind of person who thought too harshly of a person for letting himself go a bit. Croom still obviously packed more than a little muscle behind the flab. The hardwood grips of the handblaster he wore in a shoulder holster beneath his left armpit were well worn. Sure, middle age and years of ease had softened him up—his outlines, anyway. But his face hadn't got that weatherbeaten—nor his knuckles that scarred, nor his wrists so thick—by spending his whole life behind a counter. The man had been well-hammered by this hard old world.

And by the looks of things, he'd done his share of hammering it back.

The oil smudge on one cheek and the stains on the olive-drab T-shirt that was all he wore above the belt despite the day's early spring chill made clear he had no fear of getting his hands dirty. Likely had some idea how to use them, too. Both counted as pluses in Ryan's book.

"May I introduce my younger brother, Mortaugh Croom?" he said. "You'll pardon him for his hasty judgment, I trust. He's not led quite so active a life as I have. He has the finer sensibilities of a civilized man who grew up in a well-ordered ville. So he has a reflexive mistrust of coldhearts, and who can blame him?"

"And you don't?" Mildred asked in a voice that suggested that she could.

Ryan reckoned being called coldheart irritated her. She was funny that way, sometimes. Touchy.

Bass shook his head. "I've knocked around a little myself, and I know well that the sort of men, and women, who are going to be of use for the job I need done are going to be pretty rad-blasted case-hardened. Even if they don't all look it—like the professor, there. And the charming ladies."

Mildred still looked mulish, but she murmured, "Flattery will get you everywhere."

Morty Croom looked unconvinced. Ryan reckoned he had his measure now: the sheltered younger sibling, spoiled by an older brother who likely raised him in place of dead parents. There were other explanations, but these were the Deathlands, and dead was a good default. The kid was good-looking, in a ville-rat sort of way. If he wasn't a total stupe he might be able to be charming, when he wasn't sniveling to his big brother, which might make him dangerous.

Ryan glanced at J.B. Placing his glasses back on his nose, J.B. gave his head a slight dip to the side. Ryan read that as a shrug.

Which in turn read as, *We've had worse gigs.*

Ryan nodded back slightly. If he had Croom sized up correctly, the man would be one of their better bosses, all found. And if the task he had in mind, shepherding a flock of temperamental, fuel-hogging power wags clean across the Deathlands' savage heart to the coast, was entirely crazy, well, Ryan and his friends had done crazier.

Another man came in from the back room, so fast and purposeful that he brought a waft of chill air from a back door that hadn't yet fully closed behind him. This man was built along the lines of Ryan himself, with a shaved head, a gold ring in an earlobe and a close-cropped blond beard. From the black T-shirt, the lean muscles and flat stomach packed into it, and the obvious military-issue 9 mm Beretta M-9 handblaster in a holster slung down his right thigh, he was a sec man. Sec *boss,* from the way he carried himself.

He stopped just inside the door when he saw their visitors. His lean features hardened.

"Heard you had visitors, boss," he told Bass. "Came as fast as I could."

The fact he hadn't got the word first, and scoped out the visitors first, clearly bugged him. But Bass waved the apology away.

"This is Dace Cable," he said. "My head of sec. Dace, meet Ryan Cawdor and his crew. I think they'll be joining us on our trip."

"Working for me, huh?" Cable gave Ryan a hard gaze with his green eyes. Ryan met his gaze calmly.

Cable looked away first.

"That's not quite how we work, Mr. Croom."

It was Krysty who spoke up. As a general rule Ryan spoke for the group, but as always, the rest were free to take the lead when they had the best applicable skill. And Ryan knew full well Krysty was far better at handling sensitive masculine egos than he could ever be.

She handles mine triple well, he thought with amused affection.

Cable's face predictably got even harder, and he started to swell up—as Mildred would put it, "like a stepped-on toad." But Bass merely looked a bland question at the redhead.

"We're independent contractors," Krysty said. "We will happily work *with* Mr. Cable and his sec team. We answer to you."

"Listen here—" Cable began.

Bass laughed. "Ease off the trigger, there, Dace," he said. "I hear what the lovely lady's saying. You and your crew are ace at your jobs. You've done me well in some triple-tight spots. And none of you has just the experience we need for the trip we're going to take. These people have run the transcontinental roads before."

"They claim that," Cable said.

"And I believe them, Dace. Remember, I've got more time on the road under this too big belt of mine than any of your people. I know what it takes to survive out there. And I know the look of those who have. So I need to ask you to trust me on this call."

Cable nodded with no more show of reluctance. Ryan let a brow raise slightly in appreciation at the neat way Croom had managed to rein in his guard dog—without cutting his nuts off in front of strangers, and potential rivals.

If he's as straight as he seems, Ryan determined, he'll

be one of the best we've ever worked for. If he's a snake inside, he'll be one of the deadliest.

He looked at Krysty, who smiled encouragingly at him.

Ryan had an ability to read her. That smile wasn't without a shadow of doubt. She sensed something deep inside Croom that troubled her.

But Ryan didn't know of one single person alive—except perhaps somebody as young and cherry as Ricky Morales—who didn't have some deep, dark secret. Least of all Ryan Cawdor.

"This chain of command thing, though—" Cable said.

Bass nodded. "Understood. Think of these folks as specialists we've hired to work with you. They've expressed a willingness to work with you and our people. I'm sure they'll prove most cooperative."

"We'll all be on the same side out there," Ryan said.

"True," Cable agreed. He stepped up to Ryan and stuck out his hand. The one-eyed man took it.

He tried the hand-crushing game. Ryan had hoped for more from the man, but he'd expected this. He had no doubt Cable was more than good at his job, or he wouldn't be working for a man as shrewd as Croom. But once a sec man, always a sec man.

Ryan knew a dozen ways, top of the head, to deal with the hand-crushing game, ranging from the discomforting to the crippling.

He needed none of them. He merely matched the sec boss, pressure for pressure, until the sec boss grinned in acknowledgment that this was a game he couldn't win. Nor did Ryan miss the way he swung his hand behind his hip to loosen it when they let go of each other.

"So," Croom said, with a lopsidedness to his grin that

suggested he knew perfectly well what had just taken place, "that's settled, then. All that remains to discuss are the terms."

Chapter Seven

"Those are pretty generous terms the big boss signed off on," Mildred said as the group stood in the warehouse being used as a fleet garage. She was relieved they'd dropped their packs by the door. Her shoulders still ached from toting the damn thing all over the Ouachitas. "Kind of surprisingly so."

"Mebbe too generous," J.B. said, rubbing his jaw. "I'm smart. Ryan's smarter. We learned more than a thing or two about negotiating from a master."

"Trader," Ryan said.

"The one and only. And one thing we learned was, as good as we were at dealing, we were gonna get outdrawn eleven times out of ten throwing down against a man like this Croom dude."

"What do you mean?" Ricky asked.

"That Mr. Croom is paying us better than we could normally hope for," Krysty said.

"If he plans to honor his compacts," Doc said.

"I believe he does," Krysty replied. Both Ryan and J.B. nodded. Mildred wasn't so sure, herself, but she had to admit the others knew way more than she did about commerce.

"So that means he's scared," J.B. told Ricky.

The kid's black eyes went big. "He's scared of what we're going to run into?"

"Don't worry, kid," Ryan said. "That just means he really knows what we're getting into out there."

"Oh." Ricky smiled. He hero-worshipped Ryan. The pack leader's calm assurance soothed his fears.

Momentarily. Then he clearly realized what Ryan had really said. Mildred couldn't suppress a snicker as his eyes turned to circles again, his jaw dropped and the olive color fell out of his cheeks.

"So I hear you're our new convoy sec," a young man said, walking up to them scrubbing his hands on a shop rag.

"That's right," Ryan said.

Mildred's first impression was that the newcomer looked like Jesus—or Charlie Manson. He was a little guy as well as long-haired and bearded, but he had an affable manner and lacked that crazy cult-leader gleam to the eye. Also, since they were clearly going to be working together, Mildred just naturally preferred to think of him as looking like Jesus.

"This is the fleet you're going to be escorting to the Northwest," the little dude said. "I'm Dan Hogue, and I'm the man in charge of keeping them running. Aren't they beauties?"

"Cool," Ricky said. He was standing next to Jak.

The albino had his arms folded over his chest and a disdainful look on his face. Nonetheless his new friend's unabashed admiration for machines seemed mainly to amuse him.

Then Mildred was struck at the sheer number of people running around inside the big structure. Most of them seemed to be doing…mechanicky type things. She didn't need to know anything about the specifics of what they were doing to realize, with no little trepidation, the scale of the enterprise she and her friends had got themselves involved in.

Has Ryan bitten off more than he can chew this time? she wondered.

"But how will you find the gas to run them?" Ricky asked.

"Don't always need gas," Dan said over his shoulder. He was already walking toward the wags at a bandy-legged roll. Obviously assuming the new crew would follow, which first Ricky and then J.B. did. Then the rest.

"See, I rebuilt the engines and rebored the carburetors so's they'll run on anything from high octane to pure alcohol. We can even run 'em on Towse Lightning, comes to a real pinch."

Mildred shuddered. "Glad *somebody* finally found a use for that stuff," she said.

"Plus we got a real live tanker full of gasoline. It's parked in the yard out back."

Ryan looked impressed, which in itself impressed Mildred. She knew that even for a prosperous—and obviously resourceful—trader-merchant like Croom to get his hands on either the fuel or a tanker was an incredible feat.

Not as if people're making either of those things these days, she thought.

Ryan did hang back when Dan bustled forward to show off the engine he'd just been bolting back in one of the wags. So did everyone but J.B. And Ricky.

"I wonder how far that lad's knowledge extends to motorized conveyances," said Doc. "He is not evinced much sign of interest in them before."

"He and J.B. are both completely gadget-mad," Krysty said with a smile. She herself was anything but, but she appreciated anything that gave pleasure to her friends.

Krysty had a generous heart. "Anyway, Ricky'd get interested in breeding slugs if J.B. did it."

"But not you, Ryan?" Doc asked.

Ryan shook his head. "I've seen an engine," he said.

"So what do you think?" Mildred asked Ryan. "Is our new employer nuts for thinking he can get his precious convoy all the way up to Oregon or Washington or wherever he's going?"

As she spoke Mildred was struck by the fact that Ryan had no more asked their exact destination than Croom had supplied it.

"Completely," Ryan said. He showed a slight grin. "But that doesn't make him much worse off than the rest of us."

"As you can see," the little wrench was saying, practically aglow with pride in the wan afternoon sun, "we even installed hardpoints up top of the fuel tanker. Since we know it's a primo target, and all."

Ryan and his friends had moved to the yard out behind the garage, which proved surprisingly spacious despite the storage and other buildings of less apparent purpose dotted around the perimeter, inside the fairly impressive fence.

"'Hardpoints,'" J.B. echoed. It wasn't exactly a question, then again, it wasn't exactly not one, either.

The tanker was utterly normal for the breed: a long low steel tube, ovoid in section, a wheeled trailer with a long-nosed Peterbilt tractor hitched to the front. It was bare metal, no longer shiny, but Ryan saw no obvious signs of rust, corrosion or even patching.

He also saw no sign of anything about it he'd describe as a hardpoint.

Dan laughed nervously. "Well, you're not gonna make a baby like this a war wag, no matter what. But we did set up a couple sandbag nests on top, front and rear, which'll provide some protection. Right?"

J.B. looked at him with something like pity. He took his hat off and scratched his head. Ryan said nothing at all.

He did hope that Dan knew more about wrenching than he did about battle.

"Moving on," Dan said, "we got our other big wag."

"A school bus?" Mildred said. "Seriously?"

The mechanic nodded.

"You got sandbags on top of it, too?" Mildred asked.

"He does," Krysty said.

Dan shrugged. "Mebbe they won't be necessary. Since the off-duty sec folks will be riding inside, along with some of Bass's and my assistants. And me sometimes, likely enough."

"You're coming with us?" Ryan said.

"Try to keep me from coming along! Anyway, how would you people ever get these things across a couple thousand miles of Deathlands without me along to keep 'em patched up and rolling?"

"I don't rightly see how we're gonna get them all that way, period," Ryan admitted. "But I take your point."

He was starting to wonder himself how he'd get this whole traveling circus across the continent. There were going to be a dozen wags in the convoy, minimum. That meant drivers as well as sec men and the wrenches Dan talked about bringing along. Just keeping them from wandering off to pee at night and getting eaten by muties was going to be a handful. To say nothing of keeping them all safe in the face of what were certain to be concerted efforts to wipe them out by wild animals, coldhearts, and the furies of Nature. And the problem of feeding them all....

"Sure glad logistics aren't our problem, huh?" said J.B.

Ryan grunted. "When rations start to run low, it's gonna become our problem in a nuke of a hurry."

J.B. shrugged, then tensed like a hunting dog spotting a pheasant.

"What're those wags there?" he asked Dan, peering the tail end of the well-used bus.

"Under the tarps? Well, yeah, I reckon you gents would be interested in those. Ladies, too, mebbe. We moved 'em out here this morning so's to have more room to work on the cargo trucks."

"What are they?" Ricky asked.

"Come look."

Dan rolled on to the second of the trucks parked nose-to-tail and started yanking at the tarps.

J.B. looked at Ryan and nodded. "That an M-249?" Ryan asked.

"Guess so."

"You guess so?" Ricky yelped.

Dan shrugged. "Well, you know. It's a blaster. They told me to mount it good and solid, so we did. Got a pillar bolted to the bed. Got it fixed to the pillar with a pintle setup. Should be able to shoot all around."

"You'll want to mount some kind of stop up front, if you haven't already," J.B. said. Like the mechanic, he was ignoring Ricky's look of openmouthed outrage at Dan's characterization of the 5.56 mm machine gun as "blaster." Especially since Ricky was probably familiar with the piece only through illustrations in old books or brittle magazines. "Stop your gunners from blasting your own cab by accident when things get interesting."

Dan's eyebrows crawled up toward the center part of his long brown hair. "You're right, man. Never thought of that."

"You do what you do. You know wags better than blasters, right? That's your job."

J.B. meant that at sincere praise, Ryan knew, and Dan took it as such. Ryan reckoned those two were going to get on ace in the line.

Himself and Cable, he wasn't so sure about.

"Thanks," Dan said with a big smile. "And since you seem to appreciate blasters as well as wags, you're really gonna love this other little gem. It impresses even me."

With a certain dramatic flair he whipped the tarps away from the lead wag.

"Whoa," Ricky breathed.

"I see what you mean," Ryan said.

"Ma Deuce," J.B. said with something akin to reverent joy. "Ryan, I'm starting to think we just might be able to pull this off after all."

"Gives us a leg up," Ryan admitted. "This boss of yours seems to have put a lot in building up for this little trip to the coast."

"Oh, yeah." Dan clambered over the side of the pickup bed to wipe some condensation from the boxy receiver of the heavy machine gun. "Worked for it for twenty years, I hear. Course, I ain't been with him half that long. But I seen it, too. Put everything he could squirrel away toward building up for the big day. And now I reckon it's about to come."

J.B. climbed in after him to examine the blaster. Given the joyful look on the Armorer's face, Ryan reckoned the piece met his approval, from a mechanical and weapon smithing point of view. While he knew a thing or two about blasters himself, Ryan was more than content to trust his friend's assessment. So he didn't climb up in the truck bed himself.

"What happening?" Jak asked.

Ryan turned to see the albino youth frowning toward the door that opened directly from the rear of Croom's store to the yard. A short-haired woman in an apron had come out and was talking to a couple of workers. By the way she waved her hands she was agitated.

"Trouble," Krysty said.

J.B. straightened from bending over the .50's receiver and turned, frowning.

At the same time Ryan felt a tingle creeping down his spine. Jak had a keen nose for danger.

"Gather up, people," Ryan rasped. "I think we're about to start earning our keep."

KRYSTY SENSED the tension as soon as they entered the shop from the storeroom.

She sized up the tableau they found in a glance. Bass stood behind the counter with Cable by his side, both tense and frowning. Confronting them across the glass-fronted case stood a man almost as tall as the merchant, and much rounder—seriously fat, not merely lugging a middle-aged paunch. He was dressed in fancy scavenged clothes, with a white shirt and a string tie and a little black hat. Two obvious sec men stood flanking him.

Monty Croom, slouched in front of the fat man in the dapper duds looking like nothing so much as a dog caught pooping on a rug.

"Kid works fast," she heard J.B. mutter behind her. "We met him here less than an hour ago, and now he's gone somewhere else and got his ass caught in a crack."

The four sec men gave hard eyes to the newcomers. The men were extra large, with necks wider than their mostly shaved heads. Krysty was glad neither Croom nor Cable's taste ran along those lines for their sec crew: they were well-muscled bullies, who'd eat like boar hogs and whose guts would turn to water when real, live stickies started dropping on them from the trees.

Their obese boss's little glittery dark eyes never flickered from Bass's face. Clearly he paid his bullies to deal with riffraff like Ryan Cawdor and his friends.

That thought put her at serious risk of laughing out loud.

"All right, Morgan," Bass said steadily. "I paid up the debts Morty ran up on your tables. That means we're square."

Morgan smiled beneath an oily-looking mustache. He looked at Krysty as if he had made careful study of villains in popular predark entertainment. Then went all out to emulate them.

"That's not the way I see it," he said. "I think you need to fork over a lot more."

"And how do you reckon that?"

"Easy, boss." That was Cable. "Morgan's got a big crew backing him, too. With us already lame ducks in Menaville, could be the balance of Baron Billy's favor has shifted."

Krysty felt surprise. That was a shrewder assessment of the situation than she'd expected from the goateed sec boss. Also, since he seemed to have a bit of insecure swagger about him, she hadn't expected him to advise caution. He apparently took his job seriously, meaning that he owed what he saw as the hard truth to his employer, no matter the cost to his pride.

"You got it, Earring Boy," Morgan said.

He turned to Croom. "You ain't the Big Fish in Menaville no more. You paid Baron Billy for his permission to leave. Now you're gonna pay me. Plenty."

"I don't think so."

That was Ryan, stepping forward around the counter.

"Who asked you, scumbag?" asked the goon to Morgan's right. He was dark, with a mustache even grander than his boss's, and more black stubble on his heavy cheeks than on his head.

Ryan ignored him. Planting himself firmly in front of the gambling-house owner, he said, "Mr. Croom paid you what you're owed. Leave, now."

That was Krysty's cue. She stepped up, grabbed Morty by the collar and yanked him bodily away from his captors. She passed the kid back to Mildred, who towed him behind the counter. It wasn't so much a matter of keeping him safe. It was about keeping him out of the way.

The richly dressed fat man had definitely noticed Ryan now. Fixing him with a red-eyed glare, he said, "Who the *fuck* do you think you're talking to, you scabby-assed, one-eyed cocksu—"

Ryan shot a straight right fist into the middle of the man's fat face.

Chapter Eight

Morgan's nose squashed like a boot-stomped tomato. It felt good beneath Ryan's fist. So did the hot blood squirting over it.

Plenty happened at once.

The Mex-looking coldheart turned, cocking a fist to blast Ryan, who was waiting for just that—he seemed the most self-aware of the quartet. He gave the man a swift shin in the crotch. The mustached and stubbled man bent over clutching himself and groaning.

The big lighter-skinned guy on Morgan's other side, who had tribal tattoos all swirled up the sides of his own shaved dome, closed quickly on Ryan from the right.

As the one-eyed man tried to turn in time to counter his charge, something zipped over his shoulder and hit Tattoo Head in the mouth. Something crunched, and the sec man sat as emphatically as his boss had.

Ryan stepped back, looking for other threats, and found Morgan's other two goons standing stock-still. One had the tip of Jak's big bowie-bladed fighting knife pressed hard into the crotch of his jeans, and Jak giving him a big, evil grin from the region of his breastbone.

The other was staring cross-eyed at Doc's LeMat handblaster, less than a foot from his much broken nose.

"You have a choice to make, my lad," Doc said. "Do you prefer a third eye? The top barrel will provide that. The lower one will perform a clean amputation of your entire head at this range. I am willing to accommodate you in either way."

The sec man held up his hands. Ryan saw the crotch of his jeans suddenly darken as his bladder let go in sheer panic.

The man who'd been punched by Ryan was outraged. "Bastard kid took my teeth!" he roared. He seemed to be foaming at the mouth, with weird pink froth covering his beard and dripping down the front of his black T-shirt.

Mildred hurried past Ryan and swung the steel-shod toe of her right combat boot into the rising sec man's already injured mouth. He fell, stunned, onto the floorboards.

"Looks like you lost more teeth there, bozo," she said, standing over his supine form. "If you want, I can borrow some pliers from the grease monkeys and extract the rest of them for you."

"I didn't know you were a dentist as well as a healer, my dear Mildred," Doc said.

She crossed her arms and leaned against his side, being careful not to disturb his outsize revolver's aim at the bridge of the sec man's nose.

"It's more like a hobby with me, Doc," she said.

Krysty had stepped up to stand to Ryan's right. The dark-skinned dude whose balls he'd kicked in suddenly started to straighten. His right arm came up, too—with a handblaster clutched in his fist.

As the blaster rose toward Ryan, Krysty moved like lightning. Her red hair contracting to a cap around her skull, she sidestepped left, reaching across her body to seize the man's gun wrist with her right hand. Pushing the muzzle toward the general store's ceiling, she twisted her hips clockwise. Her hand yanked the sec man's arm, locking the elbow, which she continued her powerful hip turn to break with a savage left forearm bar. The blaster bounced off the floor. The man joined it at once, crumpled and gobbling like a turkey in pain.

That was everybody. Mildred had drawn her Czech handblaster. J.B. had stepped up alongside Krysty with his scattergun leveled.

Ryan turned back toward Bass Croom. Cable stood protectively in front of him.

"Wanted to see what you people could do," the sec chief said with a taut grin. "Looks as if you know what you're doing."

Ryan frowned, but he couldn't call the man out over that. His job was to protect his boss at all costs; he'd done that by putting his body between the trader and harm. And he didn't owe Ryan and his bunch jackshit, as yet.

None of which meant it tasted good on Ryan's tongue. But there was no point in pissing and moaning about it, either. Things would shake into smooth working order between them and Cable's bunch. Or they wouldn't. Dealing with either eventuality was the job they'd signed on for.

He noticed that a heavy square glass jar lay on the floor near the man with the smashed-out teeth. Its lid had come off and it had spilled white powder onto the planks.

"Who threw that, anyway?" Ryan said. "That was pretty good work. Also, good aim."

Bass Croom had recovered his good nature. He hadn't made a move during the brief scuffle, either. Then again that wasn't his job. Ryan still didn't much doubt the big merchant could handle himself in a scrape if he had to.

He showed Ryan a big white-toothed grin and clapped Ricky Morales on the shoulder. "Your boy here did that. I thought he was just a tag-along, but he showed me he pulls his weight."

Bass nodded. "I think you'll do. Dace?"

Cable nodded, but his eyes were hard on Ryan's face.

Morgan sat on his broad butt staring in sheer terror at the carnage around him.

"Listen up and listen close," Ryan told him. "Gather up your friends and leave. Now. Be glad you and they can.

"And if you think to round up more of your gaudy bouncers and try your luck again, we'll just chill them all, shoot you in the belly, set fire to your gaudy house and toss your carcass inside. This will happen. So if you want more, you'd best just step up now and face me man to man. Dying'll hurt less that way, and waste less of our time."

"I—"

Bass stepped past Ryan to extend a hand to his fallen rival. Morgan glared at it a furious heartbeat, then he wised up and took it.

The merchant hauled his bulk back upright with barely a huff of effort.

"You should hear the man, Morgan," he said. "He means it. And I think you know he and his crew can back it up. And my bunch will help.

"You got the money Morty owed you. And we'll be gone from here tomorrow morning. So you'll pretty much have the ville to yourself. You and Baron Billy, that is. So do us all a favor and head on back to the Busted Flush, now."

Morgan did that. His two injured goons supported each other. The ones who had given up without needing have anything broken took up position on either side of their master, tight jawed and narrow-eyed. They group marched right out the door into the afternoon light. Or stumbled, as the case may be.

"What is that stuff in that jar, anyway?" J.B. asked, lowering his shotgun as the door closed behind the busted-up sec men.

"Baking powder," Bass said.

Most of the companions laughed at that, but Ryan looked their new employer square in the eye.

"We roll tomorrow morning?" he asked. "That's your plan."

Bass smiled. "It is now."

"So who'd be stupid enough to ride on top of a big old rolling firebomb?" Mildred asked.

Ryan glanced at her. She stood in the yard beside the fuel tanker, squinting up through bright morning sunlight at the sandbag nests atop it without evident favor.

The one-eyed man stepped up beside her. "That would be me," he said, deadpan.

She turned him a look of wide-eyed amazement. "You've got to be joking!"

"How often does Ryan kid about that kind of thing, Mildred?" J.B. asked. "Besides, the 'bomb' part is the least of his worries. If anybody cares to take us on, one of their first objectives is gonna be the gas that puppy's carrying."

"If the stickies pull their drop-down-from-the-branches stunt on the convoy," Ryan said, "I want to be one of the first to welcome the bastards."

"You're still spouting that tree-climbing stickie crap?" Cable whinnied a laugh through his thin nose. Ryan reflected that it had apparently never been broken.

Yet.

"Listen, man," the sec boss said, swaggering close. "You got the job. You don't have to go on with all the Deathlands tall tales. Stickies in trees? Wearing camou, were they?"

Ryan said nothing. He only turned and climbed up the steel handholds to the top of the tanker. He carried a light detachable bag on his back with extra ammo magazines for his weapons, and several full canteens.

Along the top of the tank ran a flat walkway. The sandbagged "hardpoints" were near the front and rear. They didn't look any harder up here than they sounded on the ground.

Ryan went to the rear nest and deposited his bag. Then, unslinging his Steyr Scout longblaster, he stood. He wasn't concerned. As J.B. had pointed out, nobody was likely to shoot at the major prize of the whole rad-blasted convoy.

And the first enemy they were liable to face didn't use blasters.

He grinned into the early morning breeze that blew un-impeded across the top of the fence. Stickies don't have blasters yet, he told himself. They didn't used to climb trees or camouflage themselves, either.

"Hello!" he heard a voice call.

Despite the grumble of engines as the last of the cargo wags pulled into the open yard, the call was audible. It came in a female voice, high but not shrill, as crisp as a bell ringing.

He looked toward the rear of the shop. A figure had stepped out the door that led directly to the yard. It was tall and slim. The brown jacket, trousers and boots did nothing to conceal that it was feminine, albeit on the slim side.

"What can we do for you, Miss?" Bass asked, striding across the lot toward her. He wore his usual wolfskin coat and dark brown hat. It seemed that even though he was just about to relinquish his role as general-store owner for Menaville forever, he found it hard to break the habits involved.

The newcomer came to meet him halfway. She moved with brisk, long-legged strides, and a grace that made Ryan's eyebrows raise. She carried herself like a trained fighter.

The pack on her back was surprisingly small. She was clearly accustomed to packing light. Although there was nothing light about the black single-action revolver in a well-weathered cross-draw holster in front of her left hip.

"Are you Mr. Croom?" she asked, meeting the merchant right beside the tanker. She stuck out a gloved hand. "My name is Olympia. I want to buy passage with your convoy."

Bass enfolded her hand in both his own, which were made even larger by his gloves. Her hand seemed slight in comparison to the merchant's huge paws. Yet the woman herself seemed not at all overmatched by either the merchant's bulk or presence. For one thing, she stood almost as tall as he did.

"Please to meet you, Miss Olympia," he said. "And I'm afraid that's not going to work out. This isn't really a passenger run."

"I can pay."

"You look like you can handle yourself," Bass said. "But this isn't going to be a solo trip through the mountains, risky as that is for a person such as yourself. We'll be crossing the whole of the deepest, most dangerous Deathlands. And a convoy like this is going to attract trouble like a jam sandwich attracts flies."

"I'm traveling to the Pacific Northwest," she said, using the less common ancient term for the great Western ocean. "I understand what you say, Mr. Croom, but risks aside, I'd rather ride than walk."

From where he sat on the top of the tanker, Ryan saw that quite a crowd was beginning to gather. Cable had joined his boss. Morty had turned up, too, openly ogling the woman in the uniformlike clothes. Ricky and Jak and materialized, as well.

Bass shook his head. "I'm sorry, Miss. It would be irresponsible to subject a passenger to the sort of perils we're certain to encounter. Anyway, we're not exactly set up to accommodate the needs of a person such as yourself."

She smiled. From the earlier set of her olive face, just a few shades lighter than Ricky's, Ryan wasn't sure that she could. At least without breaking something.

"By the looks of it, your rolling accommodations will be substantially more comfortable than what I'm accustomed to, Mr. Croom."

She held out a gloved hand and deposited a doeskin bag in the reflexively upturned palm of Bass's hand. By the heft, Ryan gathered it had to be filled with metal coins or chunks of gold.

Bass could no more refrain from tugging open the rawhide thong that sealed the top and peering inside than Ryan could have held back from dodging or blocking a chair thrown at his face. He was just wired that way. And while his heavy bearded face was downturned so Ryan couldn't see the look on it from up there, the way his head suddenly pulled away from the bag, and the sudden hunch of his big shoulders, told Ryan that whatever he saw in the bag impressed him powerfully.

"I can carry my weight," she said. "I can do camp chores, some wrench work. And I can fight. You're going to need that. I knew before you told me."

"Well…" Bass said.

Hefting the bag on his palm, he looked around. "Dace?"

The sec boss shrugged. "If she can handle herself and that big blaster of hers, we can use her. Although a single-action wheelgun's a pretty odd choice for a seasoned shooter."

"I'm comfortable with it," Olympia said. "I don't usually need to shoot many rounds."

"You will this time out."

"I'll manage."

Cable turned back to his boss. "I don't think she's gonna

get in the way. She looks functional enough. I say let her come."

"Bass," Morty whined. That was his usual mode, Ryan had noticed; but the word had had that extra nasal edge to it that meant he was actually bitching. "Do you *really* have to take in every stray that wanders in out of the wasteland?"

"That's enough, Morty."

Bass turned to Ryan. "Mr. Cawdor?"

Ryan didn't miss the way Cable's brow tightened at his boss consulting the outlander. Gonna have to set things straight with that boy, soon or late, he told himself. Just hope his ego problems don't get us chilled.

"You're our cross-country sec expert. What do you think about taking on a passenger so late in the game?"

"As long as you think you can feed another mouth— and as long as the woman really understands what she's getting into—then I'm with your sec boss."

"We can't have too many blasters." It was J.B., ambling over from the M-2 wag to see what was happening. "Or backs bending to help heave a stuck wag out of a ditch or a mudhole."

Olympia nodded to the little Armorer. "I've done that," she said.

J.B. looked up at Ryan and nodded. Whether Croom was surprised at Ryan consulting his companion or not Ryan neither knew nor cared.

He'd made up his mind anyway on his own. But had J.B. registered a serious objection, he'd have thought it through again double-quick, and then made up his own mind again.

"I say yes," Ryan told the trader.

Bass shrugged, then his beard split in a wide smile.

"Welcome aboard, Miss Olympia," he said, shaking her hand again, to her apparent but quiet amusement. "Where would you care to ride among our princely conveyances?"

He turned to indicate the whole convoy with a grand sweep of his arm: the blaster wags, the half dozen cargo wags, including the supply truck; the cook-wag minivan; Bass's lightly armored SUV and the schoolbus where most of the off-duty crew would ride and try to catch some shut-eye.

Olympia turned and without hesitation began to climb the tanker's front rungs.

"That's not going to be a very comfortable perch, Miss," Bass called.

Olympia reached the top and stood to face Ryan, who looked from her to Krysty. The redhead had also moved up to hear the exchange with the newcomer, standing right behind Jak and Ricky, in case their young-man hormones got the better of them, most likely. She had given him a quick nod and a smile.

She knew she was his mate, and he hers, and was no less secure than Ryan himself.

Despite the fact that the newcomer was closely sizing Ryan up with eyes that, though darkish blue with a bit of green, like jade, had marked epicanthic folds. But Ryan sensed no sexual interest in that scrutiny, a thing he had more than a bit of experience at seeing. Instead it was the same kind of examination he was giving her, the kind that two obvious coldhearts made on first encountering each other.

"Liable to get more than uncomfortable up here," he said. "I'm Ryan Cawdor."

"Mr. Cawdor," she said with a crisp nod. "I realize that. I did just walk into Menaville by myself, you know."

Ryan grunted. He felt stupid. Of course she did.

"Your funeral," he said, turning back to his sandbag post.

Somebody had thoughtfully added a blanket or two to

the midst of it, both to cushion the occupant's butt against
the cold, hard steel and to provide added warmth against
the wind of passage. Well, that was an advantage of riding with somebody as smart and seasoned as Bass Croom
clearly was. He understood, bottom line, that a cold and
miserable lookout and guard wasn't looking out or guarding at peak efficiency.

"That's what I intend to avoid, Mr. Cawdor," Olympia
called to his back. "When there's danger, I feel much more
confident facing it myself than leaving it in the hands of
others."

Had he been Dace Cable—obviously smart enough,
and highly competent, but also less than fully secure—
he might have bristled at the suggestion that the sec crew
couldn't protect a paying passenger.

But he wasn't. So he simply nodded without looking
back and started to get settled in.

There were a few more hang-ups. Dan Hogue and his
two assistants, one male, one female, had to open the engine compartment of the so-called chuck wag to check
something before clearing it to roll. But in surprisingly
short order Bass Croom posed dramatically in the open
driver's door of his black command wag.

"Gentlemen," he cried. "Ladies. We roll!"

Chapter Nine

The compound gates were thrown open. The lead blaster wag mounting the M-249, and manned by Cable and a female member of his sec crew, rolled out onto the streets of Menaville for the very last time.

Only half an hour late, Ryan thought, sitting in his sandbag nest with his Scout rifle cradled in his arms and his coat collar pulled up against a chill early breeze. Not bad.

The streets were lined with gawking ville folk. They burst into cheers when they saw Bass standing upright atop his slow-rolling command wag to wave goodbye with both hands.

The man knows how to make an exit, and that's a fact, Ryan thought, craning his head out sideways so he could catch a glimpse of his boss past the battered powder-blue school bus.

He tried to ignore the fact it was Krysty riding up there, and with only Ricky with her. Ryan noticed that the youth had his own longblaster sling cinched up on his left forearm, ready to snap into firing position and take a shot. That reassured Ryan. After all, Krysty was there to provide backup to the kid with the long weapon, rather than vice versa, the way the slender, quiet woman with the long black braid was for Ryan on the tanker. A longblaster shooter could do his on her long-range work best when somebody else had his on his back. Ryan trusted seasoned veteran Krysty to handle that task. For both of them.

As for the woman called Olympia, well, Ryan would just see. What little he gathered of her, mostly watching the way she moved—and the way she scanned the crowd now, brows furrowed and eyes keen—encouraged him that if the stickies hit them, none of them would be ripping the skin off the back of Ryan's neck with their suckered fingers while he was lost in the glass of his shooting scope.

He went back to eyeing the streets, as well. He knew that Cable and his crew were all wired-up before the convoy started to roll. Anybody would have to be stupe to the point of insane to hit such a well-armed assemblage even with the full sec force of a ville this size. For one thing, J.B., playing Tail-End Charlie in the burly Toyota wag with the M-2 mounted in the bed, could shoot through any building in Menaville, even the brick ones, and in most directions the thumb-size bullets could go through all the structures in the way and keep heading for the treeline with enough speed to spoil someone's whole day.

Ryan didn't know Baron Billy Howe. Croom obviously respected him more than liked him, and didn't entirely trust him not to go jolt-walker crazy at the last moment. Ryan was leery of casino and gaudy-owner Boss Morgan. He might resent the pain of getting his nose broken and then rubbed in the dirt more than he feared the memory of how those things had happened to him.

Ryan reckoned the man was yellow deep down, a bully, nasty when he held the whip hand, and turning into runny shit when his back felt the lash. Ryan wasn't being paid to take the safety of the convoy for granted, nor did he ever take his own, and that of his friends, either.

They made it past the outskirts of the ville without incident. If the baron came out to watch them go, Ryan didn't notice.

The road west from Menaville, to the ruins of the old

postdark Fort McIlvaine twenty miles away, wound between fairly mild hills. Actually, neither the Zarks nor the Ouachitas struck any of the group as being mountains. They had *seen* mountains. Even Ricky had grown up traveling through higher, steeper ones with his father on their annual donkey-train trade trips into the Monster Island interior.

The problem was that it led through fairly serious stands of timber: big hardwoods, oak mostly, with big, strong branches reaching right out over the right-of-way.

As soon as they got beneath some, Ryan started watching above to the exclusion of anywhere else. There were plenty eyes looking around at ground level. What almost everybody did always was forget to look up, which included Ryan and his friends on their trip into town.

"Good you're watching trees."

They were the first words Olympia had spoken to him since a brief greeting on her climb to the top of the fuel tank. He had acknowledged her with a grunt then. Now he didn't even glance at her. He knew she was sitting alert in her own sandbag "hardpoint."

"Stickies around the ville climb trees," she went on.

"I know," he said. "We met up with some on the walk in."

"Cable didn't believe you when you tried to tell him about that, did he?" the woman said.

"Nope."

A high-pitched snarl of blaster fire ripped the morning air, sharp and loud above the grumble of wag engines.

"Showtime," Olympia said, mostly to herself. When Ryan glanced briefly at her she had her funny cowboy handblaster out and ready.

It was a Ruger Blackhawk .357 Magnum. It was like Jak's Colt Python, but unlike his, a single action, and empties could only be ejected and the cylinder reloaded a chamber at a time. It wouldn't have been Ryan's first choice for a blaster, nor second or tenth, no matter how much J.B. raved and Ricky nodded about what a fine and classic blaster it was. But while the blaster was slow to re-load, it spoke with way more authority than that snubby Krysty carried, and held six rounds to her Smith's five.

The Squad Automatic Weapon on the lead wag snarled again. Ryan heard other blasters thudding out single shots. All came from up ahead. Apparently J.B., who had Jak watching his back, didn't yet see anything worth burning up his own thunder-booming cartridges on.

He didn't hear Krysty's distinctive .38 Special snubby yet. He heard what he reckoned for Doc's LeMat. The older man and Mildred rode on top of cargo wags in similar sandbag nests, paired with members of Cable's sec crew. Ryan couldn't see them over the top of the bus.

Then the one-eyed man spotted motion—a big tree branch bobbing up and down right as the school bus was starting to roll under it. He caught the motion far enough in advance to actually bring the low-power Leupold scope to his eye rather than use the iron battle sights mounted below it.

It actually took a moment before his vision separated the branch from the being that crept along it. Its slimy hide, mottled brown and gray, was streaked by leaf mold and dirt and bird shit.

Who knew the little fuckers could learn to hide that well? he thought. Not to mention adapt.

Ryan had already let out half a quickly sucked-down breath, let more out, then held it. His gloved finger slowly squeezed the trigger. Well-made and better-tuned by the Armorer, the trigger broke crisply and cleanly. The longblaster roared and kicked Ryan in the shoulder, the barrel riding up in recoil.

A fresh round was chambered by the time the weapon came back online. He didn't see the creeping stickie anymore, but the branch it was perched on was bouncing vigorously up and down as if recovering from just having shed a substantial weight.

Seeing no other targets when he shifted the restricted vision field of the scope he pulled his eye away from the long-relief eyepiece to take a quick look around and grab some situational awareness. Just in time to see a stickie drop down right behind Olympia.

He didn't dare shoot. Aside from the risk that the wag might lurch in the uneven road and send a shot astray, there was the fact that at a range of not much more than twenty feet, a dead-center hit on the stickie might blow right and through and chill his companion. So he shouted a warning instead.

Most of the guards and the companions had equipped themselves with melee weapons, specifically ones that could keep a little distance between a stickie and the user's body. Even Jak had augmented his collection of knives with a hickory ax-handle. Olympia didn't seem to have one, despite the fact she, too, knew the stickies were there and likely to ambush them.

Apparently she had that covered after all. Without looking first, she spun. As she did, something shiny expanded in her hand into a four-foot-long steel rod that smashed the stickie right across its gaping mouth. Ryan could tell its mouth was open because Olympia's savage stroke snapped the mutie's head around so that its huge eyes made contact with Ryan's eye in the instant before it toppled off the catwalk to the roadside ditch.

Olympia snapped off a shot, thumbing back the hammer

and firing so fast only a seasoned shooter like Ryan could even tell she'd fully extended her arm and probably caught a flash sight picture. A shit-streaked body fell writhing in front of the tanker's tractor. The tank itself bumped ever so slightly as it ran over the stickie.

As Ryan felt it, he saw Olympia give him a quick thumbs-up from the hand that clutched the expandable steel staff she'd been carrying in a holder on her web belt. Then she turned forward and blasted again with her Blackhawk.

Ryan was already searching for more targets. As he looked right, he saw tree branches thrash along that side of the roadway. An earth-shattering roar hit his ears from the rear of the convoy as dead leaves, twigs and flailing stickies fell from the trees.

And stickie parts, along with something like black rain.

Evidently J.B. had got his driver to pull into the right-hand ditch, allowing him to cut loose alongside the convoy with the .50-caliber blaster. Since the road curved to the left ahead he had a clear line of fire. He was savaging the stickies attacking from the trees on that side.

The convoy kept rolling. Looking back Ryan saw the trail wag—J.B.'s—follow, canted to the right half in the ditch. Ryan could feel the buffeting overpressure of the Browning's colossal muzzle-blast.

He turned his attention to the left. From the way the brush on that side was dancing, and more stickies were falling from the trees, Ryan guessed the rest of the wag's blasters had concentrated their fire on the other side of the convoy from the .50, which was smart.

He didn't get another target as the convoy rolled through a wider valley where the trees fell away and the dense undergrowth turned to dry grass and scattered bushes, with hills humping up to either side.

No more targets. Dropping the 10-round box magazine out of the well of his own longblaster, Ryan winced when he thought about the ammo they'd burned up in that little encounter, especially the rare ammo for the Browning .50-caliber blaster.

But a chill spent no jack, as trader used to say. Bass Croom had stocked up well for the coming voyage. All they could do now was to try not to waste bullets, and hope they had enough to make it all the way to the coast.

The call passed back along the convoy: no one was hurt, no real damage done to wags or cargo. Ace. He was relieved that Krysty and the rest of his companions had once again escaped unharmed. He kept his gaze focused on the sides of the dirt track. Still plenty of cover out there, brush and dead ground, if the stickies for some reason wanted to try their luck again.

"We're ace back here," J.B. called out as the blaster wag driver pulled the big pickup out of the ditch and back onto the road behind the fuel wag. Ryan called the acknowledgment back along the line. The one thing all Croom's wealth and ingenuity hadn't been able to secure for his convoy was reliable radio gear. That sort of thing was at a premium in the Deathlands.

They'd drive on without it. Hardly anybody survived childhood in Deathlands without getting skilled at making do and getting by.

He glanced at Olympia. The black-braided woman was sitting in her nest of sandbags reloading her six-gun. She had collapsed her steel baton and put it back in its hip holster. She reloaded by feel, not taking her dark eyes off the landscape rolling by.

"Stickies must have a triple-huge colony," he called out. He was recalling the hurt his friends had laid on the muties on their way into town. They'd chilled a good twenty of the bastards, and figured that would at the very least have taken a major bite out of the nest. But they had to have just been hit by ten times that number.

"Lot smaller now," Olympia called back. She turned her face toward him and gave him what might have been a brief smile, then went back to her vigil.

Croom's rolling out of Menaville at just the right time, Ryan thought. The stickies are closing in on it in big numbers.

He shrugged. Not his ville. He had no people there, and all the friends they'd made during their brief stay in the ville were rolling with them. From what he'd seen of Boss Morgan and his coldhearts, and heard about Baron Billy Howe, he couldn't say they and the stickies didn't deserve one another.

The ville folk stood to get screwed, but that was always how it went. It was why Ryan and his companions chose the life they led, with all its dangers: at least they carried their fates in their own hip pockets.

He turned his lone eye to the surroundings and his thoughts to the road ahead.

Part II:

The Road

Chapter Ten

"Road gone ahead!"

From her position behind the M-249 light machine gun mounted in the lead wag, Krysty could just make out Jak as he called over the snarl of his dirt bike.

The white-haired young scout brought the little motorcycle to a halt in front of the lead blaster wag with a flourish, a quick turn and bow-wave of loose dirt from the dirt and debris that had wind-drifted across the cracked and heaved blacktop of I-40.

Krysty braced one arm on the pintle mount to absorb the impact as the truck stopped to avoid squashing the reckless scout. She waved the other to the rest of the convoy behind so that they wouldn't run into her. The lookouts atop the other wags passed the gesture back.

"Earth crack," Jak added as the rest of the convoy got stopped without mishap. "Highway broke."

Ricky brought his own scrambler bike to a far more cautious stop next to his friend.

"Do they have a lot of earthquakes around here?" Ricky called out. "There's like a ten-yard gap where it just like pulled apart. About twenty feet deep. We're not getting across."

"Does that make you homesick, lad?" Doc asked, striding up with a smile. It was a fairly warm day when the wind wasn't blowing, sunny with a few thin clouds high up. He had taken off his long coat and twirled his cane like a gent going out on the town.

Ricky laughed. "That's not part of Island life I miss that much, Doc," he called back. Tremors—and volcanic eruptions—weren't much less common than monsters on Puerto Rico, as the companions had learned during their involuntary stay there when they'd picked up Ricky.

The youth kept trying not to look at Krysty, and failing. She'd gotten used to that. She didn't like to think of herself as a vain person, but she'd have to be stupe not to notice the way men stared at her, and had since she was younger than Ricky. Though she tried not to let her kind and friendly nature encourage him too much, he tended to follow her around like a lost puppy.

For his part Ryan ignored that behavior. He was gruff with the kid, but then he was gruff with everybody. He only dressed down the kid more than the rest because he was an adolescent and got out of line.

Krysty wasn't surprised by anything except perhaps how much Ryan had actually warmed to the boy during his brief time with them. Then again, if Ryan had been the sort of man to feel challenged by a somewhat goofy sixteen-year-old kid, he wouldn't have been the man Krysty Wroth picked for a mate.

The ancient I-40 was three lanes wide here. From the traces remaining, this had apparently been the westbound side of the full highway. The eastbound lanes were simply gone, mounded over by red dirt, visible only in cracked patches peeking out of the scrub.

Bass Croom's command was pulled up on the cracked blacktop alongside the lead blaster wag. The steel plates bolted to the sides of big Land Cruiser were spattered with red from a brief rain that had left muddy puddles of the windblown dirt a few miles back. The windshield showed pink streaks behind the heavy-gauge mesh bolted over it, and bolted over all the windows.

As little attention as Krysty paid to machines in general, she had to admit it was a clever design. The plates and mesh wouldn't keep out serious blasterfire but would still provide a lot of protection to the occupants. Clever little firing slits had been built in the doors—even the back hatch, though it was usually too blocked by baggage to let anybody shoot through it. They reminded Krysty of the old-days mail slots with hinged metal covers you still found in ancient doors, sometimes.

She did wonder why a man who seemed as generally solid as Croom would want to go around forted up like that. Nobody else seemed to think anything amiss about it, though. Except Mildred, who tended to just sour on things from time to time.

The doors opened. The merchant himself was driving. Cable unfolded himself from the passenger seat where he was riding shotgun, according to some complicated duty schedule Croom had drawn out. Following Ryan's example, Krysty and the rest only paid attention to where they were supposed to be and when; it was so set up that folks stood four hours on, four hours off, four hours on for twelve hours, and then when the convoy halted for the night, no one stood watch more than two hours. Ryan and J.B. said it differed somewhat from what Trader had set up when they rolled with him, but seemed satisfied with it.

She let the sec man from Cable's crew help her down from the wag bed, where he was serving as her loader and general back-watcher. He was a young man with goggles pushed up on spiked blond hair and washboard ribs visible through the once-white wife-beater he wore under his black leather jacket. He called himself Solo, and while he wasn't visibly much less impressed with Krysty's looks than Ricky was, he seemed every bit as much terrified of her. She wasn't sure whether that was on her own account, or Ryan's, but he flushed deep pink to the roots of his hair when she smiled and thanked him for his help.

By this time J.B. and Ryan had come walking up from their own duty spots, driving the bus and riding sec on the commissary van, respectively. Mildred followed, as did most of Croom's drivers and Cable's sec force. Krysty hoped the crew of the tail blaster wag were still keeping watch, at least. But given Ryan seemed unconcerned she reckoned they were.

Bass looked up at Ryan and the Armorer's approach and nodded to them.

"I was just saying, your people can go one way along the break, and I can take my wag the other. Shouldn't be too far until the crack ends."

Cable frowned. "Now, boss, you got no call to go running that kind of risks."

Bass laughed. "Hell, son. Why else do I have the thing all tarted up with steel plates and that shit? It's not because I'm afraid of getting my wide old ass scratched with brambles."

"Not sure that Land Cruiser's the best thing to take cross-country," J.B. said. "Heavy."

As the four men discussed the merits of using the armored wag to scout, Krysty glanced toward Jak and Ricky, who sat on their light motorbikes waiting further orders. No one was suggesting splitting them up to scout north and south for a way forward, which was good—Ryan didn't like his people going solo. Jak generally preferred rolling that way, but for now he seemed content to keep an eye on the new kid, whom he'd clearly taken under his wing as much as J.B. had.

Ricky was looking along the road still, but now his

black eyes were fixed intently past Krysty where she stood beside the truck. Curious, she turned to see where he was looking.

A young woman stood beside the cargo wag right behind the lead vehicle. Krysty recognized one of Cable's sec crew who went by the name Dezzy. She was a skinny girl, medium height, with a pale face, bobbed dyed-black hair, with her right bang dyed white. J.B. said it made her look as if a skunk had sat on her head slantwise. She wore a cracked and battered black leather jacket over threadbare black jeans, and fingerless leather gloves with a reinforcing strap set with metal studs over the knuckles. She had a lever-action longblaster with a sawed-off barrel in a leather holster strapped to her right thigh.

She seemed to be looking back in Ricky's direction with her own dark eyes when Krysty noticed her. He looked quickly off toward her boss and the group clustered around him.

"—fine," Bass was saying with a bit of a frown. "I'll take Mr. Dix with me and we'll scout for a route south. The boys can look to the north."

Cable looked dissatisfied at what Krysty guessed was some kind of compromise. Before anyone could say anything more a voice hailed them from the south.

A ridge covered in some kind of waxy-leaved bushes reared maybe thirty feet, just south of the roadway. Perched atop it on an eighteen-speed mountain bike was Olympia.

"Found a way," she called.

Bass guffawed. "See, Dace?" he said, slapping his sec boss on the shoulder. "Told you it wasn't a waste, dragging that bicycle along."

"Do you trust her, Bass?" a new voice asked. Krysty saw that bass's younger brother had joined the group by the armored command wag.

"Is there a safe way for the vehicles to reach it, young lady?" Bass called through cupped hands.

"Yes," Olympia said. She pointed east to where the rise ended about forty yards behind. "That way. No track, but solid, and level enough."

Bass beamed. "Thank you!"

Then turning back to the others, he said, "Surely you won't object to my taking Mr. Dix to inspect the way for myself, Dace?"

Cable scowled, then shrugged. "Suit yourself, boss." Then added with a grin, "You always do."

He and J.B. moved to get back in the armored wag. Krysty caught Morty staring at her. When he saw her notice him he gave her a slow, wide smile.

"Don't even dream about it," Mildred told him.

Morty glared pure hate at the black woman, then looked at Ryan, turned white and walked hurriedly back to whatever wag he'd come from.

Chapter Eleven

"Sit here?"

Sitting by himself by a secondary campfire, since the big main fire had all the adults crowded around already, Ricky looked up to the sound of a feminine voice. He looked up and his heart tried to jump up in his throat.

Dezzy the sec woman stood by the fire, holding a tin mess kit with steam coming off the contents. She looked bored.

"Sure! Go ahead."

She sat on a rock. He tried not to be disappointed it was across the low blue-and-yellow flames from him.

For a few moments they ate in silence. "What's this meat in the beans?" she asked after a while. "Rabbit?"

"Yeah! You know Olympia? She shot it. Shot several of them with that crossbow of hers."

To Ricky's delight, after she'd led the convoy to a way around the crack in the world this afternoon and Mr. Croom had called a halt for the day, she had taken a breakdown crossbow from her pack. Assembling it without a word to the others, she had taken the mountain bike and ridden off into the brushy hills. She had returned as the sun set with four plump hares strapped to the rear rack.

"Seriously? That funny old-timey wep?"

He nodded enthusiastically. "It's cool!"

She shook her head. He liked the way her black bang

and her white one swept back and forth across her pallid face.

He was trying hard not to be entranced by her and failing miserably.

"Tastes good," she admitted as if grudgingly.

Then she looked at him. His heart jumped again.

"So why's that lady who's with you—Mildred—giggle every time somebody calls the cook Chef?"

Chef was a big, burly black man with a square head and a beard who apparently had worked for Bass for years, both at home in Menaville and on the road. The merchant had helped him fix dinner this night, chopping up the rabbits and some onions to flavor the beans, which were good.

"No idea," Ricky said. *"No lo sé."*

"You know a lot of Mex talk?"

He only just managed to turn his reflex laugh into a sort of half snort, half cough. "Yeah," he said. "It's Spanish. I'm from, uh, Puerto Rico. In the Carib, you know?"

That made no visible impression on her. She addressed herself to her food. Ricky wondered if he'd pissed her off. He found his own appetite, made ravenous by the day's exertion and excitement at being involved in so big and important a trade convoy, suddenly down to zero.

Her spoon made scraping sounds as she tried to get up the last of the beans and rabbit, then she mopped up the remnants with the last of a chunk of hardtack. She put her plate aside and looked at him again.

"That longblaster of yours," she said. "That's cool. What is it?"

He had it laid on his pack behind where he sat. "It's a DeLisle carbine," he said.

She cocked her head to one side. Taking that as being as good as a question, he told her about it. She actually seemed to listen.

"Can I see it?" she asked.

"Sure!" He almost dropped it, once picking it up, dropping the magazine, and then jacking the action to eject the loaded round. Then he was absurdly pleased to see her immediately crack the bolt action back open to confirm the weapon was unloaded when he handed it to her. That was what his Uncle Benito had taught him was the proper way to handle a blaster. J.B. Dix agreed, though Ricky noticed not everybody in the group was as scrupulous about handling weapons that way.

Then she went and blew most of her cred by shouldering the longblaster and leveling it straight at the middle of the back of one of the drivers who was standing by another fire.

To Ricky's relief she lowered the blaster before anybody noticed and turned it over in her hands. "So it's really that quiet?"

He nodded.

"Can I shoot it?"

"Not now!" he said, shocked.

"If it's that quiet," she said, "nobody'd know."

"You don't know Mr. Cawdor and Mr. Dix," he said. "They'd know."

For a moment she looked rebellious, and Ricky was glad he'd kept the ejected cartridge and full magazine at his side. Then she shoved the weapon back toward him.

"Mebbe we can shoot it sometime," he told her.

"Okay."

She gathered up her mess tin and rose.

"Can I see you again?" he asked.

"Mebbe sometime," she said, and was gone.

"So far," Dace Cable said, wiping his mouth from a pull at the bottle of clear liquid his boss had just handed him, "these big, bad Deathlands you been talking up aren't so much, Cawdor. Worst we've seen so far was the stickies that hit us right outside our own hometown."

Which you also said were bullshit, Ryan would have said, had he been looking to tangle with the convoy sec boss. He wasn't, though he wasn't sure how much longer them going around and around could be avoided.

Instead Ryan said nothing.

"We haven't seen real Deathlands yet," Mildred said, gazing into the flame dance of the big bonfire. "That would be what we, uh, what used to be called the Great Plain. They get going for real a ways north of here."

"Should reach them in a day or two if we keep making the kind of progress we have been," J.B. added.

Cable frowned briefly as he passed the bottle right around the main campfire to a couple of his sec crew, a man and a woman. They took hits from it, then passed it on to Krysty. She immediately passed it on to Mildred, who handed it to J.B., also without drinking.

But rather than react to the contradiction, Cable continued to give Ryan the hard eye. He was making it clear he had no particular beef with the rest of Ryan's crew.

Just Ryan.

Ryan accepted the bottle in his turn and drank. Just a sip. It was some kind of distillate, sure enough, but it didn't threaten to shrivel his tongue, fry the lining of his throat and burst like a bomb in his belly. It was actually almost smooth, with a bit of a smoky flavor.

Not too surprisingly, the merchant packed himself a better brand of alky than Towse Lightning, no matter what the stuff looked like.

He moved the bottle on to Doc, who also drank. The old man was the last member of his group seated by the fire.

Jak had wolfed his beans-and-bunny and vanished into the night to prowl beyond the circle of parked wags, as usual.

Bass sat brooding with his bearded chin on his chest, but his eyes were focused away from the fire until Morty, who had taken a long swallow, elbowed him to give him back the bottle.

The merchant blinked, then smiled and thanked his brother as he accepted it back. Ryan glanced around to see where his employer had been looking; the young woman who had taken passage with them at the last minute. Olympia sat by herself on her pack, eating deliberately and seemingly looking at nothing in particular. She was located at the very edge of the wavering, irregular patch of light thrown by the several fires, but not near any of them. Nor the circles of guards and drivers who had gathered beside them.

For a while after their exchange right before and after the stickie attack outside Menaville, Ryan had been concerned she'd turn out to be the chatty type of woman. Instead she said nothing to anybody that circumstances didn't demand. He reckoned she had to have talked a bit more to Jak and Ricky when they went out scouting together, although owing to the differing speeds of their rides, it probably wasn't much either.

It said something, also, that none of the unattached males, drivers or sec men, approached her where she sat. Ryan thought that pretty smart of them. He'd seen her fight.

When he looked back at the fire, he caught Morty giving their paying passenger a hungry eye. Ryan's lips tightened a fraction of an inch. There was trouble coming from that direction, too.

There wasn't a thing he could do about it, so he passed it from his mind.

The others were talking about their journey so far. In the two days since leaving the ville, they'd made what he reckoned pretty decent time. Most of the journey had been over back ways, especially to steer well clear of the Fort Smith nuke hot spot. But Croom had picked solid wags for his epic journey, and for a fact none of the paths they'd taken, even the ones little more than game trails or parallel wheel ruts, had been scaly. The worst impediment they'd encountered before the earth-opening rift had been big trees fallen across their path, which J.B. had happily blasted a way through with some of the C-4 plastique and initiators their boss had thoughtfully stocked for just such purposes. All of which went to show Croom knew the roads hereabouts more than a little.

Of course that also confirmed that the crack in the ancient superhighway was a new thing. Ryan wondered what other surprises the trader had in store.

Then again, there were always surprises on the road. That was one of the reasons Croom had hired the companions.

"I mean to keep going north or northwest tomorrow," Bass said. They had run a few more miles on the blacktop after Olympia showed them a path around the fissure. Then Croom had taken them off north-northwest along a smaller road that was still paved in stretches. They had made deliberate progress, about thirty miles, before pulling off and striking camp for the night.

He stood and took another long pull of the bottle. Noticing it was mostly gone he offered it to Cable. His sec boss shook his head. Without asking anyone else Croom tucked the bottle under one arm, told the group good-night and ambled off for his command wag, where he slept across the backseat.

Cable stood and stretched exaggeratedly. "Reckon I

better turn in. Need my rest if things're really gonna start getting tough here, soon. Then again, like they always say, the only easy day was yesterday, right, Cawdor?"

"Some say that, yeah."

He gave one final hard look at Ryan and walked off. His sec crew followed. To Ryan's relief Morty left, as well.

"What is *wrong* with that dude?" Mildred asked. "Cable, I mean. Not Croom the Younger. He's just an asshole."

"I wonder that, too," Krysty said. "Cable seems physically quite brave, yet somehow at the same time he seems filled with fear."

"He fears a meaner dog will topple him from the top of the pack hierarchy," Doc said, gazing into the fire. The flames underlit his long face and turned their crags and furrows into a wasteland. "He perceives, quite correctly, that our Ryan is such a dog."

"I have no intention of doing any such thing, Doc," Ryan said in some irritation.

"Crazy old coot's right for once," Mildred said. "Cable sure thinks you are."

When the other grown-ups had left, Ricky had come over to stand hovering just back from his companions. He regarded them as his family and tended to gravitate toward them. That was fine with Ryan. They'd taken the kid in, so they *were* family. Just like they were to him.

"You could take him down, right, Ryan?" Ricky said.

Ryan glared at him, but the kid continued on obviously. "You could show him who's boss and that would take care of everything!"

"Best not, son," J.B. said. "See, you're right. I reckon Ryan would win."

Ricky nodded eagerly. His dark eyes shone.

"Then again," J.B. went on, "I mind the old saying, 'when two tigers fight, one dies, the other licks his wounds.' Thing is, Ryan's got more than his own safety to look out for. Namely us. And there's no telling how Cable's people would react if their boss and Ryan went at it. Triple so if Ryan won."

Ricky's face fell. Ryan put hands on thighs and stood.

"Guess I'll turn in," he said. "Got the midnight watch. You all can do as you please, but I'd suggest resting up, too."

He frowned, rubbed the crisp stubble on his chin, then grinned.

"No matter what kind of hard-on Cable has for me," he said, "I got to admit my gut tells me he's right. I think the last easy day was today."

As he walked on to where he and the companions had laid out their bedrolls beside the parked .50-caliber blaster wag, he felt as much as heard Krysty rise and follow.

Mebbe I won't get much sleep before my watch, after all, he thought. And mebbe that's not a bad thing.

THE LAND LAY BEFORE THEM, overall flat as an eatery's tabletop, yet somehow giving the impression of writhing in torment: the surface parched and cracked, dotted with rare clumps of spiky, dead-looking growth, here and there gnarled as if long wounds had scarred over. The land had a bad, strange baked-orange look to it.

So did the sky, which roiled with clouds as far as the eye could see to the north and west, in shades that varied from flame-colored to mustard. Lightning stabbed forks like dazzling purple sidewinder tongues at the horizon from a layer of clouds that were almost black.

Ryan took it all in. He felt a muscle on the side of his mouth twitch, near where his own old scar ran from brow to jawline.

The convoy had halted on the edge of the desolation.

Croom, Cable and most of their people had come forward to stare at what awaited them as the next stage of their journey.

Doc stepped out in front of the silent crowd. Pretending to doff a top hat, he swept a low theatrical bow before them.

"Ladies and gentlemen," he declared, "I present to you, the real Deathlands! And now our show begins in earnest!"

Chapter Twelve

The acid rainstorm hit them as fast as a rattler strike, and just as hard and deadly.

J.B. saw the danger right before it came on them. Guided only by the Armorer's minisextant and Bass Croom's faded USGS maps, the convoy rolled over mud flats that had dried into hard ochre plates, and threw up thin puke-colored dust at the passage of their wheels. It looked as if it had never felt rain of any sort despite the clouds that had constantly seethed across the sky, like a stormy orange ocean upside down, since they had set forth across the true Deathlands.

From his perch in the front sandbag nest strapped to the top of the dormitory school bus, J.B. saw a new cloud mass rushing from the west, a brown so dark it was almost black and seeming to boil. Lightning bolts sizzled purple within it, giving it the look of a bad bruise that had somehow become self-luminous.

He sat cradling the M-4000 in his arms. Immediately he put it to his shoulder and fired four blasts into the hideous tortured sky, as fast he could pump the action, hating to waste the shells as if he bled them. Thankfully Croom had stockpiled ammo.

Positioned as the bus was in the middle of the convoy, the shots could easily be heard to its farthest extents. At once the wags began slowing. Four blasts was the signal to *halt now*.

He cupped hands over his mouth. "Cover up!" he bellowed up the line of now stopped wags. "Acid rain!"

Then he turned back to see the face of the sec man who rode in the nest behind him, fixed on him and white as a fresh-bleached sheet. "Got your tarp, Benny?"

The sec man nodded and began to fumble with something by his legs. J.B. had made sure that each of the so-called "hardpoints" atop the wags had a tarp rolled up inside or strapped down tight right next to it, large enough to cover the occupant or occupants. Cable had rolled his eyes. Croom had simply ordered them provided as requested, even though it meant breaking out some he'd evidently meant as trade items.

And this was why. Acid rain was coming. Fast.

Coming *now*. Something stung the back of J.B.'s left hand as he unfastened his own tarp. Ignoring the brief pain, he whipped open the rolled yellow tarpaulin, pulled it over the nest securing it to the bags with short lengths of nylon rope that were wound around them for the purpose, and huddled under it. Then he set about unpacking something from his own backpack, which he had brought up with him and carried along despite the fact it crowded the small nest.

A gust of wind hit the tarp like a giant boot. That was the prelude to what sounded like somebody blasting a stream of gravel against the tarp. The rain was coming down fierce and hard. J.B. hoped that meant it would blow over fast. Sometimes it did. Sometimes it could come down like that for days. If that happened here they were fucked, likely. So he put it out of his mind. Nothing he could do about it.

J.B. heard the screaming as he finished writhing into his blue rain slicker. Deliberately he pulled the set of old plastic swim goggles, their long-rotted elastic straps replaced with leather, down over his eyes. Then he pulled the blue hood over the frayed baseball cap hat he had crammed on his head in place of his fedora. Last he donned a pair of canvas work gloves. It took time while the agonized shrieking went on and on.

But it required time to suit up properly, so J.B. did. This was a bad acid downpour, which was obvious before the screaming began. He wouldn't do anybody any good if he went out half-baked and poorly protected. He was like as not to wind up incapacitated himself.

There were times J.B. acted without thought or hesitation. Those were the times he had to, to preserve the lives of his companions or his own skinny ass. When the situation called for it, he acted with the deliberate speed he did now. He was a man devoted to doing what it took to do the job, whatever that was.

When J.B. was covered, he loosened one end of the tarp and slipped out.

The wind spit acid into his face. The cap brim, goggles, and the scarf he'd wound over his mouth under it would keep the worst off long enough.

A steel folding ladder was bolted to the side of the bus, a means of carrying it for whatever uses may be asked of it as well as of allowing the sec crew to get up and down. It was a good multipurpose design of which J.B. approved. Now he climbed down like a man who knew how: fast, but without rushing.

The screams came from a few places back in the line of stalled wags, atop the fuel tanker. As J.B. trudged toward it, bent forward with his face averted from the acid-laden transverse wind, he realized it was the front nest.

He climbed up the rungs. Fortunately they were on the left-hand side of the tank, which put his back mostly to the wind blowing from the west.

When he got to the top he saw a person writhing in an open sandbag nest. Apparently the occupant had been caught in the midst of trying to affix his tarp over himself when the first wind gust had hit. Now the tarp flapped off the right side off the tanker, just held by ties on that side. The man it was supposed to protect writhed on his back batting ineffectually at the searing droplets with fingers already half skeletonized.

Bad one, J.B. thought.

From the shelter of the rear tarp a female voice screamed, "Help him! For mercy's sake, please do something!"

J.B. glanced back. The woman huddled in the temporary shelter was a driver named Bukowski. While most members of the crew had primary jobs, Croom set it up so many rotated through most jobs, which seemed to help keep everybody fresh. He even took occasional turns as sec or driver of another wag than his own armored wag.

Bukowski tried to stretch a hand toward J.B., then snatched it back. A glance told the story; it was reddened and covered in swelling blisters. She had tried to help her comrade. The acid rain had driven her back.

As it should. Had she persisted, unprotected as she was, the convoy would have lost two crew members instead of one.

J.B. rose and looked down at the man in the open nest. He was a sec man named Horwitz, J.B. remembered. There was no recognizing the eyeless half-melted mass of a face that the poor bastard lacked the body control even to turn away from the acid onslaught.

A Winchester lever action lay propped half out of the sandbag nest. Somehow the doomed man's agonized thrashing hadn't dislodged it. The acid was discoloring the blue barrel as well as the shiny metal of the tanker itself. No permanent damage would result as long as the downpour didn't go on too hard too long, especially if they could find fresh water to pump up to hose off the wags. But that was for the future, which wasn't here yet.

J.B. picked up the blaster.

Help him, the woman had cried. For mercy's sake.

For mercy's sake, there was but one thing to do. Fortunately it was the only practical course, as well. Taking hasty aim, J.B. put a .44 bullet through the side of that steaming disfigured head. Then carrying the blaster, he made his way back to the intact tarp shelter to do what he could for the injured woman there.

It'd go easier, he reflected, if he could get her to stop her screaming....

"WHY TAKE hard?"

Mildred saw heads turn to Jak. Ryan had told the young albino to stick close tonight. He hadn't seen fit to explain why. Jak obeyed, though he clearly chafed under the restraint.

"Yes, it's pretty clear they're all upset," Krysty said. "Mr. Croom just sits by the fire and drinks."

"He's a good man," J.B. said. "He cares about his men. Should be more like him."

"If he doesn't hit the bottle too hard," Mildred said. "Does anybody else thinks our boss has been getting moodier the longer we spend on the trail?"

"The demeanor of Mr. Cable concerns me more," Doc said, "given his consistent animus toward Ryan."

"Why would he be so upset?" Ricky asked. "I mean, yeah. It was one of his people, but sec men die. It's part of their job. I know some have been chilled working for Bass—for Mr. Croom. Dez— I heard some of them talk about it."

"New circumstances," Ryan said. "New surroundings. They've fought for Croom in the ville, and even on the trading road. But they don't know the heart of the Deathlands. Now they've come hard up against it."

"That's what they have us for," J.B. said.

"So it's the circumstances that put Cable off-center," Mildred said. "That and it's a triple-hard way for one of your people to die."

"Not every sec boss gives a pinch of sour stickie shit about his people," J.B. said. "Gotta hand that to Cable."

"He's good at his job," Ryan said. "When he doesn't let pride get in the way."

"Do you think he'll blame J.B. for chilling poor Horwitz?" Mildred asked.

Ryan shook his head. "He saw him, same as we did. J.B. did what a good boss would have for him. Or his best friend."

Ricky's eyes went wide at that. Mildred could tell he was imagining his own new friends in the awful, hopeless state the unusually virulent acid rain had left the sec man in. As hard as he was visibly trying not to, he was also struggling with the notion that he might one day be called upon to give the same mercy to one of them.

He probably wasn't envisioning they might have to do the same for him. He was still at that age when he was immortal.

"Anyway," Ryan said, "his hard-on's for me. He's smart enough to see we're good. He even said up front they needed us."

"Do you believe he will force the issue he perceives between you?" Doc asked.

Ryan grunted. "Hope not."

"You know what Trader always used to say," J.B. said, taking off his glasses and polishing them with his shirttail.

"Put your hopes in one hand and your crap in the other, see which fills up first."

"You're always such a nuking comfort, J.B.," Ryan said.

Chapter Thirteen

The sound of someone's boot soles scuffing on the rungs of the ladder on the side of the tanker startled Ricky. He was sitting in the forward sandbag nest, his whole being fiercely focused on staring out into the night. It helped keep him awake, although it also gave him a tendency to see phantom enemies in random shadows. He had learned the hard way by getting yelled at by his new friends several times to hold off giving the alarm unless he was at least sure something really was out there.

Ricky turned, reflexively bringing the DeLisle's fat barrel up to bear on the sound, and he almost died of mortification when Dezzy's pale face appeared above the steel edge.

She didn't even react to finding herself staring into the little hole in the front of the suppressed blaster. Ryan and J.B. said Mr. Cable's crew were good, Ricky thought as he hastily lowered the weapon. But what kind of gun-handling skills did they have if that didn't bother her?

The cool assessment didn't stop him getting all hot in the cheeks, dropping his eyes and mumbling an apology even he couldn't understand.

She ignored that. "May I come up?" she said.

"Sure!"

He was unsure how to proceed from there, so he gripped his carbine in both hands and turned his attention to the surrounding darkness. The moon had set an hour before.

The light of the stars from a sky blessedly free of clouds showed a black landscape that was flat except for the occasional stunted spike of vegetation.

He felt her come and slip into the nest. A thrill shot through him as her hip brushed his. In the cool spring air her body heat was like furnace air washing over him. He felt it especially on his cheek.

For a while she just sat beside him. He didn't dare look at her directly; from the corner of his eye he saw her slim legs were drawn up, her arms around them, her achingly pretty face propped on her knees by her chin.

"Ever seen somebody die?"

The question took him so off guard that he actually turned and stared briefly at her. Her dark eyes seemed fixed on the blackness and didn't so much as twitch in his direction.

"Sure," he said. The question surprised him. Even with what he now saw as his seriously sheltered upbringing in the peaceful, prosperous seaside ville of Nuestra Señora, people died. From accident or attack, and not infrequently boats put in seeking aid for mortally injured sailors. And he had killed.

"Somebody close, I mean?"

"Um." He swallowed and blinked back hot, sudden tears. The images of the shark-headed mutie Tiburón and his sec men murdering Ricky's parents in front of his eyes flashed into his mind with horrid impact. Instantly he felt a sudden wash of shame. *Yami! I have not forgotten you, my sister. I will find you and rescue you. Some day…*

"Yeah," he managed to say, turning his face away so he could dab at his eyes with the cuff of the long-sleeved flannel shirt he wore against the cool air.

She said nothing. When he looked at her again, the starlight glittered off a trail of moisture down her right cheek.

"Ever chilled anybody yourself?" she asked.

"Huh?"

Part of him wanted to answer, "lots of times," which would be true. But all of a sudden he remembered he didn't always feel good about that fact.

"Yeah," he finally said. "You?"

"Sure," she said. "Lots of times."

Somehow that rang false in his ears. He didn't have the courage to call her on it. Even though she was older than him, and pretty, she lacked Krysty's goddesslike beauty and presence, or Mildred's sometimes bullheaded bluntness. But…she was still a girl.

And he was a teenage boy.

That meant, naturally, that he had a raging boner. And, naturally, what that mostly meant was that he blushed ferociously, glad all over again she wasn't much looking at him. And especially she was pressed to his side and couldn't feel its insistent hardness.

So he held her and savored and suffered the experience in equal measure, until she abruptly rose and departed without a word of warning and farewell.

He watched her as her head disappeared beyond the steel horizon of the fuel tanker whose former shininess was now tarnished by the acid.

He stared into the hole she had left in the night, then turned his face forward.

He wouldn't have any more trouble staying awake, but he did have trouble concentrating until his raging adolescent hormones at last began to subside.

"WHY THE HALT?" Ryan asked, walking forward along the convoy.

"Something up ahead," a sec man named Marconi said. He pointed toward the west.

The land stretched fairly flat in front of the stopped convoy. They were still in the Great Plains but nearing the western edge. The land around them showed green growth and fewer signs of acid-rain ravaging. Best of all, a jagged blue line above the far horizon, just visible, indicated the relative nearness of the Rocky Mountains.

In front of the Rockies, rising up almost to obscure them from view, was a low brown cloud that seemed to stretch across the whole horizon from north to south. Seeing that, Ryan grunted. "We're going to need you to swap blaster wags," he called to Bass Croom, who stood nearby with a black Stetson hat pushed back on his head, hands on his hips, and a puzzled frown on his face behind his beard. "Bring the big blaster up front."

Bass look at him quizzically. "Sure," he said.

Glaring, Cable took a few steps toward Ryan. "Who are you to be giving orders to the boss?"

"The man he hired to get you all across the continent as safe as possible," Ryan said calmly.

And, since the loss of Horwitz to the acid rain storm just beginning to cross the Deathlands, which even Ryan had to admit was ugly, they had. Despite a few more acid showers, which caused no casualties among the crew, they'd had no more serious downpours. Otherwise they had avoided trouble to a surprising degree. Or trouble had avoided them.

Twisters had stalked the torture-scarred land but never come close to do more than elevate heartbeats. Twice cold-heart bands had been rash enough to make plays at them. The first group had broken and run from behind the makeshift barrier of an old trailer loaded with rocks and broken concrete chunks they had dragged across a stretch of blacktop at the first snarl of the M-249 in the lead blaster wag. Jak had warned the convoy well in advance, having spotted the barrier without apparently being seen himself.

A band of coldhearts had streamed down from some low hills on motorcycles. Fortunately J.B. had been manning the big .50 on the trail wag when that happened. He had blasted four of them to sprays of disassociated parts, both flesh and metal, and one into a blossom of yellow flame when they were still a good five hundred yards off. The rest had turned tail promptly and fled back the way they came, leaving their wounded behind.

In the unlikely event there were any. Those .50-caliber bullets made a mess of a body.

Leaving aside the incident of the giant Gila monster, which was too slow to pursue them, and rapidly left behind, there hadn't really been many other incidents of note. They had been lucky so far.

And now their luck, clearly, had changed.

Well, Ryan thought, it was only a matter of time.

"At ease, Dace," Bass said, turning back from passing the order along to his assistant, Sandra Watson.

The sec boss gave Ryan one last glare, then turned on one boot heel and stalked away.

"You'll probably want to get the gawkers back in the wags," Ryan told Bass. "We may need to roll fast and on a moment's notice. Not you, J.B. You stick with me."

He added the last to his friend as the man joined him. The Armorer was looking at the brown cloud, which seemed to be growing perceptibly larger. He nodded.

"Big one," he said.

"Triple big," Ryan agreed.

"What?" Bass asked.

Over the grassland between them and the mysterious cloud came Ricky Morales, riding hell-for-leather bent way down over the handlebars of his little dirt bike.

"Monsters!" he shouted, braking so hard he almost threw himself over the bars. "Big shaggy brown monsters with huge heads and horns! Hundreds of them!"

Chapter Fourteen

"Aw, bullshit," J.B. heard a man say behind him. He recognized the voice of Marconi.

He chuckled. "Buffalo bullshit, for a fact," he said. "And plenty of it."

The lead blaster wag gunned its engine and spun up some grass and sod as it lit out for the rear of the convoy. The driver was obviously aching for the chance at a little speed, given their usual glacial pace.

Bass frowned at J.B. and Ryan. "What's up ahead, exactly, again?"

"Buffalo herd, Mr. Croom," Ryan said.

"Or to be correct," Doc said, "American bison."

He stood with hands on hips blinking at the cloud. It really was getting larger now, and J.B. thought to make out a sort of surging brown line at the base of it.

"At least that is one pleasant consequence of Armageddon," Doc declared. "Good to see their numbers have so resurged, as severely depleted as they were years ago."

Cable shook his head in disbelief. J.B. wasn't sure of *what,* strictly. But his boss laughed in relief.

"So it's not monsters, then," he said. "Just natural animals."

"Likely," Ryan said. "But see, that's the good news."

"And the bad?"

"As you can see for yourself, that's a mighty big herd up

there, Mr. Croom," J.B. said. "And they're headed straight for us."

Bass nodded, then went pale as the import of the words hit him.

"Oh," he said. "Shit."

THE GALLOPING HERD of buffalo looked like a moving range of shaggy brown mountains with horns, although short and curved enough so they'd be the least of your worries if you tangled with them. Individually a buffalo was a formidable beast: one or two thousand pounds of muscle, stink and bad attitude. Ryan and J.B. had realized right off that this was a big herd, numbering in the hundreds.

Whatever had stampeded them, they showed no sign of slowing. The buffalo would smash the convoy into ruined metal chunks leaking blood, and the herd as a whole would never miss a step. They wouldn't mean to destroy the wags and their human occupants; they just wouldn't be able to help it.

Side by side, J.B. and Ryan were riding the scrambler bikes balls-out, straight at the onrushing herd.

Ryan Cawdor was a brave man. He was comfortable with the fact. But if his heart hadn't been beating almost hard enough to explode out his rib cage, and his mouth and throat dry as if he'd been gargling sand, he wouldn't have been a man at all, but a cold robot.

When they were less than a hundred yards from the irresistible flood of flesh and bone and head-crushing hooves, Ryan raised the AK-47 he'd borrowed from one of Cable's sec men. It was one of the few fully automatic personal weapons Croom had brought along, though most of his sec crew and drivers made do with bolt actions or lever blasters.

Ryan thumbed off the safety, feeling more than hearing the distinctive "AK clack." The sound of thousands of pounding hooves was like the rumble of an erupting volcano.

When he triggered a one-handed blast skyward, Ryan did hear that.

The herd closed in on him, showing no reaction to his presence.

J.B. hurled a string of homemade firecrackers ahead of him. They were big, as loud as hell and smoky. Nobody in Ryan's crew knew exactly what Croom wanted with them; his assistant Sandra assured him they were popular trade items, as were fireworks of all sorts.

The first cracker went off, louder than the drumfire artillery barrage of the hooves and the yammer of another burst from Ryan's Kalashnikov. Dirt thrown up by the blast bounced off Ryan's left cheek.

J.B. started firing his M-4000, Ryan emptied his 30-round banana mag in a final shuddering blast. The buffalo in the first rank nearest to where the riders were approaching began to falter. He saw animals behind scramble on top of those slowing as the ceaseless pressure of all the beasts behind *them* drove them forward.

Good start, but not enough.

"Turn around for another pass!" he shouted to J.B.

As Ryan put his bike sideways in a dirt-digging turn of the front wheel and a boot down on the grass, J.B. cruised by. He had let the scattergun hang by its sling and was lighting the twisted-together fuses of another cluster of a half dozen double-size firecrackers.

Ryan realized the rest of the first string had to have gone off. After the first explosion right beside him, he'd been too focused on the task—and the herd—to notice the shattering blasts.

J.B. hurled the sparking string of crackers into the lowered faces of the stampeding buffalo. Ryan was afraid he couldn't turn fast enough. He accelerated back east toward the convoy, following cautiously a quarter-mile back, but as soon as he could he torqued his head around to see his friend's fate.

J.B. was following, a tight grin on the face thrust forward low over the handlebars, his fedora somehow miraculously stuck to his head, riding flat-out. That fear alleviated, Ryan feared instead that the buffalo had stomped out the firecracker fuses.

Then the black powder minibombs went off in a sort of jittering thunderbolt.

Chaos. The boom and flash and smell of fire utterly panicked the buffalo nearby. Some shied away into their brethren to left and right. At least one reared right up and was trampled straight down by the creatures behind it. They couldn't stop, or even slow, but plenty tripped. A pile of thrashing, bellowing bodies built up around the spot where the blasts had happened. The herd began to split left and right like water flowing around a big rock.

"Yes!" Ryan pumped the AK in the air.

Luckily the bison were built for power, not for speed. As inexorable as their charge was, they galloped with a certain majesty rather than awe-inspiring velocity. Ryan was already a hundred yards away again.

He turned the bike, halted long enough to drop the spent mag and slam home another from the special ammo vest he wore instead of his coat for the occasion, and rode the bike back at the jam of bodies.

He ripped the next magazine load off in three rapid bursts. By that time J.B. was riding parallel with him about fifteen yards away. He fired off four more blasts from his shotgun, then both wheeled away again.

For their next pass J.B. left the M-4000 hanging,

switched hands and picked up the Uzi cross-slung on the other side of his body. Then he and Ryan emptied new magazines blazing away as they rushed toward the herd.

By this time the job was done. The herd had decisively split into two masses that angled away from each other. They simply hadn't had a choice: already there were dozens of animals down, some thrashing and bellowing, some barely stirring.

It was hard times for those animals. Ryan wasn't happy that they had to suffer. He wasn't a cruel man, he was a man who did what had to be done.

J.B. split left, Ryan right. By darting at the herd, shooting, waving their arms, and shouting, they encouraged the herd to keep splitting wider and wider.

Then Ryan saw open prairie stretched unimpeded all the way to the still distant Rockies.

They'd opened a passage for their friends and the wags. It should be safe enough.

Safe as anything got in the Deathlands.

The two turned back. They'd continue to ride the sides of the gap until the herd passed.

AS THE CONVOY ROLLED forward, and the two living waves rolled past a hundred yards to either side, Ricky uttered a whoop of excitement from his perch on the back of Bass Croom's improvised armored command vehicle.

He looked at his friend Jak. As usual the albino sat impassive, his ruby eyes gazing keenly ahead, white hair streaming in the breeze of passage. But his chalk-white cheeks showed unusual spots of color. Try as he would to hide it by keeping his expression impassive, his face still betrayed the fact that he was a young man and just as excited as his young friend.

Ricky had been unable to keep the disappointment from

his face when Ryan and J.B. commandeered their bikes. But now he understood the necessity. They'd had to divert the herd from the wags before the tide of moving flesh swamped them, and they'd had the knowledge to pull it off.

And the balls. Ricky thought he'd had total respect both for his mentor J.B. and his unquestioned leader Ryan. But now he found his respect ratcheting even higher.

He sucked in a deep breath and immediately regretted it. His own goggles kept the dust thrown up by the hooves of the stampede from blinding him, but nothing came between his nose and the dust. To say nothing of the stench of hundreds of hairy, musty bodies. And the urine, feces and farts they left behind.

He felt bad about the suffering of the wounded animals who had been trampled by their frenzied fellows. Fortunately Ryan and J.B. had opened the way wide enough for them to steer around the moaning, kicking animals. But he knew that his friends had had no choice. If they hadn't acted, not only would there still be a mound of unfortunate broken-bodied buffalo writhing in terminal agony from the heedless hooves of those behind them, but Ricky, Krysty, Ryan, Mr. Croom, and all the rest, along with their vehicles, would be at the bottom of it.

And Dezzy. He couldn't forget the black-haired sec woman with the white bangs. Nor the warmth of her body in the chill Plains night. Not that he tried very hard.

He heard a shout from somewhere and looked ahead. His heart seemed to seize up in his chest. A half dozen of the giant beasts had broken off from the others to the right and veered straight back toward the vehicles' path.

Right off Ricky grasped the real danger. It was bad enough that a collision with one of those half-ton or more bodies could wreck a wag. Maybe even topple the school bus or even the tanker's tractor. But the thing that caused a thrill of horror to run through his whole frame was the prospect that others would follow them, that the living tsunami would roll over them all despite J.B.'s and Ryan's heroic efforts. And with safety visible not a quarter mile ahead.

He willed the convoy to roll faster, but it couldn't. The grass was torn up by all those hard, sharp hooves, and the ground underneath. Ricky didn't know how Croom's drivers managed to stay more or less at the same speed but through some wile of his they did. Their speed now wasn't more than twenty miles an hour. If they went any faster, they'd risk collision, or a wag breaking an axle, either of which could bring disaster, with the herd still to both sides.

From the lead vehicles, right ahead of Croom's wag, came a burst of giant yellow flame and a roar of noise that overrode the thunder of the hooves. Mildred was firing the big Browning M-2. Cable hadn't even protested when Ryan brusquely ordered his own sec man out in the physician's favor, so overwhelmed had he been by the sheer immensity of the herd. To say nothing of the threat it posed, which he clearly had no idea how to cope with.

Ricky saw little geysers of earth and grass thrown up as Mildred walked a stream of big bullets toward the errant bison. The stream stopped. She was way too canny a machine gunner to risk burning the barrel or tangling the ammo belt with a too long burst.

Her second burst hit the broken-off clump of bison. The lead and two others behind it fell, tumbling away.

The surviving beasts made haste to rejoin their fellows. Whatever lay this way, they knew it was death.

And then they were through, rolling across land that had began to cluster and clump in anticipation of the still distant Rockies, extending to either side, blessedly clear of brown-pelted living missiles.

Ricky jumped as Bass Croom's arm stuck out the driver's window and loosed off four blasts from his .45-caliber ParaOrdnance. Jak showed teeth in a grin at his friend's reaction, but Ricky wasn't embarrassed. The shots had been startling. Not to mention loud.

Having given the signal, the trader—who was driving himself, as he often did—began to brake his wag. Up ahead Mildred's big blaster wag slowed to a halt. Ricky looked back as the rest of the convoy did likewise. As usual, he marveled they managed to do so in relatively good order, no collisions, although he saw one cargo wag, its driver a little less attentive or quick-reacting than the others, pull slightly out of line to avoid bashing into the wag ahead.

As Ryan and J.B. drove up to the now halted line of wags on their bikes, Croom got out. So did Dace Cable on the other side. The merchant had ordered his sec man to ride with him while they ran the herd.

Ricky wasn't good with relationships, beyond familial ones, which made the thing with Dezzy, whatever it was, even more confusing. That was why he liked machines: they were straightforward. The same with the booby traps for which he and J.B. shared a special passion. People, not so much. But even Ricky could see Croom had a strange relationship with his sec-boss, not much easier and perhaps not so much different than the one with his whiny but somehow charming younger brother.

"Why the halt?" Ryan asked, bringing his bike to a stop a few feet away from Croom. He had to shout. Although the herd was still heading east at their not-fast-but-relentless lope, thus away from them, the wind from the east meant the roar of their hooves was still strong.

"Well, the buffalo are headed the right way, thanks to you two," the trader said. He was bareheaded and in

his shirtsleeves. The day was cool, but he seemed to prefer driving without the encumbrance of his bulky coat.
"Amazing job you did, by the way."

"Yeah," Cable agreed, coming around from the other
side. He seemed stunned, and only partly by having to
praise the man he saw too clearly as a rival. But he did.

Ricky expected Ryan to remind their boss that was
why he hired them. Instead the rangy black-haired man
said nothing. He just sat there with his boot planted on the
ground, next to a lonely early season white daisy that had
somehow escaped trampling, and looked a question at his
employer with his cool blue eye.

"So now," Bass said, and from his perch high up to one
side Ricky could see the big man was grinning through
his grizzled beard, "we get to go back and butcher some
of those poor bastards who got run over by their pals. If
any of them have any usable meat.

"That way we'll have fresh meat to trade when we hit
Raker's Rest tomorrow. Not to mention feasting ourselves
fat tonight!"

Chapter Fifteen

From a distance Raker's Rest looked cheerful and welcoming, with colorful walls and gaily fluttering banners above it.

As the convoy rolled toward the ville's gates, Krysty thought it started looking rather tawdry.

The bright walls were chain-link fences with the usual concertina-wire coils rolled along the top, not much different from the compound they'd left back in Menaville, if several times larger. They had metal panels attached to them somehow, enameled in a variety of colors. Riding behind the M-249 in the bed of the lead blaster wag, Krysty quickly realized that those colors had faded in the sun. As had the pennons, which she now saw were also frayed from the wind.

Nonetheless she found it a welcoming sight after their journey across the brutal heart of the Deathlands. The gates were open wide, the guards, armed with remade longblasters, waving them straight through. The fact that the lead vehicle was a blaster wag, and some of the wags following had armed guards perched atop them, didn't discourage the occupants of Raker's Rest. They could scarcely have expected a convoy to make the perilous crossing of the Great Plains without being triple well-armed.

Fact is, she thought, they'd likely be more suspicious if we weren't showing plenty of weps.

She glanced aside. Standing next to her, bracing himself with a hand on the pillar mount bolted to the bed, was Ryan. He'd asked for the posting late when they finally got rolling. They were all a bit stiff and sore from the work of butchering the retrievable bison carcasses, and had gotten a late start. Cable had scowled and stomped, as usual. But Croom had said sure, and invited his temperamental sec boss to ride in his command wag as personal shotgun. Also as usual.

Krysty looked at her lover's face in part because, well, she liked to. It was a beautiful face, to her—most beautiful in the world. She knew well each and every contour and fold and frown wrinkle around the one eye that looked so bleakly out on the world and so lovingly on her. She loved every inch of that face, even the scar. The blows and cuts and hardships were badges of honor that had made him the man he was.

But she was a bit concerned. He was frowning even more than usual, and looking around way more than seemed necessary as they rolled between wide-open gates overlooked by obvious blaster towers. If danger was pending, it was unlikely to be from the flat ground surrounding the sprawling rest stop, or even the low hills bumping up nearby.

Nor, did she think, there was much peril to be found in Raker's Rest. She and her friends had heard about it in their wanderings over the years. The rest stop was located just far enough for comfort from the Cheyenne craters and attendant hot zone—still red-line lethal after all these years—near where the old maps said the borders of the formerly United States of Nebraska, Colorado and Wyoming came together. It was the biggest trading post and rest stop in the area and had been an established landmark for a generation or more.

"Why so moody, lover?" she asked teasingly. "Worst thing we're liable to encounter here is sharp trade."

He grunted, then gave her just a hint of a smile. Enough to make her feel all warm and fluttery in her belly, as if she were a teenager again.

I hope we actually get a room to ourselves tonight, she thought. Privacy wasn't a big issue for her or most of her friends, Doc still had some issues with it, and young Ricky still got shocked sometimes and wasn't skillful enough to hide it. But lovemaking was still personal. Personal as a thing could be. She treasured the opportunities to engage in sex in private the more for the fact they were rare as interludes of peace and relative safety.

As this promised to be.

Almost at once he was looking around. Assessing their surroundings. Her mother had taught her many useful things, not least of which was to never enter a room without knowing how she could get out of it again if the hammer came down. Preferably more ways than one. Ryan took that commendable caution and amped it levels higher.

Sure, they were likely safe here, but assuming that they really were, and letting their guard down, was a good way to end up staring up at the stars until the crows picked out their eyes. She didn't need for Ryan to say the words to hear them in her mind.

Once inside the place Krysty took in its ramshackle appearance, as if it had been thrown together hastily and maintained not much more carefully since. A lot of buildings seemed little more than shacks of random planks and scraps of plywood and whatnot.

"Not real luxurious," Ryan said.

She laughed. "But then again, lover, we've been to baron's palaces where the dogs waited under the table for bones in the dining hall, and the guests pissed in the corners, even before they got drunk."

He chuckled. "True enough. Reckon I should be glad for a chance at a real bed and a roof over our heads and sheets that have mebbe been washed in our lifetimes."

She grabbed his arm and squeezed.

A succession of sec, all wearing orange armbands, stood along the wide central street of what was, dingy or not, a good-size ville inside the wire, waving their wag driver onward. The hard-packed dirt road led to a vast central yard, with a few wags parked around the perimeter. Some more substantial buildings stood by, some adobe, some prefab, that looked to Krysty like workshops and warehouses.

A sec woman with short red hair and a face seamed with hard living waved them to a halt as they entered the yard. Ryan waved his arm to make sure the rest of the convoy knew they were stopping. The drivers were all waiting for that signal; this was all standard operating procedure, and Krysty guessed that after the horrors and uncertainties of their crossing of the Deathlands, most of Croom's people were nothing but relieved to fall back into the comforting arms of familiar routine.

In short order the blaster wag had parked and Krysty and Ryan dismounted. She was glad for the opportunity to walk on solid ground and stretch the kinks out. He seemed to be, as well.

In short order the rest of the convoy rumbled into the square yard. A mixture of Croom's people and the rest stop's sec force saw them to their assigned spaces. Krysty paid them no mind. That was their job, not that of Ryan and his crew.

Bass Croom and Dace Cable joined them. As they did so a party approached them from the building on the north side of the yard, a two-story structure with adobe walls

and a pitched corrugated metal roof. It was the largest
ville Krysty had seen in the structure. She guessed it was
the owner's, and that the man with the black handlebar
mustache striding across the hard-packed ground toward
them on long, lean legs was him. With the owner walked
an immense man with a shaved head and a striking raven-
haired woman.

"Welcome to Raker's Rest!" the mustached man declared. "I'm Bry Raker. Enjoy your stay!"

With an unerring eye he instantly sized up Bass Croom
as the boss of the convoy. He walked up to him and held
out his hand. Bass took it and shook it warmly.

"Thank you, Mr. Raker," he said. "I'm Bastion Croom.
This is my outfit. This here's my sec boss, Dace Cable.
Here're Ryan Cawdor and Krysty Wroth, a couple of my
Deathlands specialists. And this is my younger brother,
Morty."

Raker pumped Cable's hand, then Ryan's. He was about
the same height as Ryan, and built along the same lines:
rangy, bulked out by a wolfskin coat. He looked to be a
fit, energetic man in his thirties, who wore a beefy Smith
& Wesson revolver in a holster at his hip.

When he approached Krysty, she stuck out her own
hand to forestall any more familiar form of greeting and
was glad she did. His firm, dry grip lingered on hers a few
heartbeats, and his brown eyes made themselves freer with
Krysty's face and figure than she really cared for.

Giving her a flash grin he turned away. "And this is my
sec boss, Butler. And finally, my lovely wife, Katherine."

Up close Katherine Raker was even more lovely than
she had appeared at first glimpse. She was tall, only an
inch or two shorter than Krysty, and the coat and boots
she wore failed to conceal that her figure was at least trim

beneath. Her features were finely sculpted, her nose thin, and her eyes were as bright and shiny as obsidian flecks.

They in turn seemed to be far too interested in Ryan. Krysty didn't try to stifle her own grin. He's a big boy, she reminded herself, and an attractive man. And I can't very well get twitchy when some trading post vixen flashes her eyes at him, any more than he does when poor Ricky makes calf eyes at me.

Morty seemed impressed by her, which didn't really surprise Krysty. He seemed to come on mighty strong with some of his brother's comelier female employees, and to pay a lot more attention to the mystery woman Olympia than she seemed to care for. Or respond to at all, honestly; she simply seemed not to notice him. But at least he seemed to have taken Mildred's advice to heart and forgotten about Krysty, probably out of fear of Ryan.

In his case, an entirely reasonable fear, though he should be little less scared of Krysty herself, had he but the wit to know it.

Katherine seemed as immune to Morty's charms as Krysty or Olympia. She gave him a pro forma smile and turned hungry eyes back on Ryan. Krysty glanced toward Raker; she was more concerned that the husband might take a potentially inconvenient interest in her than that Mrs. Raker might harbor designs on Ryan.

But Raker was talking earnestly with Croom over fees and arrangements. Meanwhile J.B. came rolling up, then Mildred and finally Doc.

Croom and Raker seemed quickly to come to terms. Both were old hands at bartering, after all. Krysty was mildly surprised they hadn't spent six times as long haggling for its own sake; then again, Bass Croom seemed a no-nonsense sort of man. Apparently Raker was cut from the same leather.

He turned to the others and now that devil's smile came back. "Ladies, gentlemen," he said. "Make yourselves welcome. It has been years since we've hosted so large and grand a convoy. It's a pleasure for us. We want to make sure it's the same for you."

"We haven't had many visitors at all for a while," Katherine said. Her voice was a velvety contralto. Her manner seemed more haughty than anything else. "Your presence is most welcome."

From the corner of her eye Krysty caught a look of irritation ripple across Raker's face. He instantly smoothed it away, so fast Krysty could almost believe she'd imagined it.

Except she hadn't.

Raker's grin widened to show a fairly decent set of teeth, if yellowed by obvious tobacco use.

"Kit's right," he said with only a quick hint of rasp. "In fact, we'd be honored if you and your people would join us for dinner tonight. In honor of our esteemed visitors from the East, it's on the house!"

Bass gave him a big old smile back. "Speaking just for myself, I'm pleased to accept, with thanks. It'll be good to sample some down-home hospitality."

Raker clapped him on the biceps. "Great. Come with me and I'll show you your accommodations. I'll have my assistants see to getting the rest of your crew properly housed."

They walked off together: Croom and Raker talking like old pals; the immense Butler as stolid as a walking statue, having not said word one during the whole exchange; Cable hanging close beside his boss and Morty trotting after like somebody's dog. Kit Raker threw Ryan one more smoldering look over her shoulder before following her husband with what looked like reluctance.

"There goes trouble," Mildred muttered. Krysty didn't have to ask whom she was referring to. She only laughed.

"Speaking of which," Doc said, shaking himself slightly as if waking from a walking nap of some sort, "you seem troubled, my dear Ryan."

Ryan grimaced. "Just pissed," he said. "I told Jak and Ricky to meet back up with us before we hit the gates. Where the nuke are they?"

"They're just kids, Ryan," Krysty said. "Relax."

"Jak's a grown man, as he never gets tired reminding me. Anyway, they're with an adult."

"Who's riding a bicycle," J.B. said. "She probably rode farther than she thought and is having to hustle to get back. Ricky wouldn't leave her in the lurch. Jak wouldn't leave him."

"That woman strikes me more as the sort who could tell you to the foot how far she's pedaled that nuked mountain bike," Ryan growled. "She should know better."

Krysty snaked her arm around Ryan's so that they were elbow to elbow. "They'll be fine, this close to the rest stop," she said. "I don't know about anybody else, but I'm dying to see if the deal Mr. Croom drove includes showers."

"CAME BACK."

That was Jak, in his usual laconic way, summing up the giant buffalo herd that had come within an ace of zeroing them all out the day before. And true enough: the broad valley a mile or so from Raker's Rest was filled with a sea of dark brown, as the big animals grazed on what Ricky could only guess was a lush early spring growth of grass.

With a crunch of dirt under big-cleated tires that was barely audible over the low mutter of the motorcycle engines, Olympia came to a stop beside them. She unshipped a canteen from her belt and drank. Then she offered it to

Ricky, who said thank-you but declined, and then to Jak, who merely shook his head.

She only rode the mountain bike when the convoy was stopped, or moving double slow for some reason. Because Bass didn't want the two young men on scrambler bikes arriving at Raker's Rest before the rest of the convoy, he'd pulled them back a few miles short of their goal. Olympia had asked for and received permission to take the mountain bike and the pair on their dirt bikes and scout the surrounding area. Bass had apparently seen no reason to refuse and said yes. After a brief scowl Ryan had given permission, as well.

Now the shadows of them and their rides stretched far down the gentle slope behind them as afternoon declined to evening and the sun fell toward the Rockies, now a presence almost near and tall enough to feel, though still far enough to remain featureless and blue. Ricky was starting to get anxious to get back to the convoy. He suspected they'd been out longer than the adults would be happy with as it was.

"Interesting," Olympia said, gazing at the grazing herd with her blue-jade eyes. Seen up close they had little folds of skin at the inner corners. Ricky's mother had told him those were called epicanthic folds, and usually meant a person had Asian ancestry. Since they had taught him well, using cracked and ancient books his father had traded for over the years, he even knew where Asia was.

He thought Olympia was the most beautiful woman he had ever seen. Except for his older sister Yamile, who didn't count, of course, because she was his sister—and again he felt the obligatory pang of guilt and grief that he hadn't yet made good on his vow to find and rescue her. And of course for Krysty, who also didn't count in a way.

Ricky did know enough to realize in a vague sort of

way that it was to be expected he'd exist in a sort of constant simmer of horniness, self-doubt and massive frustration. He tried hard not to envision Krysty naked, made all the more daunting a task by the fact that he had seen her naked a few times, when she had stripped quite unself-consciously bare to go skinny dipping and bathing in some stream. He had similarly noticed that Mildred, stocky though she was, wasn't without her charms, but he didn't actually desire either woman. Not that that altogether stopped his body from responding to their nearness and femininity. He knew nothing would ever happen with either of them; that if he ever made a try for one the worst thing that was likely to happen was not that their menfolk would squash him like a bug, but that the women would merely laugh.

Although Ricky also knew that if he made a pest of himself to Krysty, or even Mildred, Ryan would cast him out of their band with barely a second thought. And that was all the family Ricky had now. He literally would rather die than lose them.

Anyway…he found himself also thinking of Krysty and Mildred as his mothers, somehow, which made the inevitable sixteen-year-old lust for their female flesh seem icky and disturbing. It made him guilty that he couldn't stop it entirely.

As for Olympia, he had never seen her naked. The joke around camp was that she had been born in that uniform-like brown outfit she wore. No one had seen her wash it or even change it, yet it appeared spotless and clean-smelling each morning. With her slim figure and long legs and quite astonishing height, she certainly exerted a powerful appeal on his feverish young brain and more southerly parts.

But even though she always treated him—and Jak, who really was a grownup, although only a few years older than Ricky—with the same quiet though not-deferential respect she treated everybody, the mystery woman scared the hell out of Ricky.

He found himself thinking of Dezzy, the sec woman from Cable's crew. When the adults got occupied butchering the wounded buffalo yesterday, Olympia asked for permission to take Jak and Ricky with her to put the remainder out of their misery. Because there was no shortage of labor anyway—there weren't that many salvageable carcasses—and because nobody felt all that comfortable letting Jak Lauren loose with his blades, Ryan had agreed, as had Bass.

To Ricky's surprise Dezzy had asked for and received permission to join them, too.

It had been a grim job. Despite the large stocks Bass had brought along they couldn't afford to waste ammo. They only shot the ones who were otherwise hard to reach, or still active enough to be too dangerous to approach. Otherwise they relied on knives, axes and sometimes a pickax.

Dezzy had done her part, thin-lipped and looking even paler than usual. When Ricky, during a break to breathe, drink water and make a token effort to clean the blood drops from their faces, asked why she was doing this, she answered tautly, "I like animals."

Which Ricky understood. He had the same reason. He had no compunction about killing animals for food, but he hated to see them suffer unnecessarily. Oddly enough, he knew Jak felt a variation of the same thing: in his case the hunter's ethos of the clean kill.

As for Olympia, well, who knew why she did anything? He only knew that scary or not, she was interesting to be around. And usually fun.

"Ready?"

It was Olympia herself, breaking in on his reverie in

her inevitable quiet yet somehow decisive-sounding voice. He shook himself.

"Yeah. Sorry. Uh, right. We better get back."

"Not yet," Olympia said. "Let's head up in the heights near the rest stop to scope it out first."

"Wait!" Ricky exclaimed. "No! We can't!"

By then he'd realized to his horror that he was afraid of Olympia. And that it was also just exactly too late to back down. Blood didn't go back in the body, Ryan and J.B. liked to say, quoting their long-ago boss and mentor who was known only as Trader.

Olympia didn't, however, devour him. Nor even stab him with the combat knife scabbarded on the hip opposite where her beefy six-shooter rode in its flapped leather holster. She merely looked at him and asked, "Why can't we?"

"We have to get back!" he stammered. "Ryan said we should join back up before they went into the rest stop."

"Late," Jak said. He seemed neutral in the debate. He accepted Ryan as leader, Ricky knew, but he had also learned his new best friend was anything but averse to being rebellious every now and then. Just to show he could.

Still, Ricky's heart fell.

"Yeah, I know. We're probably in trouble already," he said.

Was it his imagination or did the woman almost smile? "Then what's the problem?" she asked.

"Well, they'll worry about us!"

Olympia cocked her head to one side and raised a brow in a look that asked, *"Seriously?"*

"It's the Deathlands," she said. "Nowhere is safe. Anyway, I've sized up your friends, and seen that gray wolf of a leader of yours in action. Do you really think you're safe with them? Or do they always seem to wind up in the midst of danger?"

Jak snorted an uncharacteristic laugh. Ricky felt his cheeks burn. No, since he had joined Ryan and his crew, life had been anything but safe.

But he had to defend his new family. "Okay, sure. You're right. But there's still no place on Earth safer than next to Ryan and J.B. And the rest, too!"

"You may be right, at that. Now come on. I'm the adult. I'll take the heat if there's any."

Jak shot her a hot look.

"All right. You're adult, too, Jak Lauren. And I'm the paying customer. I'll tell them I ordered you to come along. To keep me safe from wolves."

Jak grinned at that.

"All right," Ricky said, still reluctant. Although come to think of it, he wasn't exactly eager to get back now and face J.B., much less Ryan.

She turned the bike and pushed off. "Then what are you waiting for? Let's go!"

Send For
2 FREE BOOKS
Today!

I accept your offer!

Please send me two free
novels and a mystery gift (gift
worth about $5). I understand
that these books are completely
free—even the shipping and
handling will be paid—and
I am under no obligation
to purchase anything, ever, as
explained on the back of this card.

366 ADL FVYT   **166 ADL FVYT**

Please Print

FIRST NAME

LAST NAME

ADDRESS

APT.#   CITY

STATE/PROV.   ZIP/POSTAL CODE

Visit us online at
www.ReaderService.com

Offer limited to one per household and not applicable to series that subscriber is currently receiving.

© 2012 WORLDWIDE LIBRARY ® and ™ are trademarks owned and used by the trademark owner and/or its licensee. Printed in the U.S.A.

◄ Detach card and mail today. No stamp needed.

GE-GF-13

Part III:

The Tribulation

Chapter Sixteen

"Got to hand it to you, Mr. Croom," Mildred said. "You managed to wrangle us some prime quarters. Even if it must have set you back a handsome chunk of jack."

To her it looked like an old Army barracks, even to the faded tones of green and brown. Basically a big square house with a pitched roof, in decent enough shape, had been subdivided into a few rooms with improvised walls of wood panels, most of which you wouldn't want to lean against for fear of getting splinters in your ass. It was still a big step up from the rest of the barracks, which was divided into smaller sleeping spaces with curtains, also random and improvised. Still, there was room for the thirty-five or so travelers from the master merchant's convoy to sleep with a roof over their heads, in high comfort by contemporary standards, and with at least a nod to privacy.

She looked at J.B. and grinned. He blinked at her. As usual he wasn't much for reading body language, much less hints.

Never mind, John Barrymore, she silently promised. I got some plans for later on tonight.

Bass Croom chuckled. It was a big-man chuckle, rolling up from deep in that oil-drum chest. Though Mildred had learned to be wary of most people she met in the Deathlands, and trader types second maybe only to barons, she sized it up as a genuine laugh. Croom seemed a genuine kind of guy, who genuinely cared for his people, genuinely grieved over their one fatality of the trip, itself something of a minor miracle.

That didn't account, in her estimation, for the dark circles deepening morning by morning beneath his gray eyes. Nor the fact he sometimes seemed to have a bit of a problem letting go of the bottle late at night. But despite the amazing ease of most of their journey across the worst of the Deathlands, there had to be insane levels of stress involved in shepherding his big ungainly metal-and-meat worm all the way to the Pacific Northwest.

"Bry Raker charged me an arm and a leg, you can rest assured," the trader said. "But—" he shrugged like a mountain trying to lose some annoying climbers "—I think we can all use a good rest. So it's well worth it."

"It'd be better if Olympia was here," Morty complained. As usual he was hanging behind his brother's shoulder as if to make himself part of the decision-making.

Cable swung his hot green glare from Ryan to Morty. "Listen," he said, not unreasonably, "you should just forget about her. And mebbe my sec women, while you're at it. They're sec, not playthings."

Morty puffed up. He wasn't soft, Mildred knew that, although where he got the strength and muscle tone was completely beyond her, since he never did a lick of work that she could see, or otherwise exercised. Maybe he was just one of those people blessed with a constitution that kept them fit no matter how inert they were.

"Listen," the younger Croom snarled at Cable, "you're not the boss of me."

"He's right, Morty," Bass said. With amazing gentleness under the circumstances. Not for the first time Mildred wondered why the merchant didn't just unload a good backhand on the boy, which he was, despite having adult years in her own terms, and definitely by Deathlands standards.

"Miss Olympia is a paying customer. Don't forget that. Anyway, she doesn't seem interested, and that's a fact."

"You just want her for yourself!" Morty flared. "I've seen the way you stare at her! All hot-eyed like you want to eat her up."

Bass frowned, then smoothed his craggy brow and shook his head.

"You don't understand, Morty. She just reminds me of… somebody I knew a long time ago. And while you're at it, why not give all my female employees a break? The rule back home was always no dipping your pen in the company inkwell. I haven't changed that on the road."

Morty turned red, but he said no more. Instead he went stomping off down the hall.

"There he goes in a snit," Mildred muttered, mostly to her friends, but not caring who else heard. "His favorite conveyance."

Krysty shook her head in pretend reproof. Doc stifled a laugh into an equine snort, which surprised Mildred. She'd thought the old man was off in a world of his own the way he'd been acting once they hit Raker's Rest.

"Anyway, the hard part's over," Cable said. His eyes seemed unnaturally bright, his manner crisp to the point of brittleness. Mildred didn't like the eye he was giving Ryan as they stood in the corridor outside the walled bedrooms. Then again, she never did, much.

"Over for now," Bass said, cocking his head and looking at his sec boss.

"Well, we crossed the big, bad Deathlands, right? We're at the Rockies. I mean, it's all easy from here the rest of the way. Right? A cakewalk."

J.B. gave Ryan a look. For the Armorer that was equivalent to sending up a warning flare: trouble ahead.

"Not necessarily the case," Ryan said calmly.

Cable swung around into Ryan's face. "Listen here, One-Eye," he said. "We're not on the road now. You may be the big Deathlands expert. But we're in a ville now, or the same as. This is my show. So show me some respect, understand?"

Ryan just looked at him.

Bass cleared his throat.

"That's enough, Dace."

Cable lowered his head as he turned. "I just wanted—"

"You need to take it down," Bass said as sternly as Mildred ever heard him talk to anybody. "Yes, you're good at your job. Everybody knows that, including Mr. Cawdor and his friends. And now you need to go take care of it. Just because we're in a temporary safe haven doesn't mean we can let our guard down completely, now, does it?"

And to draw the sting he ended with a smile and an avuncular hand on Cable's shoulder. The sec boss gulped, nodded and went on his way. As he did, his shoulders squared and his stride grew more assertive: he was back on the job again.

Bass sighed. Mildred understood. He'd just had to deal with both of his problem children in the space of under a minute. What she found harder to catch hold of was why he put up with their shit. Sure, Morty was blood and Cable was a good sec boss, but that didn't mean either would fail to benefit from a good slapping-down. And Bass for all that he preferred gentleness and openness in his dealings was no soft man.

"Long time ago," he said, his eyes looking at nowhere in particular, "right where I was getting my real beginning in this bad old world, after a...false start or two, I ran across a wolf cub. Young, starving, cold, whipped out of his pack. I took him in and raised him.

"And he responded. Started showing a dog's loyalty to me. I found myself with, what do they call it? A Chinese obligation to him? I couldn't just cut him loose. He's served me loyally and well and become my best friend in the bargain. So if sometimes he snarls and snaps when he shouldn't, well, I just try to correct that and move on. You know?"

"Is having your sec boss for a best friend really good business?" Mildred couldn't keep from asking.

Bass laughed out loud.

"Beats the simple hell out of having one who's your enemy," he said. "Believe you me, Miss Wyeth. And now if you'll excuse me, I want to go take advantage of those hot shower privileges Bry Raker charged me my left arm for. I'll see you at dinner, ladies, gentlemen."

He moved off, leaving the group of friends to themselves in the twilight gloom of the hall. Outside the window at one end the light had gone almost slate gray.

"I'm still nervous about this Cable," Mildred announced. "I mean, I see why Croom sticks with him now."

"A good sec man is hard to find," J.B. said. "Man knows his job, got to give him his due."

"He worries me, too," Krysty said. "He seems fixated on you, Ryan."

"Why?" Mildred demanded. "What is his major malfunction?"

"The canine metaphor our employer used of their relationship is most apt," Doc said. "Until now Mr. Cable has been undisputed leader of the security pack. Alpha, I believe the—my captors—called it. But now he perceives a threat."

"But there is none," Krysty said. "Croom hired us to

help on the journey cross-country, where even Cable admitted he didn't have experience."

Doc shook his head. "Sadly, that is not how he sees it. To him Ryan is a rival, and will a rival remain. Until the issue is resolved."

Ryan looked grimmer even than usual. "Sooner or later he'll force the issue," he grunted. "Till then I'll live."

"So how do you handle it?" Mildred asked.

Ryan shrugged. "Same as I been doing. Trying not to cross paths with him when I don't have to, try to keep pushing things down the road. Best, to where it ends and we part ways with Mr. Croom and his pals."

Mildred cocked a skeptical eyebrow. "Think it'll work that way?"

"Does it ever?"

"All right," Krysty said. "Enough dark talk and long faces. Ryan, you're coming with me. Mr. Croom paid for shower privileges for us, too. We have a party to attend, and I won't go smelling like a week-chilled skunk. You, either. To say nothing of when we share our own private bedroom tonight, for the first time in what seems like years."

She took his arm and tugged. Mildred would've thought it'd take a stronger man than even Ryan to resist the lure of seeing Krysty naked, no matter how often he got to do it. But Ryan held back, his face still dark.

"What's eating you, lover?" Krysty said. "I've been sensing it since we got here."

He shook his head. "Something's not right," he said. "Can't put my finger on it. That gripes at me."

"It's the fact Jak and Ricky disobeyed and still haven't come back in, even though it's full dark," Mildred said.

"Mebbe," Ryan said slowly.

She shook her head. "I wonder where those fool kids are?"

DINNER WAS over-the-top extravagant, even by Ryan's standards as a baron's son.

The dining hall was a frame annex to the big house at the north end of the rest stop's central yard. Ryan guessed it was a general eatery for employees who didn't have their own residences in the vast compound, as he gathered some didn't. But this night the boss himself had taken it over to provide a welcome feast for what he himself had described as the biggest convoy to come through in years.

It started off with vegetable soup made with some kind of meat stock—Ryan guessed buffalo, though he wasn't sure. Croom had gotten a decent price for a ton or so of salted buffalo meat from the previous day's adventure, so why wouldn't Raker use it? But he wasn't sure.

One thing he was sure of: it was good—would've been if they hadn't been living on road food for two weeks, although Croom's cook was all the time, since that's all anybody called him—was good at his job. Still, there were limits what even he could whip up over a campfire, like as not made of dried buffalo chips.

As he took up another spoonful of the hot, savory soup, Ryan caught Krysty's eye across the table. She smiled. She was wearing her usual clothes, but was clean. So was he.

She was sitting between their host and Bass Croom. Kit Raker sat at Ryan's left, across from her husband. Whenever her husband wasn't looking, she kept shooting Ryan burning-coal looks and twisting in her chair to give him ample opportunity to look down the chasm of milk-white cleavage left bare by her maroon silk gown. Ryan tried not to look, despite the fact she kept showing herself off a lot, owing to the fact that her husband in turn mostly had eyes for Krysty.

Dace Cable, Morty Croom and Croom himself also sat at the head table, along with a shrimpy little bald guy in rimless glasses whose head sprouted like some kind of colorless tuber from what Ryan could only think of as an undertaker's suit. He'd been introduced as Raker's top aide. Mildred said he looked like an accountant. Ryan, who had rare experience with the breed himself, tended to agree.

He glanced around at the next table down, where J.B. was peering at each spoonful as if curious about what sort of multilegged thing might be swimming in it, and Doc was holding forth in grand manner. Though sometimes when he got going he could bore a person to tears, he could also be an entertaining, even funny storyteller when the mood hit him. As evidently it had, from the reactions of the mix of convoy crew and Raker's people who sat at the much larger table. Several other tables were also arranged down the mess hall.

At first Ryan had resisted the idea of breaking up his companions. He disliked it as a rule, no less with it already broken up because of the unexplained tardiness of Ricky and Jak. Plus he hated to be put above his group in any way. He was their nominal leader, but they were still all friends, and what was good for one was good for all.

Bass had asked, politely but urgently. Ryan had gotten the nod from Krysty, who at least intuited no danger from the arrangement. And so he'd reluctantly agreed.

Maybe she sensed no additional danger. *Something* kept crawling up Ryan's back. Something he still couldn't pin down. He could only put it off to a mixture of annoyance and concern that the youngest members hadn't made it back hours since.

"Don't you find it so, Mr. Cawdor?" asked Kit Raker, turning toward him again and leaning in as a silent servant poured her cut-crystal goblet full of red wine. The wine was good, too; Ryan drank but sparingly of it and hoped his companions did, too.

He discovered that he'd spaced out and had no idea what the woman had said previously. "As a general thing, Mrs. Raker," he said, "I find I got a full enough plate just keeping me and my friends alive without poking into things that don't concern me."

He saw her brow furrow. She did it prettily enough: she was a gorgeous woman, no mistake. But he also was beginning to size her up as trouble, leaving aside the fact her husband was basically the baron of what was in effect a sizable ville. There was something dark and stormy about her that hadn't really appealed to him since he was young, single and triple foolish. If he put her shapely nose out of joint, maybe she'd at least leave him alone!

It also occurred to him that what he said may just have been such a thundering non sequitur that she was entirely confused. Good enough.

The main course was brought in: an entire roasted elk carcass, smoking grandly on some kind of wheeled cart covered in a tablecloth bleached well enough that the faint stains still visible could likely be forgiven. Ryan couldn't stop from cracking a smile as Mildred sang out, "Who even has a stove big enough to *cook* something like that?"

As the monster roast was carved up by a sweaty dude in a tall white mushroom hat, Ryan found himself listening to the talk Raker and Croom were conducting basically over Krysty's bosom. Raker was amplifying again on the theme that times had been hard. He quoted drought to the east, volcanic eruptions west across the Rockies, and general strife and disorder everywhere.

Ryan caught Krysty's green gaze again as a big sturdy ceramic plate was clunked down in front of him. It had to be sturdy to support the weight of roast elk meat weighing it down. Despite the fact he'd been hitting the soup and the bread rolls hard his stomach rumbled at the aroma.

She winked at him; he smiled back. He knew her thoughts. *Just the same as things always are.*

So the meal went: with course after savory course, for which Ryan seemed miraculously to find room. He'd be surprised if he wasn't bloated at the end of it all. But he found himself hungry, and realized how seldom, in the course of his adult life, he'd felt anything but hunger in one degree or another.

Despite his sipping sparingly, he also put down a decent quality of Raker's wine. Wines—all of which were of good quality. Not even a baron of the reasonably prosperous eastern barony like Ryan's ancestral home of Front Royal could always be that picky about what he served, either by way of food or drink. But Baron Titus always knew good wine from bad, and made sure his offspring did, too.

Too bad he wasn't as good at telling the good from the bad where his own seed was concerned. The ancient knife scar down the left side of his face panged at the brief memory. His traitor brother Harvey had put it there, cost him his eye and his birthright and doomed him to a life of rootless wandering.

By the time some kind of chocolate cake was served, Ryan could no longer muster even the pretense of eating for the sake of politeness, though for a fact it looked good. As everything had been. He was starting to feel as if his belt had shrunk a notch and was hoping Krysty wouldn't feel too frisky tonight.

Which, come to think of it, was as rare a thing as him turning down food.

Bry Raker rose, tinkling a spoon against a glass for attention. "Ladies, gentlemen, beloved employees and honored guests, please permit me to propose a toast."

Fresh wine was poured. More than a little reluctantly,

Ryan picked up his glass. At this stage he was glad he knew the trick of just wetting his lips while pretending to drink.

As he picked up the goblet, he found Katherine Raker staring at him again. This time it was a flat hot stare, and the color was completely gone from her normally pallid cheeks. She clearly disapproved of something, but he was skinned if he had the least inkling what.

"If my guests will rise," Raker said in his loud tenor. With a certain shuffling and scuffling of chairs, Croom and his people pushed back from the table and stood.

"Thank you. So now I propose a toast. To Bastion Croom, merchant prince and bold adventurer, and the brave souls who have dared to cross the worst of the Deathlands under his command—my sincere congratulations and admiration!"

He drank deeply. When he had drained his goblet of blood-red wine, Raker threw it to the plank floor, where it shattered.

"And also my sincere apologies, because you are all now my prisoners!"

And then the walls seemed to sprout sec men with orange armbands, blasters leveled at Ryan, Croom and all their companions.

Chapter Seventeen

The sun had yet to set behind the Rockies as Ricky found himself and his companions gazing down on the rest stop, but it was working on it.

It was an impressive sight, he had to admit.

"Okay, neat," he said. "Now we've got to go. We're late enough as it is."

"No," Olympia said.

Ricky and Jak turned to stare at her. She had joined them on the crest. The ground coming up had been rocky and broken-up enough that they hadn't had to stop every so often and wait for her to catch up on her human-powered ride.

"You mustn't."

Jak frowned. "Shit," he said. "Going."

He gunned his engine.

"You'll die," Olympia said.

Her voice wasn't loud, exactly, but somehow it cracked like a whip. Ricky had heard Ryan use the same voice. Well, it was completely different—he was a man, with a rough voice. But still the same. Somehow.

It commanded attention; it commanded Jak's. His engine eased back to idle as he turned a blank red stare on her.

"Your friends will die, too," she said.

"Can't know!"

"Yes," she said calmly, "I can. I'm a doomie. I can see pathways into the future."

"Talk," he said.

"That's it," she said. "I can see a short ways down different roads into the future. I see where the one your friends have chosen leads."

"Where's that?" Ricky asked. His throat was dry, and it wasn't just from eating the trail dust thrown up by Jak's bike all afternoon.

"Betrayal."

SOMEWHERE A CLOCK gonged midnight. Bry Raker, that coldhearted piece of shit, Ryan thought, liked to keep a regular compound. He stirred. His lone eye was swollen half shut. His head rang like a gong, and from far more than the wine he'd taken aboard.

He felt a strong grip on his arm. J.B. helped him stand. Actually, the Armorer dragged Ryan's still reluctant body clean onto his feet.

"You look like you've been used to hammer in half a dozen tents pegs," J.B. remarked, steadying his friend with a hand on the biceps.

"I feel that way," Ryan mumbled.

He felt his aching jaw. His tongue probed the inside of his mouth. Nothing seemed broken and he still had all his teeth.

He pried his eye open. "You don't look triple good yourself."

Both of J.B.'s eyes were black, but the round lenses of the steel-rimmed glasses perched in front of them were intact. The Armorer had made sure to slip them into his pocket before turning and making his attempt to fight free of their treacherous captors at dinner.

He'd known he'd lose the battle, as had Ryan, but they'd

both made the attempt anyway. And not because of stiff-necked pride. Trader always called a man who'd die for mere pride just another dead stupe, and they still marked his words well after all these years.

"After the beat-down you two took," called a voice from the next cell, "it's a wonder you're still alive."

Ryan recognized the voice of Dan Hogue, Bass Croom's wrench. Before Butler, Raker's giant shave-headed meat-wad of a sec boss, had personally clubbed him down with the butt of what looked like an M-1 Garand, Ryan had seen the little bearded mechanic try to swarm the cold-hearts behind him.

Ryan looked at J.B., who shrugged. Dan was the one who was lucky to be alive.

"We've been there before, son," J.B. said. "We know how to make a show of getting beat down without getting hurt triple bad."

"Brag," Morty said. The sullen young man was sport-ing a shiner of his own. He might not be worth much, but he wasn't worth nothing, it turned out. He'd fought back, too, and given the sec man who was holding down on his big brother a pretty good sock on the jaw before another laid him out with a buttstroke. "You two look like ham-mered dog shit."

"Thank you so much," J.B. said.

"Didn't say it doesn't hurt," Ryan said. "Only that we know how not to get busted up too bad."

"Not like *him*," J.B. added with a nod toward Cable. The blond-goateed sec boss for the convoy lay stretched out on the straw scattered across the packed-dirt floor of the adobe-walled cell. He only seemed now to be twitch-ing and groaning his way back to life.

Huddled in the corner of the cell, which was about twelve feet by twelve, like a terminally depressed bear,

Bass Croom stirred himself. He alone of the handful of men in this cell bore no bruises or scuffs. Even Doc was disheveled and the right side of his face was bruised from getting punched as he'd fought back.

But when Bry Raker, their host, announced his treachery, the master trader had frozen. He'd just stood staring like a jacklit deer as his hands were yanked behind him and bound.

Ryan didn't blame him a speck of dried owl shit. He knew Croom didn't have a yellow bone in his body. On the road so far he'd had plenty of opportunity to turn away from danger and never did. From his years on the road, he had to have some notion how dangerous this journey would be. Even if he couldn't *really* know how deadly it could turn.

As it had. With that smug declaration of betrayal by the man who had taken them in, taken his jack and his trade goods, and gone back on the whole notion of a trade convoy rest stop, Croom had seen himself losing everything: his goods, the people he cared about so much, his beloved little brother. His own life, though that seemed not to matter much to him now.

But his friend and sec boss, Cable, returning to consciousness, or at least some facsimile of it, roused Bass from his sunk-in despair. He rose and lumbered over to kneel beside his wounded friend and cradle his head in his lap.

"Water," the merchant said.

"Left us a bucket and a ladle," J.B. said. "Just to show they weren't total barbarians. Just back-stabbing shitbags."

Morty carried the bucket over to his big brother. The merchant ladled some over Cable's lips. They had to work a moment to break the seal of dried blood that held them together. The sec man moved his head side to side a little, but didn't open his eyes.

Croom looked up at Ryan, who nodded.

"Go ahead," he said. "We won't be needing much."

Without showing signs of wondering at Ryan's words, Bass dashed a whole ladle of the brackish water in Cable's battered face. The sec man moaned, coughed. Then his eyes opened and he tried to sit up.

"Easy," Croom said, holding him down with a huge hand to the breastbone.

"Check his eyes," Ryan suggested.

"I can see fine," Cable croaked.

"Concussion," J.B. said.

"Oh. Right," Bass said. He fumbled in a pocket for a moment, then produced a previous match, which he flicked alive with a thumbnail. Then he bent over to thumb back Cable's eyelids, one at a time, with a facility that told Ryan he was no stranger to the procedure.

"No dilation, same size," the master merchant said.

"Check for broken bones," Ryan directed. He reckoned Croom knew that. But he wasn't sure how well the trader was functioning yet, so he didn't consider them wasted words. "Doc, how about you?"

"Never better, my dear Ryan," he declared, then winced.

"Very well—that's a lie. But you and J.B. aren't the only ones who have mastered the art of rolling with a blow."

"You're kidding," Morty said. "You didn't deliberately get beat down."

"Indeed we did, lad," Doc replied.

In spite of his bruises—and his age, which his body felt even if it didn't reflect the years he had lived through—he did seem to be enjoying himself, for a fact. Action made it possible for him to forget all that he had lost, at least for a brief span.

"We had to put up a good show, you see," the old man said. "Otherwise they'd be on their guard."

"Against what?"

"Against what's coming," Ryan said. He moved to the door. It was solid wood. Even though there were no trees larger than scrub cedar on the hills anywhere around the compound they had seen, the rest stop made liberal use of timber for construction. Not all of it was scavvy. Ryan reckoned Raker did a lot of trade with logging operations in the Rockies, still about a day's drive west, if the roads held halfway decent.

There was a peephole-like opening covered with heavy metal mesh. The same covered the one window set high up on the bare mud-brick wall, through which the light of a swelling moon provided the sole illumination.

The corridor outside was lit by the faint orange glow of a lamp somewhere. A similar hefty door stood across it. There was no sign Ryan could detect of any guard in the hallway, though he couldn't see far.

"How about in there, Dan?" he called softly. "Anybody crippled up too bad to move?"

"Only if you count depression," the wrench said. "Some of the boys are taking it pretty hard."

"Where are the women?" Ryan asked.

"They stuck them someplace else," Morty said. Ryan noticed he wasn't whining even a little. Apparently when the shit hammer came down, he tightened up with the rest of them.

"This was all a spur-of-the-moment plan," Bass said. His voice still was clotted by grief and despair. "Raker told me himself before he had us dragged out of the mess hall. He still hadn't made up his mind what to do with us, which was why he didn't just chill us all and have done with it."

"Would have been the smart thing to do," J.B. agreed. "Too late now."

Bass actually reacted to that enough to give him a look of disbelief. "He mentioned slavery," he said. "Apparently that's a trade to which he's been no stranger the last few years."

The merchant shook his big shaggy head.

"Fool that I was, I offered to bribe our way clear. Anything he asked. Of course, he responded that he already had everything I possessed anyway."

Ryan turned from the door to give him a hard look.

"Listen," he said. "You feel triple-bad. You're the man in charge. I know the feeling.

"Well, face it. We're all fucked. Didn't any of us see this coming. We walked into a trap with our eyes open."

"But it's my fault," Bass said.

"It's Raker's fault," Ryan replied. "Anyway, a fired bullet doesn't go back in the blaster. What's done, is. The key thing is, we're fixing to walk out of this trap. But it'll take everything everybody's got to pull it off. You most of all."

Bass stared at him, his mouth hanging open.

"You're crazy, Cawdor," Cable croaked in a raven's caw. He forced himself to a sitting position despite Bass's reflex effort to hold him down. "Unless you can walk right through that locked solid door."

"He can," J.B. said from beside the door, where he sat on the floor with his right boot off. "And he will."

He held up a small, flat leather packet. Random moonlight glittered on little splints of metal.

"Just as soon as I open her up with my handy hidey lockpick kit."

RYAN STOLE down the jailhouse hallway. Aside from the dim waver of orange from a lantern in the room at the end, it was as dark as a swampie's heart. He carried a knife with a short, wide, single-edged blade. It was one he'd held out from the inefficient frisking by their captors.

He'd left J.B. and Doc to keep the others quiet and from wandering. Croom was still in a walking trance. Cable, though aware enough to snarl at Ryan, couldn't yet reliably stand unaided. As for Dan and the rest of the men crammed together in the second cell, Ryan had left them locked up for the moment, which was the best way he knew to keep them out from underfoot while he did what needed doing. If Croom's authority couldn't keep them from yapping about how bad they wanted let out *right now,* he reckoned his two companions could.

The ceiling was low, wood with heavy rafters that were basically just logs of similar size cleaned of bark and branch stubs. He had to keep his back rounded and his head hunched forward to keep from banging his forehead. He was glad the floor outside the cells was the same hard-trodden earth as inside. That way he didn't have to worry about a warped plank groaning underfoot.

As he reached the corridor's end, where it widened out of sight to the right, he heard soft, regular breathing. Not snoring, but what sounded like a man asleep. He heard no other breathing and no conversation.

That didn't mean there weren't half a dozen wide-awake but not talkative sec men sitting in the room. Only one way to find out. Ryan paused just at the corner, held his breath, listened. Then he stuck his head out for a three-second look.

At first he saw no one. He had to crane his head hard right to see the sec man: sitting in a wooden chair with his back against the raw adobe wall and his chin sunk to his clavicle. He had a Winchester-type lever action longblaster across his lap. The lantern burned on a low table on his side away from the door.

Ryan pulled back. Easy, he thought, which naturally raised a question. Too easy?

He ducked, stuck his head out again at about hip height for another look. No one waited in the shadows to pounce. Aside from another, larger table by the side wall and a couple of empty chairs, there wasn't even any more furniture in the little room.

Ryan slid the knife into his belt, then leaned out. Moving purposefully but without haste he grabbed the barrel of the longblaster, yanking the weapon out of the sleeping man's slack grip.

"Huh?" The sec man raised his head and turned blinking eyes to the hallway.

Ryan rammed the steel-shod butt of the carbine back into the man's forehead. He fell over sideways and didn't move or moan. The chair stayed upright.

The one-eyed man stepped quickly around, leveling the blaster at the fallen man. If he wasn't unconscious or chilled, he was a rad-blasted fine actor.

The door in the far wall opened. Ryan snapped his head and the longblaster around and found himself staring into the wide, dark eyes of Katherine Raker.

Chapter Eighteen

"What do you bitches want?"

Mildred had to fight to choke back the reflexive snarl that rose in her throat in response to the casually callous insult by the sec man outside the warehouse room. She was powerless in this situation and knew it.

So did the man outside the heavy, locked door. That was why he talked that way to the captives he was keeping watch over.

"We got a plaguer in here," she called back, trying to turn the strain she felt into fear and anxiety rather than fury, which wasn't hard. She *was* afraid. She *was* anxious. She was just pissed off hotter than nuke red at the whole situation.

I still can't believe we fell for that glib bastard's bullshit, she thought.

"Bullshit," the sec man called.

Mildred heard a moan from behind her and glanced briefly around. The eleven people—four drivers, three sec women, Dan's lieutenant wrench Randi, and Bass Croom's main aide, Sandra Watson—were sitting on the concrete floor of the storeroom between the empty shelves, or slouching on or against a stout empty table by the back wall.

Then she looked at Krysty, who was lying on the floor with just a single coat below her to cushion her from the cold concrete, and another covering her from shins to jaw for a modicum of warmth. She turned her head from side to side, moaning feverishly. Her hair, sopping wet as if from sweat, covered her beautiful pale face like lank red water weeds.

"Look through the window if you doubt me," she said through the wrought-iron grillwork. It made sense that this currently disused room of a warehouse next to the wag park should be pressed into service to hold the female captives of Bry Raker's treachery. It was clearly meant to stash valuable goods, and some of them, at least, would fetch high prices from slavers.

"All right," the unseen sec man called. "Which one of you bitches is sick?"

Mildred ground her jaw. "The redhead," she said.

"Nuking hell!" the man yelped. Krysty was clearly the pick of the lot.

"But if you want her chilled," Mildred said, striking the iron while it was good and hot, "and maybe the rest of us shitting our guts out on the floor before sunup, feel free to just stand out there and listen."

"Stand back! I'm coming in."

She heard scratching at the door as the guard fumbled his key at the lock.

"Gladly," she said. "Stepping back now." She retreated to take up position by the stricken woman's booted feet.

The door opened. The sec man was a burly guy with a shaved head, like a smaller edition of his sec boss, Butler. He was smart enough not to enter a roomful of captives with a blaster in his hand. Or his scary boss had frightened religion into him. His snub-nosed Chief's Special .38 stayed in its holster at his narrow waist. He did carry a hardwood truncheon in one meaty fist.

He looked around. The only light was what came in from outside, which wasn't much to see by.

"Here you go," Mildred called. She gestured at the prostrate woman. Krysty uttered a small whimper.

"Fuck," the sec man said under his breath. He dithered a moment, afraid to approach someone so obviously ill— and seriously so—close up. But fear of his bosses, Butler and Raker, quickly won out.

He walked to Krysty and bent over. "Wrong with you, Fire Hair?" he asked.

The hair trailing limp across the strained and sculpted features stirred as if coming to life. The sec man's big head recoiled on its thick neck. "What the nuke?"

Krysty's right hand shot up from the floor like a piston and hammered him full-force under his chin.

Mildred heard his teeth shatter under the force of the blow. Unless she summoned her Gaia power, which would leave her drained and as weak as a newborn kitten and thus unable to flee or fight further, Krysty had only the strength of a human woman. But she was a very strong human woman who knew a thing or two about close-in fighting.

The crack of his lantern jaw breaking overrode the noise of his teeth giving way. His eyes rolled up in his head and he collapsed across Krysty.

Mildred heard the redhead mutter something uncharacteristic beneath her breath. Then with a heave of strong arms and some help from her legs, Krysty flopped the dazed sec man off to her right.

Randi, Dan Hogue's big blonde Valkyrie assistant, was on him like a diving eagle. She seized the club from his unresisting fist and proceeded to hammer him about the temples with it. A powerfully built and handsome woman, who looked after her gentle boss with the same ferocious competence she brought to her trade, she also had a notably short fuse.

Apparently Mildred wasn't the only one to take the sec

man's sexist slurs personally. As strong as the big mechanic was, and as vigorously as she was pounding him, the question of whether Krysty's shot had given him a concussion would become academic once his skull gave way.

Mildred was interested in getting at the bastard's blaster. Unfortunately it had somehow worked itself around so it was now buried beneath his broad white butt, and somewhere in the course of his ongoing harsh treatment his bowels had let go. Had Mildred been squeamish she never would've survived her residency to get her M.D. Still, she needed to get that stupid snubby if they were to have even a faint prayer of getting away that was the best they could hope for.

"All right, ladies, let's move with a purpose," she heard Sandra Watson say. Croom's aide was a slight middle-aged woman who wore reading glasses and her graying blonde hair in a plain bob. She was normally quiet but had somewhere picked up the trick of making her voice crack with command at need. "We have to get moving now."

As Mildred continued to tug at the now disgustingly moist and squishy holster, and Randi continued methodically to beat the man's head in, she heard the shuffling of bodies getting into motion.

From right beside her she heard Sandi say, "Neat strike, that. Never thought an open hand shot could be so powerful."

"My mother taught it to me," said Krysty, who was sitting up now. She looked remarkably restored, glimpsed from the corner of Mildred's preoccupied eye. Not surprising since her sickness had been a sham. "Hitting bone with a closed hand is a good way to break fingers."

Krysty started to get up. Mildred managed to get a grip on the slimy wood grips of the Colt and found it still held tight by the strap.

She heard someone scream.

Her head snapped up and around just in time to see a second sec man come in the door behind a leveled scattergun whose muzzles seemed to gape like twin tunnel entrances.

"GO AHEAD AND CHILL ME if you want," Katherine said. Something in her voice and manner actually stopped Ryan from carrying through with his intent to leap, grab her and take her hostage with the Winchester muzzle against her head.

"I came here to help you," the woman declared in a voice that was at once quiet and edged with jagged glass. "I don't care if you believe me, any more than if I live or die."

Ryan straightened, keeping the blaster pointed at her. "Talk fast," he said. "I'll listen."

"I hate him," she said simply, stepping inside and closing the door. "Bry Raker."

She stopped to spit on the pinewood floor. As she did her heavy coat fell open. Ryan couldn't help noticing that beneath it she wore a filmy negligée and thick boots. The underthing had to be predark, and scavvy in that condition had to have set Raker back a fortune.

For all that jack and barter, he thought, it didn't hide much. Katherine's breasts were clearly visible. Ryan loved Krysty but was still human....

From the flicker in her dark eyes the woman seemed to notice how his attention had strayed before snapping back to her face. But she was on a mission, and not to be deflected.

"He kidnapped me," she said, as J.B. and Bass stepped up to either side of Ryan. "I was fourteen years old. His coldhearts butchered my family. He took me across his saddlebow like some kind of barbarian chief from predark books. Took me back to his camp and used me."

"I thought you were his wife," Bass said. He was sounding steadier. Ryan reckoned the fact that they could do something had a tonic effect on him. Even if realistically what they could expect to do was to die on their feet sometime in the next handful of minutes.

The woman spit again. A lock of her raven-wing hair escaped the tight bun she'd tied it into at her nape and fell in her strained and beautiful face.

"He forced me to go through a ceremony he called marriage, yes," she said. "It was a fraud. He still uses me as he will. And he is still a rapist!"

"Bullshit," Cable said. He was sounding stronger, too, though a fast side glance told Ryan he was leaning on his boss's burly arm yet for support. "She's lying!"

"Why did she come here at all then?" J.B. asked. "What's she got to gain, coming out like this? Poor girl's like to catch her death of cold, even in that coat."

"She's just hot for the one-eyed glory boy, here," Cable said, sneering.

"Back up off the trigger of the blaster, my friend," Bass said, turning to grip Cable's forearm briefly. "We're on all the same side here."

Katherine tossed back her vagrant lock of hair. "I desire him, yes," she said. "What woman wouldn't? But it doesn't matter."

"Why are you doing this, then?" Ryan asked.

"I will have an end," she said simply, squaring her shoulders and elevating her chin.

"I will end it tonight. Raker has gone too far. He and that beast Butler cooked up their treachery on the spur of the moment. He will ruin this rest stop, his inheritance, despite the fact it's built on the best water well for fifty miles. He's doomed himself. But I am the one who will bring him down!"

"I believe her," Bass said.

Ryan nodded. "Yeah. So what now?"

"I can lead you to your gear. And your arms. None of the plunder's been sorted yet. That waits for morning. After you were taken Raker got drunk and—used me. He now lies passed out snoring like the pig he is. So does Butler. I will see you armed.

"Then getting free is your own problem. I can do no more for you."

"And that's plenty," J.B. said, tipping his fedora.

"What about the women?" Bass asked a beat before Ryan could.

"They're locked in a backroom in a warehouse by the vehicle park, just like your blasters," Katherine said. "Now let loose the other men, and fast. There's little time until you are discovered. Not all the sec men are drunk or sleeping, and many others in the compound will fight you for the shares of the slaver payments Raker has promised them!"

RYAN SLIPPED OUT the front door of the jail. J.B. stood in the doorway, blocking the exit of the rest until Ryan gave the all-clear. Despite Croom's leadership some of his men were stone spooked, not too surprisingly. If allowed the chance, they might just bolt and give the whole show away, which would get everybody chilled sooner rather than later.

They were on a dirt side street, narrow, with more makeshift buildings hunched to either side. A block down he could see the wag park, the vehicles gleaming dully in the light of a waning but still-swollen moon.

He saw a shadow flit from shanty to shanty down the block. Waving a quick gesture to J.B. to hold and get ready, he raised the Winchester he'd taken from the guard to his shoulder.

A shadow detached itself from the swaybacked porch of a shack. It resolved itself into a tall figure—an obviously female one.

"You sure that's what you want to point at me, lover?" a contralto voice asked.

"Krysty?"

The moonlight hit the figure and turned shadow into the most beautiful woman Ryan had ever seen. Still and always.

"We were coming to rescue you," he said.

She gestured behind her. "Us, too."

He saw her frown briefly, then her emerald eyes go wide. He turned to see a very determined-looking Katherine Raker push her way out into the street. She had to be determined to get past J.B.

"My, Ryan," Krysty murmured, "you *are* a fast worker, aren't you?"

"Good," said the black-haired woman, striding up beside Ryan. He noticed she still hadn't bothered buttoning her coat. "This will save time. Now *move!*"

"Got it," J.B. said, straightening and slipping his pick from the padlock on the door into the warehouse Kit had led them to. He let his satisfaction show in his voice. He always enjoyed a job well done, even a small one.

The Armorer pulled the lock open and dropped it by the door. No point in trying to pretend it hadn't been cracked. One way or another that wasn't going to matter past the next five minutes.

"So then little Dezzy turned into a wildcat," Krysty was saying. She was hunched behind Ryan reporting the details of the women's escape from captivity. They were guarding the Armorer's back while he performed his break-in. The others held back crowded in a narrow alley between buildings nearby, waiting the signal.

"Dezzy?" Ryan asked. J.B. ducked inside the building. He had his hideout knife in hand.

"Little black-haired sec woman Ricky is sweet on."

"He is?"

"Men. Anyway, she jumped the sec man from the side, grabbed his blaster, shoved the muzzle toward the ceiling hard enough it broke his trigger finger without him shooting. Then Mildred kicked him in the crotch and we swarmed him."

"Ace," Ryan said.

J.B. popped out. "Clear," he said. "No one inside."

As he vanished back inside the darkened warehouse, Ryan turned and signaled. Krysty went on in as the others came forward, herded by Doc, Sandra and Randi. Bass was in the lead, walking confidently. Cable followed, still obviously a little dazed. Even though Mildred said he probably didn't have a concussion, he was obviously not near fit to fight yet. But like the rest, he was going to have to. And soon.

"Should we get people into the wags?" Bass said as he came up. At least Cable wasn't going to be puffing his chest and woofing and trying to pick a dominance fight this time.

"No," Ryan said. "They'll have sentries. We don't have time to take them down by stealth. So we need to get armed-up to fight."

As the freed captives moved inside, restrained from all rushing in at once by Dan, the gentle but well-respected boss wrench, Bass put his big bearded lips near Ryan's ear.

"We got a chance?"

"We're breathing," Ryan said. "That means we've always got a chance. Good one? No."

Bass nodded, then gripped Ryan's shoulder briefly. "Thanks."

"It's what you pay us for. Get inside."

When the last of the former captives got inside, he followed, shutting the door behind him. There wasn't much point to guarding from the outside. It was just one more person to be spotted by Raker's sec.

As Kit promised, all their personal gear and weapons were inside the prefab wood building, heaped on the concrete floor or laid on heavy tables. The actual cargo and trade goods stayed locked within the wags until morning, when the treacherous rest stop owner and his sec chief reckoned they'd be safe as anywhere.

People were sorting through stuff for their own personal weapons, kept in line by Krysty and Mildred. That wasted time, but Ryan reckoned it was worth some delay for people to use what they were familiar with. Most of the drivers didn't carry personal weapons, but got issued arms at need from a stock carried in one of the wags, where they remained. They just stood by waiting—which was safer, Ryan calculated, than wandering around outside.

J.B. had quickly donned his backpack, slung his scattergun and moved to one of the windows with his Uzi cradled in his competent hands.

"Movement," he called softly.

Ryan retrieved his weapons. Handing the lever-action longblaster he'd taken from the guard to Krysty, he slung his Steyr Scout over his shoulder and went up to peer through the mesh that covered the fly-specked glass at J.B.'s side.

He caught glimpses of people running up the block in the direction of the adobe jail where the men had been kept.

A piercing mechanical wail ripped the night air. Ryan wondered where Raker had come up with a hand-cranked alarm siren. He knew they were old-fashioned even before skydark.

"That's it," J.B. said. He turned and knelt, raising the mini-Uzi to aim out the window.

Over the rising-falling whine, surprisingly loud, Ryan heard gasps and suppressed squeals of fear behind him. He turned to see Bass hold up his hands with palms down in a soothing gesture.

"Easy, everybody," he said. "We've got to move calmly and with purpose."

Amazingly, Ryan felt the incipient panic levels drop inside the crowded room. Not go away, but far enough from redline the whole crowd wasn't about to dissolve into a terrified useless mob. The big man had charisma and his people's trust.

"Start moving people into the wags," Ryan said.

"Shouldn't we fort-up here?" Cable asked.

"They'll surround us and chill us," J.B. said, not turning from the window. "Our only chance is try to break for it."

Cable frowned slightly. Ryan saw his lips suddenly seal tight on whatever rejoinder he was about to make. The sec boss was no stupe; he'd been about to object they had little chance to get away, driving out of a roused compound.

Then he realized they had *no* chance forted up here.

The door opened. Above the siren, which had been joined by confused shouts from outside, Ryan felt it more than heard it. Or maybe he caught the motion from a corner of his eye as it parted slightly and a figure slipped through.

He spun as blasters came up. Hammers clicked back like a young army of robot crickets.

"Wait!" he called.

The figure that had entered so rapidly and shut the door behind it was unmistakable.

"Jak!" Krysty breathed.

"Where were you?" Mildred asked.

The fine pale features twisted in a flash of annoyance. "Stupe question," he said. "Came to warn."

"About what, young man?" Bass asked.

Ryan frowned. He was aware of a sound the seemed to be rising beneath the still howling alarm, a strange subterranean rumble like an approaching avalanche.

"That," Jak said.

Chapter Nineteen

"What is that?" Bass asked, big head cocked to one side to listen to the low roar getting louder.

"Buffalo," Jak said. "Coming here."

"How many buffalo?" Ryan asked.

"All."

"Shit! All right, everybody grab what you can and run for the wags!"

Nobody argued. They'd seen the unbelievable size and power of the buffalo herd.

People who hadn't gotten to what they were looking for grabbed what was nearest. The ones looking confused and hesitant got grabbed next and towed toward the exit.

The rush turned to a logjam at the door. Ryan shouted and started yanking people back by collars and the hoods of their jackets. Bass stepped up and started tossing people bodily aside to clear the exit.

Shouts cracked outside. Ryan heard screams, then several people retreated quickly back inside the warehouse.

Leaning down, Ryan dared a brief look at about waist-height around the door frame. A couple of sec men stood a block away, north, toward the jail. As Ryan looked, one fired a handblaster. The other was shouldering a long-blaster.

A body—Ryan thought male—lay facedown in the street eight feet from the door. Pulling briefly back, Ryan drew his SIG-Sauer P-226 with his left hand. Then, straightening, he stuck his left arm and his head out, took quick aim on the longblaster man and triggered three quick shots.

The two sec men jumped out of sight around the corner of a building. The handblaster guy seemed to be pulling his friend behind him to cover. But Ryan was unsure whether any of his shots had hit.

He rammed the SIG back in its holster. Unslinging his Scout, he strode out the door to kneel with his right side against the wall and the blaster leveled.

"Move 'em out!" he shouted.

He heard the rush of bodies and thump of boots behind him. He also heard the drumbeat of buffalo hooves getting loud.

He glanced to his left. He thought he saw an orange glow, just visible above the roof across the street. Using fire to spook the herd, he thought.

Looking back through his scope he saw a sec man's face poking from cover at a building's corner. He seemed to be staring toward the glow.

The only target Ryan had was the sec man's nose, so he lined up the shot and took it. He saw blood spray and heard a squall of surprise and agony. The head jerked back out of sight.

With a tremendous grinding squeal the gate and fence gave way under the impact of uncountable tons of flesh and bone. Ryan turned and raced for the parked wags.

Raker's sec men and armed employees weren't the bigger threat any longer.

RICKY WASN'T STRONG enough a motorbike rider yet to feel good about steering with one hand while shooting his big Webley revolver with the other. But accuracy wasn't an issue. The target was the starry sky, and his speed was low enough he could easily put a foot down when he started to lose control of the bike.

"Move it, you buffaloes!" he screamed. *"¡Ándale!"*

A moving wall of tails and churning rumps rolled up over the slow slope in front of him. Forty yards away to his right he saw Olympia likewise shooting her blaster in the air. By her face, she was screaming something, too.

But Ricky couldn't hear her. They weren't actually chasing the whole herd. At least, not the super-gigantic one that had menaced them earlier. As far as Ricky knew this wasn't even the same herd: it was big, though not quite the ocean of flesh the other had been. And the brushfires they'd set in the grass to the east, fortunately still dry from an arid winter, had only gotten a portion of the herd moving.

Still, it was a big portion—a lot of animals. As he and Olympia followed the stampede to the top of the rise his heart was in his throat with a sudden spasm of fresh fear. What about his friends?

He stopped. The compound lay spread out, huge and dark but for a few lights glimmering faint and yellow from windows.

The stampede was headed pretty much right at the main gate.

Stopping at the crest, he saw flashes of bright yellow flame as sec men on guard panic-fired their blasters into the horned faces of the herd. He even thought one or two went down. But they made barely a ripple in the living tidal wave as their fellows stomped right over them.

He hadn't heard the gunshots, but he actually heard the crash as the herd hit the fence. Or imagined he did.

For a moment he thought it would hold. He saw the front of the stampede start to mound up like a breaking wave, as animals behind rolled up against the ones stalled at the fence.

Then the gate went down with a squeal of tortured metal. A heartbeat later a section of fence as wide as the wave front of panicked animals was flattened. The stampede rushed on, barely slowed.

"What have we done?" he breathed. Ricky crossed himself with his thumb.

He heard a dwindling engine snarl as Olympia slowed to a stop beside him on Jak's motorbike.

"Our friends have to fend for themselves now," she said, as if she could read his mind. And truly, he doubted that took much if any of her doomie gift.

Ricky turned eyes blurred with sudden hot tears toward her. "But—"

"Not all of our people will make it," the woman said with a matter-of-factness that made him hate her for a moment, then she turned and looked him in the eye. "But I have seen that without this happening, none of them lives to see sunup. They were already starting to break out when your friend Jak was still pedaling toward that drain where a stream crosses beneath the fence I saw in my vision. They would have all been trapped and chilled. Or recaptured, tortured and sold."

He could find no words to ask if they had done the right thing. Should he have believed her?

"Only time will tell if we've done the right thing," she told him. And once again he realized it wasn't that uncanny she knew his thoughts. "Let's hurry down and do what we can do."

He risked a quick glance toward the rest stop. The dark tide had already flooded into the wag park. He saw muzzle-flashes and thought he saw a wag battered.

He couldn't watch any more. Instead he concentrated on following Olympia down the forward slope at a breakneck pace.

WITH A CRASH and multiple glass fountains from the windows that wound up on top, the battered blue bus fell over on its side.

"Fireblast!" Ryan snarled.

At least a dozen of the freed captives had managed to clamber aboard before the stampede pushed it over.

He sprinted toward the fuel tanker. For a moment at least it was clear of the living flood, but a single buffalo charged him from between two of the cargo wags.

Ryan snapped a shot at it. The creature bellowed and turned aside. He sprinted, reaching the rounded steel flank of the tank, and quickly began to climb the front set of rungs.

As he did, the tanker began to rock. It had been parked toward the center of the wag yard oriented north-south with its tractor at the northern end, meaning it would have to roll through ninety degrees to get out the western gate. He was climbing the western side of the tank, away from the buffalo, although the great shaggy animals had begun to lope by to both sides, trailing long strings of slobber from their fleshy underlips.

Can they actually turn this bastard over? he wondered.

Then he got to the top, saw over to the far side.

"Fireblast!"

The fleeing beasts didn't just fill the rad-sucking main street. They were overflowing into the east-west side streets, as well. Plus, even as Ryan hoisted himself onto the flat metal catwalk, he saw some kind of structure go down like a playing-card house halfway between the gate and here.

Between where the gate used to be and here. It was gone, submerged under a flood of bodies that was being funneled into the compound through a gigantic gap in the eastern fence.

He could see the rounded low hills a quarter mile or so east outlined against the orange glow of the likely grass-fire that had got the stampede started. He thought he saw two tiny figures on motorbikes between the hilltops and the back of the herd.

"At least there's an end to them," he heard J.B. say as he clambered up to sit on the rear sandbag nest. Like Ryan he carried his backpack.

Ryan shouldered his Steyr, aimed and fired. One of the buffalo butting against the east side of the tanker bucked, gave a bawl loud enough to be heard over the enormous racket and dropped down as if dead.

"Still more outside than in," Ryan said.

J.B. triggered a blast from his Uzi. Ryan saw several buffalo flinch and veer about thirty feet from the tanker. The Armorer was trying to get the herd to steer clear of the big rig.

Ryan risked a look around. What he saw was, if anything, worse than he imagined.

Worst, of course, was the school bus lying on its side. People were still desperately climbing out the windows. Not all were making it.

But as Ryan saw a slight blonde woman whom he recognized as one of the drivers start to slip back inside a busted-out window as a fresh surge of the living tide rocked the fallen wag, a big dark hand reached down, caught her skinny wrist and yanked her right straight out of the bus.

Ryan recognized Chef. Not that he was hard to make out, even in the starlight and confusion. He was one of three black men with the convoy, and he was the only huge burly one with a square head and massive bearded jaw. He was standing with his massive legs braced, helping people escape.

He swung the blonde woman over the west side of the downed bus, then he simply let her go.

Upraised hands caught her and eased the squirming, shrieking woman down. Ryan saw that six or eight people, presumably ones who'd already gotten clear of the doomed wag, were gathered there amid some of the gear that'd been carried aboard. For the moment, anyway, it was clear of buffalo. In fact they only seemed to be streaming around the northern end of the bus.

Ryan turned and shot another buffalo ramming into the wag he and J.B. were on. Aside from the fact they were on it, the tanker's survival was crucial to the survival of the convoy. That fuel was worth risking their hides for, and not because of its high barter value.

This time he didn't even try to luck into a heart shot, the way he had last time. The conditions were too bad and the targets in constant writhing motion. Instead he aimed to break a shoulder joint, an easier target that would reliably put one of the big beasts down. Not chill it, at least right away. But it would zero the creature out as a threat.

From the inner corner of his eye he caught a flash and heard more screams from the vicinity of the bus. Snapping his head around, he was just in time to see Chef, a ham-hock hand pressed to his side, stagger backward and topple over the undercarriage of the wag into the seething mass of terrified buffalo. Ryan heard him bellow as a huge, horned head tossed him. Then his bass voice rose in screams that were quickly cut off as he fell beneath the churning black hooves.

Just north of the wag park, in the street east of Raker's big house, Ryan saw Butler. The enormous sec man was dressed in T-shirt and jeans and in his stocking feet. He was jacking the lever of a Winchester-style longblaster for another shot at the escapees.

Ryan swung his own longblaster toward him. He didn't bother with the scope, but rather lined up fast with the battle sights. As the sec boss raised his own weapon, Ryan fired. Butler's head jerked, and blood gouted out the back of the bull neck in a black mist. He went down.

Ryan turned back and used up the rest of his 10-round mag of 7.62 mm rounds on the animals still shoving against the tanker. By the last couple of shots, it was on others trying desperately to clamber over the still thrashing bodies of the ones he'd crippled, to keep from getting trampled by those that continued relentlessly pressing from behind.

By then he had a decent barrier created. Between that and J.B.'s judicious bursts of 9 mm rounds, which would do little more than sting the giant frenzied animals—they had the herd so that it was simply flowing around the tractor-trailer combo like water around a rock.

As he pulled a fresh magazine from his backpack, Ryan took quick stock of the situation. Most of the cargo wags remained on their wheels except the pair that had been parked on the east edge of the yard and side-on to the stampede. The smaller blaster wag with the M-249 was rolled even as he watched, though.

He switched out magazines and looked for more targets.

Though blasterfire now crackled all around, at least no one seemed to be shooting at *them*. The rest of the rest stop's defenders, showing better sense than Bry Raker's late sec boss, were shooting at the great big frantic animals that were clearly the greater threat.

Pushing bison aside with its big snout, Bass Croom's command wag with its homemade armored plate bulled its way into the still clear space in the lee of the fallen school bus. Bass's right hand stuck out the driver's window and blasted with his ParaOrdnance. Morty leaned out the passenger side, his long blond hair wild, firing with a lever-action carbine.

As the running bison started to sheer away from the armored wag, Bass stuck his face out the window.

"Come on!" he shouted, waving his blaster for emphasis. "Climb aboard! We gotta get out of here!"

A big bull put its head down and started to charge full-on at the command wag. Ryan dropped it with a shoulder shot. It fell and skidded with its black snout pressed against the grille as frightened survivors dived in the opened back doors of the wag or climbed up the sides.

Ryan heard other engines snarl above the mighty thunder of the herd. The convoy was preparing to get under way, anyway. Whether they could escape the stampede was still the big question.

He glanced up at Raker's house. The stout adobe walls had simply defeated the stampede, as Ryan feared they would. The fleeing monsters simply ran around it.

"Son of a bitch," Ryan cursed. He hungered to take vengeance on the rest stop boss for his treachery, but now he would simply squat inside laughing his bastard ass off in perfect safety. Unless he did something triple stupe like run outside to try to save the rest of his business from being smashed and stomped to kindling by the stampede.

Astonishingly Bry Raker ran outside his home. He was dressed just in a pair of pants—barefoot, bare-chested, hair spiky and as wild as his eyes. He held a long black M-16 in his hands.

"Fight like a man!" he heard a woman scream. "Get out there and fight for what's yours like a man! Stop cringing like the backstabbing coward you are!"

Movement drew his eye up. Somehow Kit Ross had gotten on the pitched corrugated-metal roof of the big house. She stood atop the flat porch roof, her hair flying free in the rising breeze like black flames.

Apparently driven by her shrill imprecations, Bry Raker uttered a scream of rage and charged at the mass of running animals. He fired his blaster from the hip on full-auto, and he seemed intent on ripping through his whole 30-round magazine in one flaming, chattering burst.

Then he was knocked sprawling by a lowered head the size of an oil drum. His wife raised her fists above her head and laughed like a crazy woman to hear the screams of agony as black hooves cut and smashed him like stamping dies in some horrible machine.

"Note to self," J.B. said. "Don't piss that one off."

He looked back east. "Herd's still coming," he said. "We need to move. I'm gonna drive this baby, see if we can bulldoze a way out of here."

The animals were pressing against the side of the tractor now. Ryan started dropping them as J.B. went down the rungs on the far side to dash for the cab.

How were they going to get out of the yard? Ryan wondered. Even if they could get the show on the road before they all get plowed under, how would they get out?

No sooner had the thought crossed his mind than he heard the answer, spoken loudly and with authority.

And the yellow-orange flame tongue of Ma Deuce.

AFTERWARD NOT EVEN Ryan could have told how they got the surviving wags not just moving but lined up for the western gate of Raker's Rest.

One way was simply the .50-caliber Browning mounted in the bed of the pickup blasting a path through the bison. The thumb-size slug would chill a beast instantly; getting caught by a burst could rip an animal the size of a sedan into steaming, spattering chunks.

But even more than the carnage the big blaster wrought among the buffalo, the tremendous noise and flame the weapon generated terrified them. When the wag pulled up on the west edge of the yard and ripped a blast toward that gate, the herd parted and split north and south as if being opened with a zipper.

Apparently dodging the wags and buildings around the main yard had slowed the herd momentum. The last of the stampeding animals was coming in from the east. But they hadn't had enough head of steam to break out the west side yet. Instead the whole compound was gradually filling with slowed-down but skittish beasts.

The problem was, the wag park still got the brunt of animals galloping in terror of something their relatives already inside had already forgotten about. That was the disadvantage to the plan Jak reported Olympia had cooked up on the fly.

Ryan couldn't hold that against her. He knew the alternative was worse.

With the little black-haired sec woman with the white bang backing her up and helping her reload, and Mildred steering where her redheaded friend directed, Krysty had finished breaking the main force of the flood where it came into the yard. But now, as Bass's command wag led the way, with a couple of the cargo wags behind, then the tanker with Ryan up top and J.B. at the wheel, and then the remaining vehicles, with the wag blaster bringing up the rear, the way to freedom and safety was blocked by a few hundred tons of milling, bawling bison.

Bass kept driving through them, standing on the horn. His armored wag was more than powerful enough to push the beasts aside. They were doing terrific damage to the

less robust buildings to either side, which was most of
them—and to the rest of Raker's Rest, too, by the bellows,
crashing of collapsing walls and screams. Ryan didn't expect to lose much sleep over that.

The bison kept flowing back in among the vehicles,
slowing the convoy's progress to a crawl. The risk remained they might upset one of the cargo wags still on
their wheels, or Chef's chuck wag, which had survived.
Several wags had refugees clinging to the top like baby
opossums.

After a tooth-grinding eternity Bass's wag reached the
gate. Now a new problem developed. The sturdy metal bar-
ricade resisted the armored wag's efforts to push through it.

The tractor's air horn blared. Ryan saw J.B. gesturing
out the window, vigorously waving his hand to the right.

The driver of the wag right ahead got the idea first.
He or she pulled the wag to the right, crunching into a
collapsed wooden porch and chasing away some ambling
buffalo.

J.B. took the tractor out of gear and gunned the engine.
He kept the air horn hollering.

The other cargo wag got the idea and cleared. Then Bass
caught on. His improvised armored wag backed away from
its futile nudging of the gates and into the space between
the perimeter fence and the outermost building.

Ryan caught on, too. He began shooting ahead of the
tractor, trying to hit low enough not to endanger the wags
ahead and also kick up some dirt to help the buffalo get
the idea to clear the road.

It would have been nice to have the big .50 help out, but
Krysty didn't dare shoot along the right side of the street,
for fear of hitting the wags that had ditched that way, nor
the left, for fear of scaring the buffaloes on that side back
into the road.

But J.B. was going for it. He let in the clutch. The huge diesel engine roared and the big tractor surged ahead.

Running over a full-grown buffalo could still bring disaster, not to mention spectacular personal extinction for J.B. and Ryan if the tanker ruptured and the fuel lit off. But clearly there was a difference between driving too fast and charging. Having a roaring, howling monster bearing down on them at speed got the attention of the buffalo still wandering the right-of-way. Especially when a cow too slow on the dodge got clipped by the right front of the coffin-snouted tractor, which punted the vast beast through the front of a wooden structure that had survived intact until now.

The path cleared. Ryan clung to his blaster with one hand and the straps holding the sandbag atop the tanker with the other. He braced for impact and felt the elastic push-back of gate and fence. Then the chain or cable or lock that had secured the gate broke with a wrenching screech. The gates flew open, the right wing flying off the hinges and bouncing off the prairie with a musical-saw twang as the rig pounded on for freedom with Ryan whooping and pumping his fist on top of it.

The other wags pulled in behind as J.B. headed out for the far black wall of the Rockies.

Chapter Twenty

"I'm worried about him, Ryan," Mildred said.

It was early afternoon of the day of their escape. The convoy had put some miles between them and the compound and the buffalo herd. Then, well into the Rockies' foothills Bass called a halt.

The remaining wags had formed a circle in a bowl-shaped depression with a skinny stream trickling through it. The grass was longer here and showing streaks of green. The mountains loomed nearby.

Mildred guessed they were in what in her day had been Wyoming, some miles north of the Platte River.

She was dead tired. They hadn't had a restful night. The day of jouncing travel they'd spent after breaking out of Raker's Rest hadn't exactly been conducive to sleep. She and Krysty had taken turns dozing fitfully, sitting against the side wall of the truck bed hoping not to get bounced out while the other kept watch.

They'd made the trip without incident. Mildred had no idea how many miles they'd actually traveled. Bass had called a halt, because they were all exhausted, and in no shape to try crossing the Rockies.

So they had made a camp and lit fires. The day wasn't actually chill despite an edge on the winds that blew up from the plains and eddied here hard by the mountain wall. Now the twenty or so survivors huddled around two dried buffalo-chip fires for both physical and spiritual warmth, drank awful-tasting but warming chicory, and tried to sort things out.

She spoke to her companions, huddled by their own fire. Except for Jak, who was prowling off somewhere out of sight on the spare mountain bike, keeping watch over the camp from the heights. He could run for days like a wolf without sleep. Then again, he could also nap like a cat, wherever and whenever, and get good rest.

Heads turned to the other fire. Bass sat on a rock, his big hands cradling a half-empty bottle of Towse Lightning that he'd just opened when he'd sat half an hour ago. His eyes, sunk deep in dark pits beneath the bushy crags of his eyebrows, never seemed to leave Olympia.

Their enigmatic paying passenger stood well off to one side. Her arms were folded beneath her small breasts. Her face was turned to the wind, and her hair hung in one gleaming braid down her back.

Sitting on his haunches beside Mildred, J.B. sighed. He took off his hat and scratched the thin spot on top of his head.

"Well," he said, "hard to blame him much. He's suffered some hard hits, these last twenty-four hours."

"Seems longer," said Ricky, who sat with his knees up, staring into the low and near invisible dance of flames in front of him.

Doc cackled. "Indeed, lad! It was a lifetime to many of our companions. And even more of our foes, doubtless, for what comfort that may bring."

"Mr. Croom seems more upset about losing his people than his wags or goods," Ricky commented.

"I think that makes him a good boss," Krysty said. "A good man, certainly."

"Even if we did lose but one cargo wag," J.B. said, "it's a pain the bus got wrecked. And losing that blaster wag could come back to bite us in the butts before we reach our destination."

"Croom knew enough not to expect to make it all the way without losing wags and goods," Ryan said.

He stood by the fire. By the slight slump to chin and shoulders, Mildred knew he was feeling fatigue as much as the rest of them. But he clearly felt restless.

"That's why he brought so much," he finished.

"Couldn't expect to cross the Deathlands without losing people, either," J.B. said, putting his hat back on his head.

"Ten people killed or missing is a lot," Ricky said. "Just over thirty to begin with. And we lost poor Horwitz right out of the gate."

"Eleven," Mildred said. "Marconi died before we halted."

The wrench had been knocked sprawling by a rogue buffalo bull. Fortunately, or so it seemed at the time, he'd actually been knocked back into the clear space beside the fallen bus. Friendly hands had dragged him on top of Bass's wag, and he'd been transferred to the passenger seat of the chuck wag while the convoy got sorted out to make its break. But he'd never regained consciousness.

"I think he drowned on his own blood," Mildred reported grimly.

"Bullshit!"

Everyone turned and looked at the other fire. Dace Cable had been squatting on his haunches next to his boss, talking. Not quietly but Mildred hadn't exactly been listening.

Now he started pacing back and forth, not quite breaking the circle around Ryan's fire before turning back to his own bunch. His eyes were bright, his thin cheeks flushed.

"He's hyper," Mildred muttered.

"Do you blame him after last night?" Krysty asked. "He lost two of his own people, remember."

Mildred shrugged. "I'm not thinking of blame. Thinking trouble."

J.B. put his hands on his his khaki-clad thighs. "Yeah. Storm's been a spell brewing. Reckon it's due to break."

"It's all that bitch's fault!" Cable shouted, pointing at Olympia's back. "No wonder you're obsessing on her now! She comes out of nowhere. She's nothing but trouble. Then she brings that whole fucking herd of buffalo stamping down on us and kills a third of our people."

The woman in question showed no sign of even hearing him, but Bass was roused to protest.

"Now, Dace," he said, clearly trying for a conciliatory tone. But instead the words came out in a raven's croak.

"No, boss! No more excuses! That triple-stupe stampede came within an ace of chilling us all. Even that white-skinned mutie should've had more sense than to go along with that dreck!"

"Here now," Mildred said. She stood.

"Now, Mildred," J.B. said, trying his best to sound conciliatory.

But she was hot past nuke red. She hated injustice, wherever and whatever form it took.

"That doesn't come within a longblaster shot of being fair, Dace Cable," she said. "Bry Raker and his bastards had us dead to rights. Without the buffalo herd hitting the camp all we would've done is died a lot. Yeah, we lost a shitload of people. That's what happens when we all—you included—walk into a trap with eyes wide open. She, Jak and Ricky are the only reasons any of us are still breathing."

Cable turned bright red, then white. He advanced on her with fists clenched by his sides.

"You're no better than any of them, bitch," the sec boss snarled. He was close enough she could see spittle flying from his lips. "Just another fucking coldheart, wanders in out of the Deathlands and spins a line of lies and bullshit—"

J.B. stepped between the two. "Easy now," he said. As always, he didn't raise his voice.

"No."

For some reason everybody froze. Cable turned his head to look at the speaker as if it were a massive tank turret being cranked by hand.

"It's me you've got a beef with," Ryan said. "I hoped we could get past it."

"You mean you been dodging me!" Cable almost screamed.

Mildred saw Sandra Watson over by the fire leaning close to Croom, whispering urgently in her boss's ear. Mildred guessed she was trying to get him to step in and call things off. But he just sat and stared as if he'd been hit between the eyes with a pickax handle.

And truth to tell, Mildred doubted the showdown could be averted any longer. Some wounds—of mind and body—festered until they got broken open and debrided.

"Not now," was all Ryan said.

"Listen, son," J.B. said, leaning his face close to Ricky's ear. "Whatever happens, don't try to horn in."

Ricky stood practically dancing from one sneakered foot to the other. His cheeks burned and his heart raced so fast he feared it would explode. He actually thought he might die of anxiety.

Ryan and Cable had stripped to their shirts and squared off in a circle formed by the members of the convoy. The remnants of Cable's sec crew stood on the far side from Ryan's friends. Bass and Morty stood to the left, with Sandra looking anxious by her boss's side. The wrenches and drivers were spaced out right and left.

"What if they try to help him?" Ricky asked.

"Relax," Krysty said from Ricky's other side. He felt a different kind of rush—the thrill he always felt whenever she spoke to him.

"If they do, we'll let you know when to move. But I don't think they will. Look at them."

He swallowed and nodded. The fact was the sec men and women didn't look eager at all. They looked mostly glum.

He did notice Dezzy was missing, and wondered where she was.

Standing upright with fists raised, Cable advanced on Ryan. The one-eyed man stood calmly with hands about the level of his breastbone. With a swiftness that shocked Ricky, the sec boss's leading left hand flashed out in two quick jabs. Both struck Ryan's jaw with a smack the boy winced to hear.

Ryan moistened his lips with his tongue and just stared at his opponent.

Grinning so wide it looked as if the top of his head was in danger of falling off, Cable waded in. Ricky didn't know much about unarmed combat, but he started unloading what looked like very powerful punches on Ryan. Straight shots from his right hand, mean-looking out-and-in blasts with his bent left arm.

Ryan held up his forearms and bobbed from side to side. Still a couple of the blows landed with sounds that seemed to hit Ricky in the gut.

"Ryan!" he screamed. "Do something!"

Over among the sec men somebody shouted, "Go, Dace! Show him!"

To Ricky's astonishment another sec man turned and muttered something to his cheering comrade. The first one slumped and looked sheepish.

J.B. chuckled. "See? They've fought beside us. They're willing to let their boss work out his problems with our boy."

"But J.B.!" Ricky almost moaned. He had to blink back tears. "Cable's pounding him!"

"You think?"

Ricky sensed motion from his other side. Glad of the excuse to look away as Cable stepped in to hammer at Ricky's beloved leader some more, he saw to his amazement the slight form of Jak Lauren, squatting on his haunches beside him.

Jak saw his friend glance his way. "Olympia," was all he said.

Ricky nodded. He was getting used enough to his friend's clipped speech that he reckoned he understood. The tall, mysterious woman had spelled Jak on his one-man patrol so he could come support his companion Ryan.

He heard gasps from the far side, and some from Mildred and, worse, Krysty. Then he felt something take hold of his left hand.

He looked quickly around and controlled his reflex to snatch his hand away.

Dezzy stood close beside him. She looked at him with dark eyes big in a pale, expressionless face.

Ricky felt himself blushing hotter and looked back at the fight—in time to see Cable whip through some kind of spinning kick that slammed his right boot heel against Ryan's left cheek.

Ricky nearly screamed as Ryan went down.

Chapter Twenty-One

Krysty held her breath. So, it seemed, did everybody else, as the man she loved toppled backward in slow motion, but not all the way to the ground. He mostly turned his upper body and went to one knee. His left fist went to the ground to halt his downward progress as Cable danced back.

The sec boss turned and strutted around the circle, his chest pushed out and his fists in the air. But his own people didn't join in his celebration.

"Uh, boss…" said Solo, the sec man with the spiky yellow hair.

Krysty saw the side of Cable's expression turn into a frown, then he followed his subordinate's gaze.

Ryan was kneeling as if in perfect relaxation, with his left arm propped on his knee. Despite the trickle of blood that ran from the corner of his mouth beneath his eye patch, he smiled.

"My turn," he said.

He rose. Looking a bit bewildered, if Krysty was any judge, Cable turned back toward him and dropped into his hands-high fighting stance.

The sec boss was as game as he was fast. He fired two more quick jabs as Ryan approached. The one-eyed man deflected both with his upraised right forearm.

Cable unloaded an overhand right meant to smash full into Ryan's face and drop him then and there, either stunned or out cold.

Ryan ducked, turning his hips and upper body to the right. The massive punch skidded off the top of his head and glanced off his shoulder blade.

At the same instant Ryan landed a palm-heel hook to Cable's short ribs. Krysty heard bone give way with a loud crack.

With a gasp scarcely less loud, Cable stepped back. His eyes were wide. While Krysty knew how much that shot had to hurt—she'd felt her own ribs break before—he seemed mostly reacting in surprise. Things weren't going the way he had expected.

Even as the sec boss backpedaled reflexively, Ryan advanced, without haste, yet inexorably. Like a man going to work.

Which, Krysty knew, was exactly what he *was* doing.

Out of nowhere, seemingly, Ryan launched his right fist in a straight punch so fast that Cable's arm was just moving to intercept it when the fist crunched into his jaw.

Cable staggered back. Ryan came on, unloading shots so fast that all of Cable's responses came too late, and all landing with crunching impacts on his face. He was already staggering.

He skipped back adroitly, gathered himself and actually countercharged. Ryan kept coming forward, too. Ducking under his jab, he doubled the sec boss over with a punch to the man's washboard gut. Then he stood him back up with a palm-heel uppercut beneath the goatee that made the sec boss's teeth clack together.

Krysty heard neither teeth nor jaw break, but the shaved head snapped back. She thought the sec boss was already going down. His body fell back, while his hands dropped forward as if he could no longer hold them up.

Yet so panther-fast was Ryan that he unloaded a spin

kick of his own, blasting the outside of his vertical right boot full into the side of Cable's face before he could fall.

Then he did fall, full-length on his back, so hard Krysty felt the vibrations from thirty feet away.

"Yay!" Ricky Morales shouted.

"Hush, child," Mildred said sternly.

Nobody else said anything at all. Morty kind of frowned and rubbed his jaw. Krysty wasn't even sure whether he was pleased or displeased by the turn of events. Likely, neither was he.

There was no doubting his big brother's reaction. Already hollow-eyed with regret and incipient despair, Bass Croom's big face was slack and bleak with the look of a man who saw no possible outcomes to what he was witnessing but bad and worse.

Ryan stood a few feet from Cable, who lay prostrate with arms outflung. The sec boss was moving and moaning. He wasn't out cold, but he wasn't altogether attached to his body, either.

"Now that's what I call a surgical beat-down," Mildred murmured from Krysty's elbow. "Wonder if that poor man appreciates how much trouble Ryan took not to hurt him too bad?"

Behind the women, Doc said, "I doubt he appreciates anything at all just now!"

Ryan stood calmly, his arms relaxed by his sides, knees lightly flexed, weight on the balls of his feet. If Cable was somehow feigning being stunned and launched himself off the ground in a fresh attack, the first thing he'd find out was that Ryan was a mile from as open as he looked. In fact, Krysty knew, he was in the perfect state to defend or counterattack.

Of course, if somebody went for a blaster, well, that was a story that wouldn't have a happy ending. But the sec men and women just stared at their fallen boss with a mixture of wonder and concern. The drivers and wrenches mostly just looked worried. Bass looked as if he didn't dare breathe.

Cable shook his head and raised it to see Ryan leaning over him with hand outstretched as if to help.

Krysty bit her lip and held her breath. Mildred grasped her arm firmly for support and reassurance.

Things could turn to blood and death right now, if they broke wrong.

Dace Cable's right hand came up to grip Ryan's forearm. Ryan clasped his opponent's arm in turn and hauled him to his feet.

The lanky sec boss rocked back on his heels momentarily, then he got control of his sense of balance and got himself upright on his pins. He rubbed his jaw, turned aside to spit blood on the grass. He turned to Ryan and grinned.

"All right," he declared in a loud voice. "You beat me fair and square! And I'd be proud if I could call you bro!"

Of all people it was Dan Hogue, the mild boss wrench who looked like predark pictures of Jesus, who raised the first cheer.

Ryan nodded.

Cable threw out his arms and came forward to embrace his former foe. Krysty still didn't let herself breathe. She didn't know whether to trust the man's abrupt conversion or not.

Yet Ryan made no move to pull away or to defend himself. Instead he let Cable enfold him in a full-on hug and for one of the few times in their life together, Krysty saw her life mate do something halfheartedly.

Ryan raised both hands and patted vaguely back at Cable's shoulders as if suspecting he might be red-hot.

"So," Mildred called to Krysty at the front of the fuel tanker. "Why do you think Bass Croom has gotten so fixated on our mystery lady lately? Is he hot to trot with her, or is there something else that I don't see?"

For a moment Krysty looked blank. Her long red hair was blowing behind in the wind of their passage through the western foothills of the Blue Mountains in what Mildred still thought of as northeastern Oregon. The day was sunny and warm enough neither woman had a coat on despite the fact they were moving at maybe twenty-five miles an hour along an ancient dirt road.

Damn, Mildred thought. I used a slang phrase that's been dead for like two hundred years. Hard to tell even now what's still comprehensible, and what's not.

Then Krysty laughed. She had to have worked it out by context.

"It could be," Krysty said. "She's very pretty. I can see how he might become overly attached. But he seems a pretty confident man, too. If he wants to be with her, why not just ask?"

"Because he's too old for her, maybe?"

Krysty laughed again. "That doesn't always slow them down. Believe me."

Spring was coming on fast if not yet hard. The sun was halfway up the sky and warm on Mildred's face despite the crisp edge to the breeze. Wildflowers sprang out of everywhere, white and blue and yellow, in the flats and hollows and on the hillsides like tiny explosions.

They were ten days out from the fateful stay at Raker's Rest. After pausing to breathe and lick their wounds, they had had it surprisingly easy. They passed through a relatively low point in the Rockies, then on across the Wasatch Mountains into the Snake River Plain. They followed the course of the Snake for generally smooth rolling past where it turned north toward Hell's Canyon. Everybody said the canyon was a dangerous region to be avoided at all costs, both because of the lashings-out of a tormented nature, and the wildlife. Two-legged and otherwise.

Instead they kept heading west across the Blue Mountains, into northeast Oregon by Mildred's consideration.

That passage hadn't been so easy.

Now they rolled west down a decent dirt road through dwindling foothills between high ridges, whose heights Mildred and Krysty watched carefully. As they hoped did everybody else.

They were actually getting near the point Bass had pointed out on his ancient U.S. Geological Survey map as their destination—rather, as close to their final objective as he would divulge. Krysty reckoned they'd keep on west across the Cascades to the Cific coast. Mildred thought north into southeast Washington, into the heart of the Inland Northwest, maybe even across another bend of the upper Snake, which was earning its name at that point by sidewinding toward Hell's Canyon.

"Bass may be obsessing more because he's boozing it up pretty hard," Mildred said. "He hasn't recovered from losing a third of his people at Raker's Rest."

"Mebbe," Krysty said.

She kept scanning the high points. The nature of the convoy restricted it to what J.B. called "high speed routes," meaning low stretches between high points such as streambeds and river valleys. Unfortunately that meant they had to put themselves at risk of ambush to advance at all. Like now.

"It doesn't explain his hang-up on Olympia, though." Mildred chuckled. "I still can't figure that one."

"Me, neither," Krysty said. "When we started out I was worried she might make a play for Ryan."

Mildred laughed out loud. She couldn't help herself.

Krysty glanced toward her. Mildred noticed her friend's motion from the corner of her eye. *She* was watching those ridges, too, like a hungry dog eyeing its humans at the dinner table.

"It makes sense," Krysty said a bit defensively. "Ryan is the strongest man around. It would be natural for her to gravitate toward him."

"Not that," Mildred said. "It's just the notion any woman could ever compete with you. You're a goddess, Krysty. And least of all could anyone else compete in Ryan's eyes. Uh, eye. Even a long, exotic drink of water like that one. She does have a look to her, I've got to admit, even if she could stand to pack some more meat on her bones."

It was Krysty's turn to laugh. "I'm not worried about Ryan, silly," she said. "It was her. Olympia showed herself formidable right out of the gates. She could cause trouble if she turned things into a woman-scorned situation. Chilling trouble."

"Could somebody that smart and strong really pull a stunt as stupid as that?"

"What do 'smart' and 'strong' have to do with her heart?"

Mildred bobbed her head to the side and sighed. "You got me there, Krysty."

"Mebbe it helps that Olympia seems as fixated on something as Croom is on her."

"Yeah. But what?"

Krysty shook her head. "No idea."

She turned briefly to Mildred. "At least Cable's been acting like a sweetheart."

Mildred frowned. Wasn't that kind of a flying subject change, there? Still, if her friend wanted to talk about something else, Mildred would honor that. Krysty did very little lightly.

"Yeah," she said. "After Ryan pounded some sense in his fool head. Of course, who knew that'd work."

"Ryan suspected it might."

"Yeah," Mildred said. "But it doesn't always pan out that way. We all know that too well."

"That was one of the reasons Ryan was hoping to avoid the showdown," Krysty said. "Also why he had to give Cable his shot first, so that he couldn't delude himself the outcome was a fluke afterward."

"Yeah. So Ryan let Cable pound him in the head for what seemed like an hour, after Ryan and J.B. have rattled on for years how letting yourself get hit in head is stupid."

"You treated Ryan after the fight," Krysty said. "How badly hurt was he?"

Mildred sighed. "Not at all. A few bruises and contusions, a fair amount of facial swelling, the sort of thing that looks way worse than it is. Yeah, it took a truckload of skill to keep from getting hurt bad while giving the appearance of taking the best the sec boss had.

"But I may be even more impressed with the fact Cable didn't get hurt worse. Ryan's skill was so sure—and he was so sure of it—that he'd held back while beating Cable. Also contrary to his usual advice."

"Good advice is to be followed always," Krysty said. "Until it isn't."

"Did Trader say that?"

"No idea. But it sounds as if he might have, doesn't it?"

"Yeah. I guess Ryan figured he was more use to us all alive than staring up at the stars. And better fit to fight than crippled up."

"Wasn't he right?"

"Yeah," Mildred admitted. "Cable's a good man. Maybe not the swiftest arrow in the quiver, but not stupid."

She frowned at the heights. They were rising again to both sides, into long hogback ridges. For some reason that made her more uneasy.

"Speaking of showing pretty good," she said. "I sure wish Morty stayed the way he acted when we had to fight our way out of the rest stop. He fought like a champ along with everybody else."

"Danger focuses the mind," Krysty stated. "I get the impression Morty doesn't have much focus in his life the rest of the time."

"No," Mildred said. "Bass plays mother hen to the boy so much, I kind of wonder if he's smothered him some."

She gritted her teeth and shook her head. "Still, I wish Bass'd get back to doing a little more mothering of the boy. Rein him in some. But with big brother all distracted, Junior is starting to really act out. Acting real entitled and pugnacious because everybody else won't do what he says."

"At least he hasn't worked up the courage to start serious trouble," Krysty said.

"He will if he ever gets the nerve up to try to force the issue with Olympia."

"True."

"The boy'll bring trouble down on all our ass— Shit."

"You see them, too?" Krysty asked in a tight voice.

"Uh-huh," Mildred said.

It wasn't hard to miss the dozens of warriors on motorcycles who'd appeared suddenly on top of the ridge to the north like bad Indians in a predark Western.

Chapter Twenty-Two

At Ryan's urging Bass hit the horn of his Land Cruiser four times. It was the signal to stop.

As soon as Ryan saw the wags following begin to slow, he told Bass to pull over and stop.

The trader's heavy sunburned face had gone dead pale behind his beard, which even in the moment Ryan could hardly help but noticing showed a lot more white than when they started out from Menaville. He obeyed.

Ryan opened the door and stepped out before the big armored wag stopped rolling. He waved his arms vigorously above his head in what he hoped everybody would take as a "stand easy" signal. Of course it'd be straight-up self-chilling to start shooting at a hundred or more heavily armed biker nomads who had them unmistakably dead to rights. But even after all they'd been through there was still a chance somebody might panic and do something stupid, especially that fool Morty Croom, if he thought it would impress Olympia.

To Ryan's relief, no shots cracked out from the convoy. Everybody stopped without dinging anybody else, although the driver of the tanker rolled close up enough on the cargo truck ahead of it that Ryan's throat sort of seized up for a moment.

The bikers continued to sit, outlined against the sky. So were their weapons, which were abundant. Now that he was no longer riding inside the armored wag, Ryan could hear the muted growling of their engines, like a multitude of hungry beasts.

Bass mopped his face with a handkerchief, although the morning wasn't yet warm.

"Boys sure know how to make an entrance, don't they?"

Ryan nodded. "Stone Nation," he said. "I knew we were getting near their territory."

"Why haven't they attacked us yet?" Morty asked, tumbling forward like a panicky puppy.

The others were approaching, too, as if seeking safety in numbers. Not the best practice if the enemy opened fire. Still…

"If they were going to attack us, they'd be all over us already," Cable said, striding up from where he'd been manning the .50 in the tail-end blaster wag.

"Then why are they doing that?" Morty demanded. He was embarrassed and his response was to get angry.

"I've heard of this bunch," Bass said. "Other traders talk about them. Bad bunch to cross, but I hear if you deal with them straight, they deal straight back."

"That's the fact," J.B. said as he joined the growing crowd. "What you got here, is what you call a strong negotiating posture."

"Welcome to the Stone Nation," said the man with the pyramid of kinky black hair cascading over his wide shoulders as he swung off his bike. It was a big bastard, heavy for off-road use, but solid-built, powerful, its only real concession to biker flash being the tall ape-hanger bars gleaming chrome in the sun.

"I am Speaker for the Stone Nation," he said, walking forward to where most of the members of the convoy stood waiting near Bass's wag.

Ryan looked at Bass as some of the two dozen or so

other bikers who had ridden down with their boss dismounted. About half remained astride their rides. The rest stayed up there, silhouetted against a painfully blue sky brushed with red feathers of clouds. "And that's just the ones we can see," J.B. murmured from Ryan's side.

"Ace on the line," Ryan replied.

The trader roused himself as if from a standing sleep. "Hi," he said. "I'm Bass Croom, straw boss of this traveling circus. What there's left of it."

On that note he seemed to deflate a little. Ryan felt his jaw tighten. The Stones by reputation weren't coldhearts by any stretch. But you did *not* want to show weakness in front of them.

But Speaker grinned. He had a handsome face that looked years younger than Ryan reckoned it could be, a sort of reddish tan, with a straight nose, flashing black eyes and startlingly white teeth.

He stepped forward to embrace Bass with arms twined with spiky tattoos and braided bracelets.

"I heard what you and your crew did to that snake Bry Raker," he said.

"You did?" Bass asked, sounding as surprised as Ryan felt.

Speaker laughed. He seemed good at that.

"News travels triple-fast out here in the West," he said. "Stones do, too. I'll give you a big discount on passing through our lands and water rights for chilling that slaving bastard."

He turned to the others. "These are my family. This is Morning Glory, my right hand."

One of the tallest women Ryan had ever seen stepped up beside her chief. She was about six-eight, dark-skinned, with jet hair that hung in braids in front of her burly shoulders, and halfway down her imposing frontage, across a gorge made of some sort of skinny bleached bones. She wore an eagle feather at her nape, and was built to match her height. Not fat by any means, but wide. She had a face like a slab of beef, a nose like an eagle's beak. Her eyes were like black diamond drill bits.

Ryan wouldn't like to face her in a fight.

"And Pit Bull, my left."

The man who stepped up to that side of the Stone boss looked to be a handful, too, but less formidable in Ryan's seasoned estimation. He was an inch or two shorter than Ryan, built broad, with a short patch of scalp-lock dyed magenta on top of his shaved skull, a matching soul patch under his outthrust underlip, and tattoos of skulls and dragons and hatchets all down the huge arms he obviously left bare to show off. The hatchets were much like the four he had hanging from his vest and belt, all predark steel models, forged of a single piece for strength. His eyes were blue and glared at the newcomers as if daring any to meet their furious gaze.

Ryan did. The man's jaw set and his neck muscles visibly swelled, but he did nothing. He wouldn't, with Speaker right there; that was clear.

At the same time, clearly Speaker was making a point by having him there.

Pit Bull could be a handful. Ryan sized him up as more dangerous than the giant Plains Indian woman, but not more formidable. More dangerous in the way a yellow jacket was more dangerous than a diamondback, but less formidable. The wasp looked for an excuse to tangle. The rattler didn't, but would chill you fast if you forced the issue.

Bass introduced Cable. Speaker gripped him forearm to forearm, then he turned to Ryan and his gaze grew calculating.

"This one yours?" he said past Ryan. From the flicker of his gaze Ryan knew he was talking to Krysty, who had taken up her customary position at her man's right elbow, a half step back.

"Yes," she answered. "I'm Krysty Wroth."

Speaker nodded. "You, big fella?"

"Ryan Cawdor."

"Pleased to meet you! May your shadow never diminish."

Instead of the forearm to forearm thing he gripped Ryan hand to hand. Ryan wasn't much surprised the Stone Nation boss failed to try the crushing game. He had already sized Ryan up, and he had nothing at all to prove to anybody.

Ryan was just as glad he didn't try to squash his paw. The man had a grip like a vise.

"Welcome, Ryan Cawdor, and welcome Krysty Wroth!"

He stepped to shake Krysty's hand, then turned it and kissed its pale back.

"Always nice to meet a real gentleman," Krysty said. Ryan tried not to roll his eye.

"If you want to trade this one to us, we can give you plenty bucks in exchange," Speaker said with a broad wink as he straightened. "If all parties agree, of course. We don't hold by slavery."

"I'll think over your generous offer," she said, "after I size up the merchandise."

Speaker's eyes widened, then he laughed. He was a handsome devil, she thought, and charismatic.

He looked at Ryan with new respect. "You're either the unluckiest hombre on legs," he declared, "or the luckiest. Haven't yet made up my mind, to talk straight."

"I'm the luckiest," Ryan said.

Speaker laughed again, then moved on while Bass, who

had automatically shifted to merchant mode introduced his brother and the rest of the crew.

As he did, Ryan sized up those who had accompanied Speaker. They either stayed astride their rides or leaned against them. They were a colorful bunch, sporting lots of tattoos, face paint, feathers and what were clearly strands of scalps. Most of those seemed to hang from Morning Glory's belt. The ride she'd dismounted sported plenty, too, dangling from the handlebars. Pit Bull had at least half a dozen.

Speaker displayed none of the grisly trophies, but not, Ryan reckoned, because he had no kills to his name. He wore a simple double-action revolver in a flapped holster on his left hip, a Bowie knife in beaded scabbard counterbalancing it on the right. Their wood grips looked well worn.

They had weapons, too, everything from AK-style longblasters to swords and spears, which might be useful against a foe on foot if you were riding down on him on a powerful bike.

Bass introduced his people in the order in which they happened to be standing near him, closest first, which meant it took him a few to get to Morty. His blond younger brother was scowling and stepping from one foot to another when Bass introduced him.

For once Bass gave his junior sibling a hard eye, with his face turned where Speaker couldn't see. Morty's eyes went wide at his brother's expression. They flickered left and right, to see Ryan giving him a cold stare, too, as did Cable, both from the sides just within his field of vision when he glanced around.

Morty swallowed, mumbled something and meekly shook hands. Likely getting a gander at the Stone Nation boss up close settled him down some. It would be easy at first glance to dismiss Speaker as a pretty boy. He *was* pretty, almost to the edge of feminine. But even Morty could see, if not the steel and flint behind the ready smile, then the sort of hard-asses who acknowledged him their leader. And whatever Mortaugh Croom was, he wasn't stupid.

Still, Ryan allowed a twist or two of the tension in his gut to unwind. When the convoy first stopped, Morty actually agitated to dust the Stones off the ridges with the .50, which they could've done. After waiting a beat for Bass to say something, Cable pointed out that the survivors, including however many might be hanging back out of sight, would be on them like angry hornets. And they knew the country.

The sec boss had actually deferred the issue to Ryan, who agreed, since Cable only spoke straight fact.

As Speaker and Bass stepped a bit apart to commence their palaver, Ryan still felt nagged by unease, like a rat gnawing at his belly lining from the inside. He understood the Stones plenty well. While they seemed inclined to friendliness—and they had a reputation as honest but tough traders—they also had a savage name when crossed.

Plus they were volatile. Ryan knew them for the breed that could flash over into not just chilling fury but an outright sadism inferno in the last beat of a heart. And he wondered if Morty, who'd been acting increasingly erratic with Bass having pretty much abdicated all responsibility, really, since their betrayal and escape, might do or say something to strike a spark.

That was out of Ryan's hands for now. All he could do was stay loose and ready to jump whichever way he had to, to protect himself and his friends—and his employer and his people and his wags, sure.

But for now it was all smiles.

"So," Speaker said to the master trader, "once more, I bid you welcome to the Stone Nation. As I believe I mentioned before, naturally there are a few fees to discuss."

"Naturally." Bass Croom actually grinned. "So let's talk turkey."

Chapter Twenty-Three

"Isn't she cold?" Ricky asked.

"Hush up now, boy," Mildred muttered.

"But she's—she keeps losing her clothes," he protested. "She's lost…most of them already. Um."

In fact in the process of dancing around the big "council fire" in the center of an octagon made of long folding tables where the dinner feast was being served, the young woman with the night-black hair falling free clear to the tattoo at the small of her back had lost everything but a pair of silver-studded black boots with matching spurs, a black leather sort of bikini bottom, and various trinkets scattered about her tanned but generally well-put together person. The knife scar down her right cheek gave her a bit of a rough look, though.

But Ricky wasn't looking there anyway, and his throat had suddenly gotten too dry to pass any more words.

"Pipe down," J.B. said. As usual he didn't raise his voice.

Ricky deflated like a shot tire and sank in on himself, almost dragging his chin in the remnants of the last course cooling on the chipped pottery plate on the folding feast table in front of him. Off to the left where another table was set at right angle to this one he saw Dezzy's inscrutable black eyes on him.

He sank his head even farther between his forward-hunched shoulders.

Some of the bikers watching from the far side of the fire were hooting and cheering the unsettlingly revealed dancer. Not all were men.

Most listened as Speaker did what his name implied: animatedly told Bass—and by extension his companions—the story of the Stone nation.

"It all began centuries ago," the handsome chieftan said, "in the bombed-out, burned-out rubble of Chi-town. There a great, great man named Ranger gathered up the survivors under the banner of what was then known as the Almighty Black P. Stone Nation. He accepted everyone who was willing, the stoned and the straight alike. For he knew their travels would be long, their travails many, and their suffering would outlive many if not all of those who dared follow."

Speaker's gestures, Ricky noted, swept left and right and up and down as if molding the figures, the very history of what he described, out of clay. He was a good storyteller; his telling entranced Ricky, though not so much that he failed to notice that even the bikers, who had to have heard the story a hundred times before and had a nearly naked dancing girl to look at besides, fell silent. Indeed the dancer stopped, bowed to Speaker—who acknowledged her with a grin and nod—and taking up her things retreated into the night that had gathered around the sprawling Stone Nation encampment.

"For many suns' journey Ranger led the people west. Many moons', too, for they all felt the urgency that burned within him. And soon they knew the cause, for along with the shaking of the tortured Earth the skies grew black with clouds that didn't disperse."

Sitting at the pack leader's right, Bass Croom listened as if entranced. He looked livelier than Ricky had seen him in days, since the horror at Raker's Rest, in fact.

Though he complained loudly about how much Speaker was gouging him for passage and water rights, Ricky, who knew a thing or two about negotiation despite his tender age, thought the master trader sounded gratified. His gray eyes positively sparkled.

Though their mannerisms were different as moon from sun, the big, bluff, bearded *gabacho* and Ricky's own late father—small, soft-spoken, deferential in manner—had a common core. They were good at driving good deals, each in his own way. And they loved doing so, perhaps, as much as any actual profit they made from their transactions.

"Eventually the refugees, haggard, exhausted, cold, their numbers depleted by plague and fire and enemy attacks, stumbled in among the Plains people—the Lakota and their allies like the Sutaio, and the Kaui-gu and their brothers the Numunu. Those whom you white-eyes still know as Sioux, Cheyenne, the Kiowa and Comanche. They considered themselves free from the white man's oppression by the war.

"Though they were hard, those free-riding Indian men and women, their hearts were not made of stone. They were filled with admiration for the Stones, their suffering, and their endurance. And their leader.

"Not at first. First the invaders had to prove their mettle, to be worthy of friendship. That entailed plenty of chilling and dying on both sides. But once their cred was established the Plains folk adopted them and their magnificent leader, Ranger."

He paused to drink from a mug of dark, frothy beer. If it could be called a mug. It was made out of a short, massive buffalo horn. Jak, sitting down the table from Ricky, drank despite occasional warning glances from Mildred and Krysty. But sparingly, Ricky noted. They didn't want

Ricky drinking beer, which was fine with him, since he didn't really like the taste.

As he listened he took stock of the Stones themselves. They were a scary bunch, and no mistake. But some of the things that frightened Ricky most at first, the bizarre haircuts, the gaudy, glittery decorations, the face-painting and the tattoos, began to exert a fascination on him as the evening wore on. Some of them were really impressively well done, when Ricky looked at them closely—or as closely as he could at the other tables. The beadwork on scabbards and clothing particularly impressed him, as did the tattoos, which could either be stark and bold, like the rearing, highly stylized dragon on Morning Glory's left biceps, to patterns as intricate as clockwork.

Their weapons were often decorated, as well. Some had painted furniture, or carved bone grips. Some of the lever-action carbines stacked next to their owners showed engraving on the receivers, though Ricky was too far away to make out detail.

Ricky felt ambivalent about that. On the one hand he didn't hold with tarting up a good weapon, a good machine of any sort. On the other hand, like his uncle before him and his new mentor and idol, J. B. Dix, Ricky was a sucker for good workmanship, wherever and however encountered. Also, none of the embellishments looked to interfere with the weapons' utilization.

He wasn't that happy about the bikers keeping their weapons on them or close to hand. Even he, who didn't consider himself at all good with people, could sense undercurrents of latent violence beneath the hearty joviality of the bikers. That some of them were hitting the brews pretty hard concerned him.

Then again, none of the Stones seemed to be getting as drunk as hard and fast as Morty Croom. He sat at the table directly to the left around the octagon from Ricky's, where Speaker was holding court to Bass and Cable, Ryan and Krysty, and Sandra Watson. For his part the Stone Nation chief had Morning Glory and Pit Bull at his side, as well as a mousy little guy with a pot belly, goatee and wire-rimmed specs not too different from J.B.'s. who seemed to be called Running Shits, for some reason Ricky couldn't fathom and wasn't sure he wanted to.

Despite Speaker's great skill at yarn-spinning, Morty didn't seem to be paying attention to him. Instead he seemed to be staring fixedly at a Stone Nation girl at the next table left. It was the slight woman with the skinny dark-blonde braid hanging by one side of her pretty, pouty face. She had on a black-and-white vest that seemed to be made from the hide of a pinto pony, and it seemed like nothing much beneath. She was talking rather languidly with the bikers around her. Ricky noticed she was occa-sionally catching Morty's eye and even throwing a smile back his way.

Ricky worried Morty might do something to cause a scene. He figured that would cause the violence he sensed flowing under the surface of the festivities to erupt full-on. Still, he was at least halfway glad Morty was so keen on the nomad girl. Mebbe she'll distract him from Olympia, he thought. Stop his buzzing around her like a horsefly.

Even Ricky, who knew he knew nothing about women, could see the younger Croom would never get anywhere with their mysterious passenger. In fact Morty had been caught spying on Olympia when she was bathing in a stream, the woman completely heedless of the frigid tem-peratures. His older brother yelled at him, though Bass lapsed quickly back into his depths of funk. And Morty went right on being Morty.

Ricky wasn't sure how Morty even had the nerve to

keep trying his luck with Olympia, much less spy on her naked. She scared Ricky spitless, and she had always been friendly to him, in her distant, distracted-seeming way. They were comrades in arms, they had fought together. And she still terrified him.

The youth was only surprised Morty hadn't made a real scene yet, the way he'd been getting drunk and carrying on in camp. Others in the convoy were starting to grumble, as well. Why didn't the master merchant put his younger brother firmly in line, especially since despite his depression he was growing visibly more anxious to get wherever they were going.

Ricky saw Dezzy, who was sitting with big blonde Randi, her boss Dan and Little Feather, looking straight at him with her big black eyes. He swallowed and stared down at his plate just as it was whisked away, to be replaced by, of all things, some kind of yellow curry with vegetables and some slightly stringy meat in it. When he tasted it he found surprisingly good, though the curry made his tongue sting so that he gulped from his ceramic cup of water.

"The Stones and the Plains people rode out the cold, long night together," Speaker was declaiming. "And over the harsh decades the two groups grew together.

"Ranger grew old and died. The sky cleared. The Plains tribes, with the Stone Nation now an accepted member of their alliance, rode forth to claim the Plains once more. If sometimes the acid rain chilled them, and horrible muties, the buffalo had sprung back, allowing the nations to feed and grow big and strong.

"The time came, many suns later, for a parting of the highways. A descendant of the great Ranger named Diabla took leave of the alliance, and led much of the Stone Nation west to seek its own destiny beyond the Rockies.

The parting was a friendly one. The time had simply come, as such times do."

"And so we staked our own claims and rode our own range, with our goat herds and scattered plots where the sick and old and slow grow crops. Not that they're easy marks themselves, as many cougars, coldhearts and stickies have found to their sorrow!"

Ricky's attention wandered. What was it between him and Dezzy? Or was it even a thing? Since wordlessly holding his hand at the Ryan-Cable showdown, she had hardly talked to him. She had gone whole days without meeting his glance or acknowledging his presence.

Yet sometimes she did look at him. Like now. He caught her. He couldn't help thinking that now, like before, she seemed somehow expectant.

Of what? He had no clue. He didn't know what to do.

"Now we Stones range free across the Plains and mountains to trade, seek visions, or just—you know—cruise. We're all about freedom."

Suddenly he seemed to draw in on himself somehow. "Which, my friends, is why we hate slavers so much. That's why we grew to hate Bry Raker. Even more than the fact he kept getting more and more inclined to sell us the weight of his thumb on the scale along with the flour. Raker's ancestors were a pretty good lot, built the place up.

"Bry was a bad fruit all along. And when he started dabbling with slavery he made us his blood enemies. Stones do not cotton to slavery, and the slavers are many as well as powerful. They got a whole trade network of their own, from sea to shining sea. But we're always ready to mix it up with them. We give those slavers a triple-hard time when we run into them, which they commonly do not survive."

The way he said those last words chilled Ricky's blood, but it heated right back up in sudden excitement.

"Yami!" he yelled.

Faces turned. Speaker frowned at him.

"Ricky!" Mildred whispered.

He couldn't contain himself.

"Sir? Excuse me, sir? There's something I have to ask you. Please."

Speaker's brown eyes had narrowed. Now they widened slightly, though his expression didn't soften from the stone-statue aspect it had taken on at the interruption. He glanced at Bass Croom.

"The boy lost his sister to slavers," the trader explained. "He often talks about it, and who can blame him? He hopes to find her someday."

"Luck with that," muttered the huge and forbidding Morning Glory from her seat near Speaker. They were the first words Ricky had heard come out of her.

Some of the other Stones laughed. Speaker frowned at them. He didn't speak or even make one of his sweeping melodramatic gestures, but the snickering stopped as if he'd chopped it off with that big knife in the beautifully beaded scabbard at his hip.

"There's no disgrace in pursuing a quest," he said, "only honor. No less if it's hopeless. We Stones know that. Ask your question, boy. Your loss and your seeking earns you that right."

Ricky looked at Ryan, who nodded once. He seemed relaxed, which took Ricky off guard. Quickly the tale of the murder of his family and Yami's abduction in front of his eyes tumbled from Ricky's lips. Speaker listened with his head tipped slightly to the side.

Some of the Stone muttered comments when his tale ended. None of them laughed.

Speaker looked at Ryan. "I can see why you took this one into your tribe, One Eye," he said. "But you still haven't asked your question, young man."

"Well, we didn't exactly get to question anybody at Raker's Rest, sir. So I was wondering—have any of the slavers you've…talked to…mentioned her? A tall, beautiful girl—young woman? Long black hair, skin and eyes like mine?"

Some of the Stones guffawed at that. Speaker raised a forefinger. They stopped.

"The slavers traffic in many such women," Speaker said, not unkindly. "They've stolen no few like that from us, over the years, although Stones make poor slaves, and look only to kill as many of their captors or purchasers as they can before they end with dirt hitting them in the eyes. But I fear your quest is hopeless."

"But a girl from the islands, Speaker," said Running Shits, who despite the name got the nomad chieftain's respectful attention. "From the Carib. They're not common on the mainland."

"True words, my friend." He looked at Ricky again. "I wish that I could help you. Your sister's plight cries in my heart, as it does in that of any true Stone, by blood or adoption. But we have heard nothing such. If it will help, we'll keep our eyes skinned and our ears open for sign of this Yamile Morales.

"The odds are against you, boy. You know that. But this is your quest. So, go for it! Keep riding that road. In spirit you are one with us."

Chapter Twenty-Four

"Not a good sign," J.B. said at Ryan's side.

He stood on the edge of their camp, in a little hollow among hills just big enough to park the remaining wags in a circle, about a quarter mile southeast of the vast main Stone Nation encampment. Ryan had insisted they stay in a separate area, and all return to it after the feast. The potential for friction between them and the Stones to strike sparks was just too great.

Cable had backed him, as he did these days. Ryan was glad of that. Cable was a good man to have fighting at your side, and better once he'd gotten his insecure bullshit out of the way at last.

Had he done so earlier—or had Ryan been willing to risk the lives of his friends to force the issue himself—they might've taken fewer hits on their long and grueling road. But that bullet wasn't going back in the blaster, any more than any other. So Ryan didn't bother himself about it.

But something *was* worth bothering about. Had Ryan believed in omens, J.B.'s bad sign would have been a triple-bad one. A volcano was erupting, far away to the northwest. Though it had to be dozens of miles distant, they could clearly see its cone shape, by the hell-glow of the molten lava spilling from vents in its sides, and the fires burning in its throat that illuminated the pillar of smoke it puked up at the stars in flares and sullen glows of red and orange. They could hear it occasionally, booms and cracks like distant cannon, when the wind turned right.

Their path led them east of it. Ryan thought. The problem was that Croom had revealed no more of their road than the Upper Snake, about a day's drive north of them with middling surfaces to drive on. As far as Ryan knew, the volcano *was* their destination.

"Reckon we'll just have to play the cards we're dealt, best we can," he said. "Same as always."

J.B. emitted a brief laugh. "It's not as if anybody leaves the game alive," he said. "Take more than just a frisky smoker to slow us down, anyway."

Somewhere off toward the hills a night bird called. Somebody whooped wildly in the Stone Nation camp. It cut off abruptly, followed by catcalls and the sounds of applause. The wind whispered through the grass and ran playful fingers through Ryan's shaggy hair.

"You gentlemen should get some rest."

They turned. Bass Croom was walking up on them with his bulk silhouetted by the low buffalo-chip fire at his back, where most of the others sat and talked softly.

Despite the fact his face was to the night, Ryan thought he could see the man's eyes burning brightly by sheer starlight. He was in an upswing. For the moment.

The trader was clearly manic-depressive, as Mildred had told them before Ryan tuned her out. Naturally enough she had gone all doctor-technical on them, but that was all Ryan needed to hear. He could see the truth of it, and none of the rest, he reckoned, would load any blasters for them.

"We'll roll in the morning," Bass said, rubbing his hands together. Ryan smelled the sourness of stale Towse Lightning on his breath from six feet away. "Bright and early."

Ryan shook his head. "Not a good idea," he said. "We're

riding the thin edge of exhaustion as it is. Everybody needs at least a day of rest. Better two or even more. And we still need supplies they can get from the Stones. Even fresh food like goat's milk and eggs will help sustain us. And help morale."

Bass reared back with fury plain in his eyes. "What's this bullshit?" he all but bellowed. "You work for me, Cawdor!"

"Yes, I do, Mr. Croom," he said levelly. "That's why I'm telling you this, man to man. You may not get wherever you're going faster if we rest a day or two, that's true. But you're triple more likely actually to make it."

"Why, you—"

"Bass!" It was Sandra Watson, running up to grab at his forearm. "Settle down. Step back and take a deep breath."

"And he's right, Bass," Cable said, striding up. "If my people can't shoot straight for their eyelids falling shut, they're not going to be worth a bent spent shell case protecting you. And how do you think our drivers will do when they're falling asleep at the wheel every ten minutes?"

Bass glared around, looking like an old buffalo bull brought to bay by wolves. Then he deflated a little. His big tongue came out to moisten his lips.

"You—you're right," he said. "I just, well, we're so close. It's been so long. And I— There's so much I've had to live with—"

"Bitch!"

It wasn't a shout so much as a scream of fury. They all looked back at the campfire.

Even the hubbub of laughter and drunken singing from the Stone Nation camp seemed to dwindle for a breath or two.

Morty stood right by the fire, his fists knotted at his

sides. Even from sixty feet away Ryan could see his face was flushed, pulled all out of shape by his passion and the booze, which he'd continued to punish triple hard since they got back to their own campfire.

Standing facing him with her head tipped slightly back was Olympia. Even in the dark and this distance, Ryan could see the posture of her wiry frame was relaxed. He could also tell it was the relaxation of a big mountain cat that could spring into slashing violence in an eyeblink.

But Morty couldn't.

"You've held out on me too long, you bitch!" the younger Croom shrieked. "You've been flashing that ass of yours and teasing me all this time. Well, it stops now! You're giving me some of what you promised me all along."

"I have promised you nothing, Mr. Croom," she said. Though not raised her voice snapped like a whip. Ryan had a fleeting sense she had been trained to that somehow, along with her other fighting and scouting skills, which seemed impossibly advanced, since she had to have seen no more than twenty winters, if that many.

"But I promise you now—you will regret it if you force me to—"

He grabbed her and pressed his mouth to hers.

Ryan's jaw dropped. He would never have imagined Morty could make a move that fast. Especially not with a woman with the steel-trap reflexes that Olympia had shown. Maybe he had taken her by surprise.

Olympia wasn't a woman to waste time being stunned by a mere twist of events. As Ryan could've told Morty and saved him plenty of pain. Her head rocked back away from his, breaking the sloppy open-lipped contact. Then she snapped forward. Ryan heard Morty's nose crack as her hard forehead smashed into his face.

He reeled back.

She started to turn away, but once again Morty showed surprising speed. He caught her arm midturn and spun her back to face him. He had his other fist cocked back over his shoulder to punch her.

"No!" Bass bellowed, lumbering into a run.

Not even Ryan Cawdor, no slouch himself where speed was concerned, could have intervened in time to stop what happened next.

Olympia spun into the pull as if it was her own idea all along. Her right hand came up as her rapid hip turn torqued that arm out of Morty's grasp. She caught his wrist, then continued her turn. Her momentum yanked his arm out straight with the elbow visibly locked.

Ryan winced. But instead of shattering the locked-out elbow with her upraised left forearm she pressed it against the vulnerable joint, using that pressure along with pulling his wrist around and down to throw him facedown in the grass by the fire. Olympia then stood with one hand on the back of his elbow and a boot on the side of his head. The face turned toward Ryan was chill white, but for the dark trickle from his dented-in nose.

"Touch me again," she said, "and I kill you. Nod if you understand."

After a moment in which even Ryan didn't breathe, he saw the downed Morty nod.

Olympia let him go and stepped back. Without seeming to hurry at all she wound up a good six feet away, far enough that he couldn't tackle her by surprise if he was set on self-murder.

He wasn't. There was murder in his blackening eyes as he jumped to his feet. For a pair of shuddering breaths he glared at her.

Cable started walking toward him, purposefully but not briskly, so as not to provoke anything. Ryan stood his ground. This wasn't his fight, for which he was heartily glad.

For her part Olympia simply stood looking at Morty as if nothing had happened. She wasn't even breathing hard and seemed utterly calm. Ryan was utterly sure that if Morty moved on her she would keep her promise, regardless of the consequences.

Before Cable could reach him and restrain him, Morty spit blood on the grass between them. Then, whirling, he vanished into the night at a stumbling run.

"Morty!" Bass cried after him, and started to follow.

But Sandra held his arm from one side, and the considerably more substantial Randi, who had appeared at his other elbow, took him from that side.

"Easy, Bass," she said. "Let him blow off steam."

He sucked in a long shuddering breath and nodded.

Ryan sensed a familiar presence at his side. He put his arm around Krysty's shoulders as she leaned her head against his chest. Her warmth and firmness by his side comforted him.

Rubbing his beard, Bass stared at Olympia. He didn't seem to bear her any ill will. He wasn't that unreasonable. No matter how crazy he was making himself he was sharp and seasoned enough to realize that Olympia had let his sheltered younger brother off not just lightly, but with astonishing mercy.

Even Krysty, gentle soul that she was, would almost certainly have broken the boy's elbow for treating her that way. Or just dropped him flat with a broken jaw. Olympia had hurt him just hard enough to sober him up enough to pay attention.

"She's scary good, isn't she, Ryan?" Krysty said.

"Yes," he said, because it was true. "And I hope she's really on our side."

"Me, too."

Olympia turned and started walking away. Ryan thought she was headed to where she'd unrolled her bedroll by itself beside the commissary wag. Instead she went around the little fire to where Dezzy sat on her backpack. Her eyes were wide at the whole spectacle. Like the rest of the party, Ryan's people as well as Croom's, sec men as well as drivers, she had made no move to interfere in the confrontation between Morty and Olympia.

Ryan knew Morty had been bothering the little sec woman with the one white bang as well as every other female in the party, except Krysty and Mildred. As far as Ryan knew he'd never gotten anywhere, boss's spoiled sib or not. But Ryan didn't think Dezzy minded the prospect of seeing Morty get the wind knocked out of his sails. And like everybody else she'd seen Olympia in action enough to have little doubt she could do the knocking.

Olympia knelt briefly beside the young sec woman. She had to have said something, as Dezzy frowned slightly.

Olympia rose and walked with her usual stalking-panther grace to her bedroll.

Ryan stood with his arm around Krysty, feeling her heartbeat against his ribs, watching. Dezzy sat for a moment, head down, gazing at the low yellow dance of the flames. Then she got up and walked around to where Ricky was sitting. He was still obviously wired up by what had just happened. He jumped a little when he noticed her approaching.

Without a word as far as Ryan could tell, she reached down and took Ricky by his hand. Urging him to his feet, she led him off into the darkness.

Chapter Twenty-Five

"Trouble."

Jak's low, urgent voice snapped Ryan from deep sleep to total instant wakefulness, even before the single long-blaster shot shattered the dawn stillness.

Ryan jumped to his feet and grabbed his Steyr. The hills overlooking their little camp all seemed to be lined with Stones on bikes. They had to have pushed them up there to keep from rousing the convoy with engine sounds.

The shot had come from the highest hill, by chance the one nearest the big Stone Nation camp. Atop it Speaker was just stooping to lay his longblaster in the grass. A staff that looked suspiciously like a spear haft stuck up out of the thigh-high grass beside him.

Ryan, backed by Krysty, had convinced Jak into taking no more than a four-hour turn on patrol overnight. As a normal thing Ryan didn't reckon it was up to him to make personal choices for his people, all of whom were adults except for Ricky, who could also shift for himself as far as Ryan was concerned, or for the most part. But Jak sometimes had a short fuse, especially if he was fatigued. Ryan wanted him alert when he was awake, so he made him go to bed.

Now he might have cause to regret that, because the two men who'd had last watch, Doc and the slight and gentle head wrench Dan Hogue, were being held captive by angry-looking Stones on the foreslope of the hill right

below Speaker. The brutal-looking Pit Bull hung on to
Doc negligently by his upper arm, completely disregard-
ing the possibility the gawky, frail-looking old man could
pose any threat to a stud like him. Especially backed by
two eager-looking young Stone Nation warriors. Doc's captors hadn't even found it necessary to deprive him of his
ebony swordstick, though Ryan saw the oddly shaped butt
of Doc's LeMat sticking out of the waistband of Pit Bull's
black leather pants, pressing in against the pudge of his gut.

Morning Glory, vast, silent and grim, held a knife with
a great big bowed blade against Dan's throat. The wrench
looked resigned. He didn't lack courage, anyway.

The members of the convoy were rousing from their
bedrolls around the cold campfire and near the circle of
parked vehicles. The armored wag, the three cargo wags
and the chuck wag were on the outside. The prize stra-
tegic pieces, the huge fuel tanker with its burly coffin-
nosed Peterbilt tractor and the pickup blaster wag with the
.50-caliver weapon, were parked inside the outer circle.
The smell of dozens, maybe hundreds of idling bike engines had begun to seep down into the hollow and cover
up the fresh smell of dew-wet grass.

Krysty stepped up to stand by Ryan's side. "Get the gear
and start loading it on the wags," he said quietly. "When
we have to move, it'll be in a triple hurry."

"What if it sets them off?"

"Then we die quicker. Move."

It was a tone he seldom used on her, and he heard her
utter a slight gasp. Then she was gone, moving with her
own liquid grace.

J.B. joined Ryan. He pushed his hat back on his head
and scratched his balding crown.

"Gonna be a long day," he said. "Scorcher."

"Yeah."

With Cable walking at his side, looking around the mob of bikers surrounding them with slitted eyes, Bass walked toward the hill on which Speaker and the captives stood.

"What's going on here?" the master trader asked in a clear, strong voice. "This doesn't look any too neighborly, I got to admit."

Even though forty or fifty yards separated them Ryan saw Speaker's face, as impassive as a tan statue, twist slightly in reaction to Croom's words. When he spoke, his voice, projected almost as if from a loud-talker, was clotted with barely suppressed emotion.

"Now that I have your attention," the Stone Nation boss said.

He stooped. From the long grass by his legs he picked up something in both his bare, muscle-twined arms.

Ryan heard a woman behind him stifle a scream. Speaker held in front of him the nude body of a young woman. Her head lolled limp, trailing a single long braid into the grass as well as her unbound dark gold hair. From that alone Ryan recognized the one called Little Feather.

Her face and bare body bore the chalky, slightly-blue tinge of the well and truly chilled.

"We found her like this before dawn," Speaker said. "Our sister. Our daughter. Raped. Her rapist strangled her to shut her up."

Bass bowed his head. "My grief is yours, Speaker," he said, touching himself over the heart with a flattened palm. "But—"

"To death, he thought," Speaker continued relentlessly. "He thought wrong. She named her murderer before she let her spirit go up to the Great Sky. So strong was her spirit. She spoke it in my ears with her last breath. And the monster who did this to her was one of yours."

"Fireblast," Ryan muttered beneath his breath.

"She's not rigored up yet," J.B. observed. "Fresh chilled. He's not lying."

"Surely there's some mistake," Bass choked.

"You must deliver the chiller up to face Stone justice." He raised his head and smiled a terrible smile. "Stone vengeance. For we know the crime, and we know the criminal. Little Feather's courage has convicted and condemned him."

Bass shook his head. "We…we have to think about this."

"No." Speaker didn't shout, but the word tolled like the single beat of a mighty drum. "There is no thinking. We will have our vengeance. The only question is whether we take him alone, or all of you because you foolishly tried to protect him."

The noise was so shatteringly loud and close in the cool morning air that even Ryan flinched at its sudden eruption. He turned, not so see what it was—that was triple clear—but who.

Dace Cable had slipped away from his boss's side, a fact Ryan had absently noticed and wondered at, but hadn't allowed to dwell in his consciousness longer than an instant. Not with more pressing things to think about. Such as not dying.

But it had been no cowardice that impelled the sec boss's actions. For all his foibles Cable had never shown the slightest strand of yellow.

"Stand back!" the sec boss shouted from behind the spade grips of the huge blaster. Its perforated barrel gave off wisps of steam in the still humid air.

A small, dark figure eeled into the truck bed beside him—Dezzy, come to back her boss and load for him.

"We're rolling out of here, and if you try to stop us—"

Cable's shaved head exploded.

Ryan saw a flash from Speaker's hill, then the sun glint

off steel was obliterated by a spray of red as Morning Glory, her face as unmoving as slate, slashed Dan's throat to the neckbones with a single stroke of her big Bowie knife.

With a speed no one could have expected from someone of his apparent age, Doc whipped the slim triangle-sectioned sword from the cane he clutched in a knuckly right hand and under his right armpit stabbed Pit Bull in the hip. Though clearly not badly injured Pit Bull hollered and relaxed his grip.

Ryan was already moving with a purpose. He had seen a flash from a hill to the left—the south. He brought his Scout up fast, slipping his left forearm through the shooting loop of the sling, and looked through the glass. It was set on its lowest power: two. That was enough and more.

The shooter lay belly-down in a patch of blue flowers on the hilltop, about seventy yards away. Her hair, tied back from her dark, keen face in two braids thrown over her shoulder, was dyed a darker blue. She was startlingly young.

She was concentrating on the main threat, to her tribe and to their chieftain: the big blaster. She had just thrown her action to rechamber another shot in what looked like a scoped deer rifle. From the sound that had slapped Ryan's ears about the time Dan got chilled, he made it for a .270 or thereabouts.

The sniper was good, but as she sighted in on her next target—without needing to look Ryan knew the slim black-leather girl with the one white bang had leaped to take her dead boss's place without hesitation—she moved a trifle slow.

The Scout longblaster roared and its butt kicked Ryan's shoulder hard. When his glass came back down on target after he rode the recoil—and by reflex chambered a fresh

.308 cartridge—the spray of blood and brains was still visible out the right side of the sniper's head.

He dropped the glass from his eye, spinning toward Speaker. As he did, he heard the man's voice ring out above the sudden tumult. *"Chill them!"*

Other Stones leaped to place their bodies between the enemy longblaster and their chieftain. Ryan looked toward Doc.

Pit Bull was staggering back, bent over and squealing like a pig, a shockingly high note from such a bulldog body. He was clutching, not his punctured belly, but his face. Blood squirted between his fingers.

Doc, who had clearly followed his gut poke with a slash across the Pit Bull's face, was turning back with his sword and cane both clutched ungainly in his right hand. In his left he now held the LeMat.

The young warrior on Doc's left, who had fallen back a step when the oldie exploded into action, now closed in, fumbling at his waist for his knife. Doc stuck the long pistol barrel of the LeMat up under his victim's chin and literally blew the man's face off with the shotgun beneath.

As the corpse fell back, Doc turned and raced down the slope toward his companions, his coattails flapping behind him.

With Doc having freed himself, and Speaker masked by zealous guardians despite his roars for them to clear away and let him fight, Ryan turned and raced for the best vantage point he knew.

As he did he heard a savage snarling of engines and ten or more big Stone Nation bikes came surging between the western and northern hills. He kept running.

Ryan reached his goal and heard the Browning M-2's mighty voice speak again. Three shots, four, three. He heard screams, metal crashing, and then a whomp as a ruptured gas tank exploded into flame.

That wasn't Dezzy, he thought as he began to climb the cold steel rungs. She'd never practiced on the .50. Not even Croom for all his wealth and cunning preparation could afford enough of the huge .50 BMG cartridges to burn on anything but saving the wags and their occupants' asses. As smart as the sec woman was, cool in a fight, and triple brave, shooting the big beast for the first time in a firefight she would have mashed the butterfly trigger and held it down until either the belt of linked ammo tangled in the big box hung on the side, or the barrel melted down. Sure as she breathed; it was just what people did when they weren't trained, like their vision narrowing to a tunnel and their fine-manipulation skills turning to crap. Reflex.

No. That was a pro shooting Ma Deuce.

When he reached the flat catwalk atop the fuel tanker, Ryan was startled to see J.B. crouching in the aft sandbag emplacement.

"That wasn't you?" Ryan asked. His ears were still ringing from the big blaster going off, but he could hear well enough to notice there was little shooting going on, and that mostly outbound. The motorcycle engines noises were dwindling.

Not being one to waste words J.B. didn't bother answering.

As Ryan settled into the forward fighting nest, he heard Morty's voice crowing from down on the ground. "Run, you cowards! We whipped 'em, Bass! We whipped 'em good."

"Dark night!" J.B. exclaimed in disgust. "That young jack fool. The Stones aren't beat. Not by a .50-cal shot. That's what you call a tactical withdrawal."

"Yeah," Ryan grunted as he cast a quick look around.

At least the younger Croom was right as to what had happened, if not why. No Stones remained in sight, nor their bikes. Healthy ones, anyway. Several badly cut-up wrecks sprawled, one still blazing, where the Browning had shattered the first Stone Nation charge. But all Ryan could see on the low heights around were bodies, still or barely moving.

At least two forms lay on the grass around the camp-fire. A glance confirmed none of them was his friend, so Ryan looked back at the blaster wag.

Standing as firm as a teak statue behind the huge blaster and its pintle and pedestal mount was Mildred, looking not the least little bit like a fully trained predark physician. Ryan had guessed it was Mildred when J.B. proved not to be the shooter. On more than one occasion the Armorer had instructed his lover on the finer points of shooting a big blaster.

How she'd convinced Dezzy to relinquish control of the piece Ryan had no idea. When she was rolling Mildred tended to steamroll any opposition. But the little sec woman crouched at Mildred's side, her sawed-off lever blaster in hand and looking alertly around, ready to guard Mildred's back or to reload her piece at need.

Ricky did well there, Ryan thought. Hope the kid made it.

"We're all fit to fight, anyway," J.B. said as the tractor's engine grumbled into life. "Doc made it back intact."

Three fast blasts of a horn announced Bass Croom's armored wag was ready to roll. The other wags all answered with a single horn shot each. Whoever had taken the wheel of the tractor let loose a blast from the air horn.

"Hope Croom's people know the Stones will be back," J.B. said. "Just as soon as they calculate how to take out the big blaster."

Glancing back, Ryan saw his best friend's mouth set. He was concerned about Mildred. Right now she had a big red target glowing right in the middle of her forehead. The same as Cable had.

No matter how otherworldly and naive Mildred was, she was battle-seasoned enough to know it.

The Peterbilt wag bellowed, and the rig lurched into motion. Croom's vehicle and one of the cargo wags were already headed out the saddle between the northern end eastern hills. The tanker turned to follow.

Looking all around in case the Stones should get bold—or triple stupe—Ryan saw motion near the wrecked bikes. He swung his Scout to cover.

Across the scope of the not-yet-shouldered blaster he saw Olympia wrestle a motorcycle upright. Like all of them it was a huge road bike, a BMW, he thought. Like most it showed little modification, although he knew the Stone Nation tribe heavily tinkered-up their machines for extra endurance and durability. Surprisingly the motorcycle showed no decorations Ryan could see.

A form lurched up from the grass by Olympia's right leg, eyes staring out of a bloody mask and a right hand raised up with a knife to strike her down.

Her right hand whipped around, her telescoping staff snapping open. Ryan saw the biker's head whip as it was knocked sideways on his neck. A heartbeat later heard the click of it locking out and the sodden crunch of skull giving way.

He heard Olympia gun the bike engine as the tractor-trailer rumbled up and over the gap. She could take care of herself. He turned his attention to watching their surroundings for the inevitable next attack. Not that he expected it for a spell.

Speaker was too damned smart. As angry as he was

over the horrible crime committed against the girl, he wouldn't lose his head. He'd rein in his people until they could plan a strategy, one he was sure would chill his targets at minimal loss to the Stone Nation.

It wasn't as if those bikes couldn't catch the lumbering convoy any time their riders wanted to.

"I just hope one thing," J.B. called as the train lined out down a long flower-dotted slope toward the still distant Upper Snake.

"What's that?" Ryan asked.

"The Stones keep on letting their greed for all this nice fuel get the better of their hunger to see us burn."

"You're always a fucking comfort, J.B."

His friend gave him a brief grin and tipped his hat.

Chapter Twenty-Six

Ryan already expected the hit by the time it came, about an hour after they fled the campsite.

After flattening into a wide basin for a spell, with no more relief than a tabletop, the country had started to become hilly again. The road ran between two series of ridges, not high but close, with rocky caps and steep slopes.

It was a good road—two-lane, blacktop still mostly intact despite earthquakes and frost heave—enough so the convoy was averaging about thirty-five miles an hour.

It was also an unavoidable death trap.

Ryan's first warning of the shithammer coming down was when Jak came flying down the face of a ridge ahead and to the left, zigzagging the rapid decline with crazy speed and raising a rooster tail of yellow dust in his wake. He waved one arm frantically despite the risk entailed in taking a hand off the bars.

As he wobbled brutally on the bike, blasterfire crackled from the ridgetops, muzzle-blasts winking like sun glints off glass.

Ryan raised his Steyr but didn't target. He didn't dare fire until he knew what was actually happening.

"Going for the blaster wag," J.B. muttered.

It was true. Twenty or more nomads flowed from the ridges to both sides. Their big bikes came straight down the slopes, but their riders were masters of handling the machines off-road no matter how unwieldy. None of them went down.

They were whooping and brandishing weapons, spears and hatchets and blasters. Leading the pack from the northern heights was Speaker, his kinky black hair flying like a flag behind him, an AK in his hand.

The M-2 roared. Its big bullets cast up a series of earth geysers slanting across the face of the slope that led from the caprock. Several bikes went down; one blew up. The rest came on.

Using their intimate knowledge of the terrain—their home range, after all—the Stone Nation had picked an ambush site that would give the convoy's ferocious firepower only the briefest of openings to have any effect.

A blur passed the tanker on the other side, heading toward the rear of the convoy. Olympia, Ryan knew, on her scavenged ride. He reckoned that was nothing but suicide. Then again, what else could she do but fight or flee? She'd already shown she meant to share the fate of the convoy, even if that looked black as a stickie's soul right this instant.

Ryan lined up a shot on Speaker, but he was a triple-hard target, jouncing over obstacles and slewing around others. He fired but missed. By the time Ryan cranked the action and readied the longblaster to shoot again, the nomad bikers were swirling around both sides of the pickup like a hornet swarm. Mildred had the receiver of the M-2 shoved way up over her head, trying desperately to bring the blaster's deadly bullet stream to bear on the fast-moving attackers. At her side Dezzy was firing shots from her sawed-off carbine as fast as she could work the lever.

The almighty blast and flame from the M-2's barrel seemed to be having more effect than the half-inch slugs. The bikers sheered away from both. Some were knocked over bodily, to fly into spinning tangles of limbs and frames and wheels.

But the surviving riders always pressed back in to attack from another angle. More were streaming down to join the fight. By this time Ricky and the sec man with him were shooting at the Stones, as well, from their nest atop the chuck wag.

Jak's scout bike flashed by to the north side of the convoy. His giant chromed Python handblaster flashed in the sun. Like Olympia, he was bound to help his friends no matter how hopeless. Unlike Olympia, his motives at least were clear: he lived and died by and for his companions.

Ryan didn't even need to look around to know that none of the nomads was attacking the rest of the convoy. They were focusing on the one thing that could otherwise ruin them: Mildred's .50-caliber blaster.

He saw Speaker pull up alongside the cab of the blaster wag. He held up his Kalashnikov and triggered three fast shots obviously semi-auto.

Through his scope Ryan actually saw blood from the driver splash the inside of the windshield. Another rider, with eagle feathers waving from a spiked Mohawk, took the shot Ryan fired at the chieftain.

The blaster wag slowed, slewed violently and ran into the ditch to the south. Ryan grunted as he saw Mildred thrown clear of the bed. Whooping Stones circled it, waving their feather- and scalp-strung spears and firing shots in the air in celebration.

Ryan shot a biker who closed in on Mildred's supine, motionless form out of the saddle. Then to his surprise the Browning bellowed again, its terrible voice subduing all other sound.

The knot of Stones following the one Ryan had shot was blasted to gleaming, spurting, flaming parts. Dezzy had taken up the grips of the M-2 and was trying to support her comrade.

A bike came from the west. Ryan instantly recognized the whipcord shape of Olympia in her tan uniform-looking jacket, pulling up alongside Mildred. While Dezzy blasted any enemy bikers who tried to close in on them, she coolly dropped the kickstand, which like most Stone Nation bikes had an outsize pad to slow it sinking into dirt, dismounted and half dragged, half helped Mildred to her feet.

Ryan heard J.B. utter a single grunt from the front nest, then he went back to triggering single shots from his Uzi, though the range was too long to have much chance of hitting anything. In between bursts from the Browning, Ryan heard Jak's Python cracking off from the north side of the road.

Olympia manhandled Mildred onto the back of her bike, then got it going and turned it to ride for the convoy. Ricky was shouting and waving his arms at Dezzy to make a break. Ryan willed the boy to shut up and shoot.

But it wouldn't make any difference. The slim young sec woman blasted apart a swarm of bikes that formed to pursue Olympia and her rescuee.

Ryan shot a biker rolling in behind Dezzy. The bullet hit her in her left arm but had enough impact to knock her off her ride. Jak was closing in on Dezzy, waving his blaster in the air and shouting. Ryan had no chance of hearing him over the roar of bikes and blasters and the majestic intermittent roar of Ma Deuce. But he knew the albino was trying to get Dezzy to bail and jump on behind him.

Instead Ryan saw her stiffen, saw the silver glint off the steel of the thrown hatchet that had buried itself between her shoulder blades.

Pit Bull rode past the stalled-out blaster wag, down

the blacktop, pumping both fists in the air at his triumph. Jak pointed his handblaster at him and pulled the trigger.

The hammer fell on a spent casing. The cylinder was empty.

Ryan's shot at Pit Bull's garish skull-strip missed as he wheeled his bike abruptly to the right. Stones were swarming over the blaster wag now. Ryan hoped the hatchet had chilled Dezzy fast.

On the chuck wag, the blond sec man named Solo was holding Ricky in a bear hug from behind with his skinny arms to keep the kid from jumping off the still rolling wag in a futile attempt to help his friend.

A pack of Stones gave chase to Jak. While they were more experienced motorcyclists and knew the ground, the albino was as cunning as an old coyote. He was now an experienced dirt bike rider. He knew that no matter how skillful they were, those vast and massive motorcycles could never keep up with the scout cycle on any kind of bad surface.

He rode after the convoy right along the slope from the ridge caps. Where the Stone Nation machines slogged through the loosely packed soil, he seemed to skim over it. The fact that he was smaller than most of the bikers— who tended to be tall even when they weren't as beefy as Pit Bull—helped him leave them in his dust.

Olympia rode past with a seemingly unconscious Mildred slumped against her back. She made brief eye contact with Ryan through her goggles as she flashed by.

He gave her a nod; she rode on. Turning his head, he saw her pull up alongside Croom's armored wag. Not for the first time, Ryan felt a surge of respect for the master merchant's skill in keeping the powerful wag moving no faster than the less wieldy trucks could travel. Its engine was burly enough to leave them all in the dust despite the added weight of improvised armor plate it carried.

He also had to admire Croom's balls in not doing so. He could have saved his ass—and his precious younger brother's—by simply clearing out and abandoning the others to their fate. For all his faults and flaws, that wasn't something Bass Croom would do.

It would possibly get him chilled with Ryan and his companions and his own employees, but at least he'd die a man.

He saw the passenger door of the Land Cruiser fly open just as Olympia pulled alongside. Somebody reached out and with a bit of help from Olympia's left arm—she was still driving the bike at speed down the uneven highway—dragged Mildred into the lead wag.

And that's one for that little bastard Morty, Ryan thought. As far as he knew the blond-haired young man was the only other occupant of Bass Croom's wag. He had his suspicions about the boss's younger brother, and they were ugly ones. But he put himself way out to help a helpless Mildred.

That put Ryan in his debt, and he wouldn't forget.

As for whatever injuries Mildred had sustained getting thrown from the blaster wag—well, she'd get over them, or she wouldn't. Just as she'd get the chance to, or she wouldn't. She had risked her life and damn near lost it to cover the others' escape. All Ryan or anyone outside of the command wag could do was their best to save her sacrifice from being futile.

"Here they come!" he heard J.B. shout.

"I'M ALL RIGHT!" Ricky shouted to Solo. "You can let go now."

The death grip around his chest relaxed.

The wrecked blaster wag was shrinking rapidly with distance. Just at the edge of visual detail Ricky saw a nomad—he couldn't tell the sex at this range—stand spraddle-legged atop the cab of the pickup, brandishing a round, dark and light object overhead. He shuddered and closed his freely streaming eyes and hoped that wasn't Dezzy's head.

Then he opened to eyes to see the hornet swarm buzzing in pursuit of the convoy. He jumped as he felt a hard grip on his shoulder. He turned to look into Solo's face.

"Sorry, kid," the spiky-haired sec man said with just the slightest hitch in his voice. "Don't zone. Right now we've got troubles of our own."

Ricky looked around. The Stones were coming fast in pursuit now, up the road and on both sides. They began to speed past the last cargo wag and the chuck wag. Ricky ducked as one rider loosed a shot at him from a stretched-out, low-slung bike. But it wasn't aimed and came nowhere near.

As they had a moment before, when they took down the dangerous .50-caliber blaster wag, the Stones were concentrating on one target at a time, and this time it was the tanker.

Settling back down among the strapped-down sandbags, Ricky raised his DeLisle longblaster to his shoulder and took aim. It wouldn't be enough, he knew. They were doomed.

But he'd die doing what he could. It was all he could do.

Chapter Twenty-Seven

"Things are heating up," J.B. said.

The Armorer could smell the sulfur in the air, like a razor cutting through the road dust and engine fumes. The smoke pall from the volcano to the northwest covered the whole western horizon. It was the sort of thing he noted because details mattered. Not because it mattered now. As serious as an eruption was, it wasn't their actual problem at the moment.

J.B. wasn't in the habit of wasting words hammering down the obvious. The comment to Ryan was his notion of a joke.

That seemed to him as practical a response to certain death as anything, along with chilling as many of the enemy as he could before they chilled him. But that was a given.

Ryan laughed. He rocked back as his Scout longblaster roared. A bare-chested Stone Nation biker with black chevron marks covering his face, riding up the left side of the tanker, threw up his hands and fell off his ride sideways.

Ryan ducked as shots cracked at him from a Mini-14 held by the rider right behind the man he'd shot. J.B. pointed his Uzi at the shooter and squeezed off a 3-round burst. The rider uttered a raven croak of pain and dropped out of sight beneath the silvery swell of the fuel tank.

"Just keeping our heads down," J.B. called out over the crackling of blaster fire on all sides, and the different crack of bullets passing overhead at a speed faster than sound. He and Ryan had swapped nests again, so that J.B. was in the rear and Ryan's longblaster could support the front end of the convoy. "These boys and girls like to play face to face."

"Yeah," Ryan called back to his friend.

That was the rep the Stone Nation carried. They used blasters when they had to, but they preferred fighting foes hand-to-hand, where they could look into their enemies' eyes and feel their blood spurt hot over their knuckles. If it got them chilled, well, who left this world alive?

That wasn't Ryan's way of fighting. He fought to win; he fought only to win, to gain survival for himself and his friends, which were the stakes he was likely playing for now.

He wasn't interested in debating combat philosophy with the Stones or anybody else. That wouldn't load him any blasters. But he knew it was key to know how his opponents liked to fight.

He was momentarily out of targets on the left side of the tanker. He didn't like the implications, but he took advantage of the opportunity to take quick stock of the situation ahead of the fuel wag.

A half dozen or more nomad bikes buzzed around Bass Croom's lead wag. They might have shot out the tires—or tried, since the makeshift armored car had run flats—but they preferred playing it this way. In fact Ryan sensed they were mainly keeping Bass—and the other convoy blasters—busy while they focused on their prime target: the tons of gasoline riding in the big fat steel bladder beneath J.B.'s and Ryan's asses.

Still riding her Stone Nation bike, Olympia was right behind the armored wag, going knee to knee down the heaved pavement with Morning Glory, Speaker's giant shadow. The Plains woman was swinging what looked like a samurai sword, of all things. Olympia battled her with her telescoping metal staff held one-handed. She seemed to be holding her own.

Meanwhile Ryan saw Jak duck beneath a hatchet swipe of a Stone Nation rider as they rode down the ditch head-on. His white hair swirled as he twisted in the saddle of his dirt bike. Apparently he had a blade in his hand; Ryan actually saw red spurt from the nomad's weapon-arm as Jak gashed him in passing.

Frantic movement took Ryan's eye back where it always longed to go—to the cargo wag ahead atop which Krysty and Doc rode in a double-size sandbag nest. Doc had his outsize LeMat broken open and was stuffing in fresh .44 Remington cartridges. Krysty was making the motion that had captured his attention: waving madly at the left side of the fuel tanker.

Still holding the Scout in his right hand, Ryan let go of its fore end with his left hand. Turning, he drew his SIG-Sauer P-226 blaster and extended his arm. Over the three-dot front sight he saw a very surprised-looking face that had just appeared above the edge of the metal tank to the left of his nest.

He fired once. A hole appeared over the left eye, wide, staring and blue. The head fell away without a sound escaping the man's mouth.

Feeling a warning sensation prickle down his spine, Ryan kept twisting in his seated position. A biker who had scrambled up the rear access ladder loomed above J.B. with an ax handle upraised to flatten the little man's fedora and smash his helpless skull. Ryan gave him a double tap right through the elk-bone gorget that hung in front of his breastbone. He spun and fell away off the rear of the tank.

Letting his Uzi fall to dangle from a long sling over his left shoulder, J.B. grabbed the pistol grip of his M-4000 scattergun, which was slung from his right side to the level of his short ribs, just above the dubious protection of the sandbag rampart. He blasted a biker who was lunging up the rungs welded to the right rear side of the tank, so close Ryan could see the yellow muzzle-flash lick against the black-painted upper half of the shouting face before the charge of double-00 shot smashed into it and the shaved skull above.

Ryan sensed movement to his right. A Stone Nation warrior popping up on that side actually grabbed the barrel of his Scout and yanked at it, ignoring the fact the barrel was hot enough from the shooting to burn his flesh. The one-eyed man smelled cooking skin.

He didn't fight the tug. Instead he turned, helping the biker swing the longblaster toward his own face before triggering it. The 7.62 mm bullet smashed into the man's lower jaw. The craggy black face, twisted with lunatic glee, started to deform from muzzle-blast as well as impact. Then the face went away as the owner fell off the tanker.

Anticipating as much as sensing an attack from the left, Ryan wheeled back that way, driving with his left heel against the inside of the sandbag wall. He smashed the butt of his handblaster against the nose of the biker who was lunging for him with a needle-slim commando dagger.

The man reeled back. Ryan was about to jam the SIG-Sauer back in its holster when a weight landed on his shoulders from behind. He was crushed onto the sandbags by a mass of bodies. The person on top of him was a woman. Her face was painted green, the irises staring from wide white eyeballs were bright green, and he could feel the heft of the breasts bound in by a cloth band crushed against his own chest. She held a big knife icepick-fashion that she was driving toward Ryan's eye.

He jammed the muzzle of his SIG-Sauer against her side

and blasted twice. Her body jerked, and her eyes turned to glazed green marbles.

The tip of the knife sliced his right cheek as he turned his face away. It buried itself to the hilt in the sandbag beneath his head.

There were at least two more bikers in the dog pile, who were for a brief interval unable to get at Ryan for the quiescent body of their late sister. The one-eyed man jammed the handblaster into the waistband of his jeans, ignoring the way its metal scorched the tender flesh beneath.

He managed to worm the panga out left-handed and ram its steel butt into the nearest person's face. Teeth splintered. Cursing, the biker rolled away.

Another bare arm was poised overhead. A tomahawk-style hatchet with feathers tied beneath its steel head was silhouetted against high thin clouds. Ryan sliced his adversary's biceps with a drawing cut of the panga blade. The man screamed. The ax fell from his hands to bounce off the top of the wag with an oddly musical ring.

Using the deadweight pressing down on the weapon as well as his body, Ryan quickly worked the bolt action of his Scout. Then, with his body already twisted clockwise, Ryan shoved his right leg free, swinging it up and to the right to clear both the chilled Stone Nation woman and the man whose arm was spraying blood on his face, so hot it felt scalding. He tasted the copper in his mouth.

Then he was clear. Ryan jumped up, panga in left hand, Steyr in the right.

Hopelessly entangled with the dead woman, the man whose arm Ryan had sliced rolled with her off the east side of the tank and out of sight. Ryan wheeled back to his left.

The man whose mouth he had shattered with his panga butt had managed not to fall off to his likely doom. He was on his knees and cursing from a mouth that spilled blood like lava. He hacked wildly at Ryan with a Bowie knife.

The one-eyed man used the momentum of his turn to slash him across the face with his panga. Blood shot out of a crimson slash in his face. He fell back and off the tanker.

Shrieking a cry of rage the Stone Nation biker whose nose he'd broken with the SIG-Sauer flew at him from the middle of the tanker, where he'd apparently been recovering his self-control after the sudden shock and pain. He had his slender double-sided knife held point-down from his upraised fist.

Ryan shot him with the Scout one-handed. He spun away, the knife falling from his hand. He landed on his face, his body slanted across the fuel tank's center line. He didn't roll off, but he didn't seem likely to move again.

Beyond him Ryan saw J.B. surrounded by a mass of flailing bodies and flashing steel.

As Ryan shifted weight to charge back to the rescue, a desperate cry rang out from one of the wags still following the big rig.

"Ryan! Behind you!"

RICKY CURSED himself.

Both his beloved mentor and his adored and feared leader were in immediate chilling danger, and he was holding two empty blasters—the most useless items in the entire known universe. He had nobody to blame but himself.

He'd fired the last cartridge from the DeLisle's 10-round box just as Stones began to scramble onto the chuck wag with him and Bert. Proper practice, as drilled into him by his lost Uncle Benito for years, and then by both J.B. and Ryan since he had joined his new family, held that you reloaded an empty blaster the instant you emptied it, no matter what.

Both their teaching and the sheer press of necessity said a person also did what he or she had to to survive. He just hadn't had time, but had been forced to let the carbine fall on its sling, whip out his Webley and gut-shoot a burly bear-shaped warrior before the man split his head with a machete. Then it had been a mix of clubbing attackers with the heavy handblaster—something else he hated to do— and blasting them with it until the hammer clicked empty when he tried to shoot one of the nomads swarming J.B.

Ricky was still numb from seeing Dezzy die. The prospect of losing J.B. made sour puke fill his mouth. He could only watch helplessly and do nothing.

He heard a gargling dry sound from behind, then a blaster went off almost in his ear.

A figure pitched forward across the sandbag to his left, the wag's west side, as he'd turned forward to see the awful scene on the tanker. As it flopped on its side away from him, onto the flat top of the wag's box, he saw it was a young woman—Indian—by her features. She was no older than Dezzy had been. A trench knife was held in place by her outflung hand as it relaxed into death.

Ricky looked up into the eyes of Solo, his sec man partner on the chuck wag. The young man's eyes were wide and staring—down at the bloody spear head sticking eight inches out of the middle of his chest.

A giant biker grinned at Ricky from over Solo's shoulder. "You're next!" he called, though with all the shooting and screaming and commotion—or maybe just the thunder of his own pulse drowning his ear—he could only make out the words by reading the man's lips.

Solo raised his head. His eyes met Ricky's, and he lifted his right hand, as if to shoot Ricky at contact range with the Model 1911 semi-auto handblaster still gripped in it.

He'd used it to blast the woman about to take Ricky's life, at the cost of his own.

Time seemed to slow to a tortured and torturing crawl. Solo gave the blaster a funny little shake that incongruously reminded Ricky of trying to wag his penis dry after taking a piss. Then Solo's eyes rolled up in their sockets, and his chin slumped down to the notch of his collarbone.

Ricky understood his final message an instant before it was too late.

As the Stone Nation biker yanked his spear out of his victim's back, Ricky let the DeLisle drop. Its sling yanked his shoulder, but he ignored the impact. He grabbed the .45 from his comrade's hand. Fumbling with fingers that still held the empty Webley, he turned the big angular blaster in his grip.

The enormous biker cocked the spear back by his waist to stab Ricky across Solo's fallen body. Ricky thrust the sec man's blaster to the full length of his arm and pulled the trigger.

The big blaster roared and did its best to buck free of his hand. It had double the recoil of his wheelgun, caused by the big mass of machined metal, the slide, that slammed back and forth after each shot to eject the empty casing and drive home a fresh cartridge from the magazine in the well.

His first shot went wide. The big Stone biker's eyes grew large in surprise. The second shot hit him right under the right nipple. The blaster was rising inexorably in response to its powerful blasts.

On Ricky's third shot the slide locked back. Empty.

But the nomad head was rocked back. Ricky got a glimpse of his mad dark eyes seeming to cross as they tried to look up at the fat blue hole that had just appeared in the middle of his forehead above them, then he toppled like a felled tree off the rear of the chuck wag.

Ricky turned. As he did, he cracked open the Webley's top-break action and fumbled in a pouch at his waist for a fresh full-moon clip of .45 ACP rounds. Though the Stones attacking J.B. hid the Armorer from his sight as well as whatever was happening to Ryan at the tanker's front end, the very fact the nomads were still there confirmed that the little man in the battered hat and glasses was somehow holding his own.

Ricky slammed the reloaded cylinder shut. His jaw jutted with determination. I'll save you, J.B.! he thought.

Sensing a rush of motion behind him, Ricky wheeled back to blast a lunging biker in the body at face-spitting range.

He saw others clambering up, with that same crazy courage they'd showed all along. Ricky would have to save himself first, and that was going to be a full-time job for a spell.

The rest of his life, maybe.

Chapter Twenty-Eight

Ryan wheeled right, bringing up his Scout as he did so. Not to shoot—its chamber was empty, and he'd had no chance to throw the bolt, especially not with his big panga gripped in his left hand.

An impact caught the weapon as it crossed in front on his face. The pressure ran up Ryan's arm and drove him back a step. He recovered, then gazed past the curved blade buried in the Steyr into Speaker's face. Though his jaw was thrust out with determination, something like delight glinted in the chieftan's black eyes.

"Just you and me, One-Eye," the Stone Nation boss said. "Just like it was fated to be."

Ryan yanked downward with the longblaster as he got his hips behind a whistling panga cut at the oddly calm face.

The heavy but razor-honed blade of the panga clipped a lock of black hair from Speaker's head as the Stone Nation warrior turned his body right, away from the blow. He kicked the Steyr's receiver, barely missing smashing Ryan's finger on the trigger guard. He used the impact both to wrench free his weapon and dance back a step.

Ryan let the Scout fall to hang on its sling.

"So what's it to be, then?" Speaker said. He was actually grinning now. "Will you whip out your SIG and blast me? Or will you face me blade to blade like a man?"

I'd shoot you on the spot like a man who intends to go

on breathing, Ryan thought. If I didn't know triple well you'd cut me down with that fancy-ass pig-sticker while I was trying to draw.

He tugged at the Scout's sling with his thumb so that the longblaster rode muzzle-down along his back. That way it wouldn't foul his fighting form. Then he lunged forward. The panga whistled overhand toward the apex of Speaker's hair pyramid. Ryan was done with words. Now he'd let steel do his talking.

He saw Speaker's thin lips twist in a smile of contempt for the sheer blunt obviousness of Ryan's attack. His own weapon swept up. It was actually a full-on saber, the old cavalry type, with a steel basket hilt guarding his hand and everything. A sword—the kind of weapon that'd been obsolete for like a century before the Big Nuke. It was still serious steel, with a lethal edge, and Speaker knew how to use it.

He'd already made a mistake, though. Ryan tucked his own blade in as he let his body drop. He put the knuckles of his knife hand on the flat ribbed-steel catwalk and let that take his weight as he scythed his right leg around in a sweep at Speaker's legs. The Stone Nation chieftain went down sideways.

The man didn't lose his bearing or his balance and fall off the fat steel tank, as Ryan hoped. He landed hard on his side and without a beat rolled toward Ryan, launching a wicked saber cut at him overhand.

Ryan already had his boots beneath him to get up, and simply jumped back out of the way, out of his sandbag nest.

The saber split the sandbag nearest the front. Speaker recovered instantly to a guard position as it began to bleed yellow sand.

"You're good, One-Eye," he said. "But good enough?"

Good enough not to underestimate you again, Ryan

thought. He'd had a pretty high assessment out the gate of the combat skills of a man who could be acknowledged boss of the vast, contentious Stone Nation. Now he had to lever it up a few notches.

He still didn't aim to lose.

With the empty sandbag nest between them, his backpack lying inside, he risked a quick glance over his shoulder to see how his friend was making out. He was in time to see the Armorer's body snap forward, catapulting a woman with blue-dyed braids into the bearded face of a Stone Nation warrior wielding a ball bat with nails sticking out of it. Both fell howling off the tanker.

J.B. held his own. For now, at least. The little man was easy to underestimate, too. Especially the wiry strength wound up in that compact body of his.

Ryan turned to meet a furious leaping attack by Speaker. He stepped back as the chieftan landed on the rear sandbag. His panga easily parried the cavalry sword.

Shorter than Ryan's blade, it wasn't that much lighter than the saber. Nor did Speaker have the strength simply to power Ryan—a bigger man—down.

Still, he had plenty of strength. Ryan felt it, right enough.

Blades rang like wicked bells as they traded fast and violent strokes. Speaker did love flair—he had a flashy style that wasted energy and time, two vital commodities in a fight, as that jumping attack over the sandbags showed. But triple fast, enough so that his flamboyance didn't give Ryan any obvious openings for counterattacks.

After what felt like an hour to Ryan, it was clear that straight-up, blade-to-blade fighting wasn't giving a clear edge to either, which meant his opponent likely noticed it, too.

Instinct guided him. He sprang back a step as Speaker unleashed a horizontal slash forehand at his blind eye, and then used his momentum to whirl into a spinning back kick.

It was the sort of move that almost always ended in getting the man who made it chilled. Though sometimes crippled up first, if the intended recipient grabbed the over-exposed leg and threw his opponent down. Or simply dislocated the hip. Ryan had done all those things to foes.

It was a stupid move to throw at a fighter with the skill and rattlesnake speed of Ryan Cawdor, if you didn't have the skill and puma speed of Speaker.

The sheer unexpectedness of the kick, which while relatively slow to develop was as powerful a strike as a human body could deliver, would have nailed Ryan in the chest with rib-crushing force, but Ryan's instincts, and likely his ability to read the shifts of his opponent's balance, had saved him and won him the chance to slash at the back of Speaker's lower leg.

Speaker's boot and his own quick reflexes saved *him*. He rechambered the kick immediately, then put his foot down and went back into a sensible fighting stance.

He showed Ryan a big grin, the one-eyed man had felt his blade bite flesh, even if not deeply. He saw red gleam on the wide blade as he held it up in front of his face.

"You don't trick easy, do you, One-Eye?" Speaker asked.

Ryan said nothing. He was judging the other's injury by his weight. It wasn't serious. He knew that from the fact the Stone Nation chief was able to put weight on his injured limb.

The difference between a sword fight, which this functionally was, and a fight with smaller knives was that a single cut or thrust could kill a combatant and frequently did. It was a rare battle that could be stopped by a single knife wound, cut or thrust. Whereas a blade as big and beefy as the panga's—or the saber—could split a skull or even lop off a limb. Just like that.

In a knife fight, the most common outcome was for both combatants to get cut, and for the one who bled less to win as his opponent weakened and allowed him the fatal upper hand.

That dynamic could play in a full-on sword fight just as easily. First blood had gone to Ryan. Now, given their close match in fighting ability, all he had to do was to hang and bang until Speaker weakened. The problem was that was still a minor cut. A man like Speaker could lose a deal of blood and still function at peak, especially with adrenaline supercharging his system like an overdose of jolt.

The worst problem was that Speaker knew it, so he'd be looking to change the odds back in his favor, any way he could.

The conventional move was for Ryan to press him hard and let him bleed. At the moment Ryan had no better tactic than to do that. He came on hard, driving the smaller man back with a flurry of blows that took advantage of his edge in height and strength.

Just when he let himself hope he could get Speaker to stub a boot heel against the fighting nest and fall over backward, Speaker threw himself right at him. He parried high, letting the panga blade slide down his upthrust saber, then clacked Ryan's teeth together and rocked his head back with a savage left uppercut.

Red exploded behind Ryan's eyes. His body reacted on its own, yanking his left knee up almost to his chest, then pistoning his boot forward with his hips behind a massive thrust kick.

Speaker hadn't been expecting that any more than Ryan had anticipated that punch. The two fighters flew away from each other.

Still fuzzed by the blow to his jaw Ryan lost his balance and had to turn clear around. As he caught himself with his left hand on the catwalk he saw a Stone Nation woman, her back to him, raising her spear for an overhand stab at J.B., whom her body hid from Ryan's view.

The Deathlands warrior knew that Speaker had recovered his balance and poise fast and was undoubtedly springing to attack his opponent's back. So he did something the nomad boss wouldn't expect. He sprinted fifteen feet toward the rear of the tanker and slashed the spear woman across the back with his panga.

She shrieked and arched her back like a cat hit by a speeding wag. The spear flew away from upflung hands, and then a savage sideways stroke of the M-4000's butt smashed the side of her face and toppled her off the truck.

J.B. stood there, his hat and glasses still in place. He held his scattergun in both hands like a riot baton. The pair of foes left to him were keeping a respectful distance behind.

"I had it," the Armorer said mildly. "Mind your own knitting, Ryan."

Ryan saw a figure suddenly loom behind J.B., a figure not that much taller than the armorer, though significantly broader. Its head, which seemed to flow up out of the huge sloped shoulders without much intervention by a neck, was shaved to a short scalp lock, dyed a brighter red than the droplets of blood drying on the grinning face.

Speaker's lieutenant Pit Bull had joined the fight.

J.B. was already turning to face his earlier foes as well as the new arrival.

Ryan wheeled and slashed. J.B. could take care of himself, as his mild reproach—the equivalent of another man cussing Ryan up one side and down the other for his damn foolishness—had indicated.

And he needed to, because the timer in Ryan's mind had reckoned a man like Speaker would've just had time to reassess the situation and charge to take advantage of his foe's turned back. As usual it was right.

Ryan's backhand panga swing deflected a whistling cut from the saber, but it was a glancing contact.

With a wrist undoubtedly strengthened by hours working a wrench, Speaker was able to twirl his long blade around like a willow wand. As Ryan's knife hand rolled over for a swing the other way, the long curved sword gashed his arm, just over the ulna and about three inches above the wrist.

Driving with all the power in his long, strong legs, Ryan threw himself forward. His dropped shoulder smashed into Speaker's chest.

Once more Speaker's cat reflexes saved him. Instead of letting the bigger man power him down, he sprang back. He almost overbalanced and went over the side for the long fall to the road streaming by a dozen or so feet beneath.

But he didn't. He caught himself and backed away, waving his saber in the air between his face and Ryan's with deceptive gentleness.

"Like your friend said," the Stone Nation boss called. "Keep your mind on your own troubles. I told you—this is between just you and me."

He wasn't even breathing hard. Then again, neither was Ryan.

But Ryan had troubles now.

Speaker's white teeth flashed. "So we each have scored a hit," the nomad said. "Let's see whose hurts worse, first."

Ryan felt his lips skin back from his teeth in a grimace. Having either a leg fold up or having your weapon-arm drop could get a person chilled pretty fast in a fight like this; kind of a toss-up which was worse, really. But while

Ryan's wound was superficial—he could feel by the fact his grip stayed strong that it hadn't cut muscle or tendon, but mostly skin and maybe veins—he suspected it was bleeding harder than the nick he'd inflicted on Speaker's hind leg. An arm would weaken faster than a leg, being smaller.

So now Speaker pressed his advantage hard. The saber turned into a steel whirlwind with Ryan at the center of its concentrated fury.

The one-eyed man felt his arm begin to weaken. The blood was flying freely from his cut. He had to keep ducking his head to keep a drop from flying in his eye and blinding him for the split second that would be all it would take for him to wind up with that eye staring up at the sky from the ditch by the road.

He was still able to match Speaker's speed, but his strength was draining like gas from a bullet-holed tank.

Just when he was thinking about trying to use his superior weight to try to regain the advantage, Speaker lunged for him.

They caught each other's weapon wrist. Grinning like a fiend, supercharged by the advantage he knew he held, Speaker forced the long blade of his sword toward the taller man's face.

Sunlight glinted off the wickedly honed edge of the saber inching toward Ryan's eye. Sweat streamed down his face and the muscles of his shoulders and back screamed from exertion, as the blade kept getting closer and closer.

Ryan's right arm buckled.

Chapter Twenty-Nine

Ryan went with it.

Speaker was trying to push his body against Ryan's with all his strength. Instead of fighting that any more, the one-eyed man lunged. He pushed up hard with his left hand, using the sudden shift of position to stop opposing the power of Speaker's sword arm with his own, moving hand and weapon skyward. His forehead snapped forward and down, right onto Speaker's right collarbone.

The bone snapped with a sound like a glass rod breaking.

Speaker howled and sprang back. He let go of Ryan's failing panga arm and used his body's momentum to rip his other wrist free of Ryan's grip. He landed lightly clean on the front side of Ryan's sandbag emplacement, but his sword arm dropped as if it had turned to a used gaudy bar rag. The saber dropped from his fingers and slid, clattering, over the swell of the fuel tank's side and away out of sight.

Speaker stared down at his limply dangling arm, which no matter the strength of his muscles, he couldn't force to rise. That was what a broken clavicle did to a person.

The leader of the Stone Nation raised a look of sheer horror to Ryan's face.

"You bastard," he said.

"And then some," Ryan agreed, then flew right up and

over the sandbags in a flying sidekick, because Ryan Cawdor had some flash of his own.

It should have been easy for Speaker to deflect the kick and send the man hurtling onward to his doom with a faceful of cracked asphalt.

But Speaker's reflex was to use his right arm, which didn't work.

The sole of Ryan's right boot thudded against the flat-muscled chest left bare by Speaker's buckskin vest. He flew backward and vanished down the gap between the front of the tanker and the tractor's overcab compartment.

Ryan almost lost his own balance on landing. Fireblast! he thought. *Wouldn't* this be a dip shit way to die? But he caught himself and turned right down to see how his friend fared.

Not well. Two Stones were holding J.B. by the upper arms from either side. While just beyond him, Pit Bull, grinning like a stickie with a can of gasoline and a lighter, raised one of his hatchets high over his head for the chilling stroke.

Ryan heard a sharp pop, that rang with supersonic harmonics.

Pit Bull roared in pain and reeled back a step. Lifting the hand he'd clapped to his belly, he stared at the palm in horrified shock. He had a fresh hole in his ample belly and it was hosing blood.

J.B. kicked him in the balls, and he fell off the back off the tanker.

Ryan was already in motion, drawing his SIG left-handed from the waistband of his jeans. He threw the handblaster to the full extension of his arm, lined up the sights and squeezed two quick shots, aimed at the blurred image of a head propped like a balloon atop the front-sight post.

Despite the close focus Ryan saw bright fluid spray from his target.

As he snapped his vision back to take in the scene with clarity, and switched the blaster toward J.B.'s captor on his own left, he saw that figure double over.

The Armorer had driven the muzzle of his shotgun into that Stone Nation biker's lean belly. As neatly and business-like as if he were chopping wood, J.B. raised the longblaster and brought the buttplate down hard on the exposed back of his opponent's neck.

The nomad dropped flat on his face. That blow had sounded like an ax splitting wood, too; his neck was broken.

The body slid backward and dropped off the side of the tanker. Ryan didn't see whether J.B. had helped the man along with a nudge of his boot.

The nomad Ryan had chilled had fallen, too. They were alone atop the long steel sausage. J.B. slipped into his sandbag nest, sat, and began feeding fresh brass and green-plastic shells into the receiver of his shotgun.

"Sit down and stop admiring your handiwork," J.B. said. "You're making yourself a target."

He was right, but Ryan frowned as he heard a sound: the powerful snarl of a Stone Nation motorcycle engine, rising to distinguish itself from the general roar of engines, blasters and voices raised in anger and pain.

He saw something streak up the dirt flank of the ridge that still rose to the tanker's left—the west side of the road, which continued to unwind north, straight as a blaster shot.

It was Morning Glory, riding her huge outlaw sled full-throttle. A figure slumped against her broad back: Speaker. He looked semiconscious—he'd probably banged his head on his fall between tractor and trailer. But he wasn't rag-doll limp, meaning he wasn't yet chilled.

Ryan began reeling up the sling of his Scout. He meant to take care of that.

It'd be a pure shame to chill a warrior as brave, skilled and resourceful as Speaker was, but shame wasn't an engine that exerted powerful motivating force on Ryan Cawdor's life. Not compared to survival.

Ending their capable and charismatic leader probably wouldn't cripple the Stone Nation. It wasn't even likely to cause them to call off their vendetta against the convoy.

But if putting a 7.62 mm boat-tailed hollow-point bullet through Speaker bought Ryan and his friends even a minute more of life, well, he valued that minute a thousand times more than the Stone Nation chieftain's whole heroic life.

Before he could even get hands on the longblaster the Peterbilt tractor swerved left.

For a moment Ryan froze. He was unsure whether the trailer would run up on the tractor and jackknife, or whether the whole rig would turn sideways and simply roll over. Neither of which would be good for the continued health and well-being of the two men atop the giant can of highly inflammable—indeed, explosive—fuel.

The swerve corrected. The Peterbilt tractor's coffin snout turned straight north along the road again. A fresh motion snagged Ryan's gaze and pulled it down to the ditch, where a pale form was rolling and flopping over the grass. The face was a mask of blood, he could see that, but the long braid of hair, almost white-blonde before the blood had dyed much of it bright red, told Ryan the whole story. That was Randi, the convoy's chief wrench since the death of her boss Dan Hogue a couple hours before.

She'd been driving the big rig, which meant a nomad now held the wheel of the fuel tanker.

Ryan looked back at J.B., who was hitching his back-pack over his back.

"Time to go," the Armorer said.

As RYAN CLAMBERED down the rear rungs on the right side of the fuel tank, a nomad woman swung her bike close. She had a Mohawk spiked with grease, and her hawklike features, painted black, were contorted in a scream of rage as she cocked a spear to impale the one-eyed man.

Hanging from the same rungs a few feet above him by his right hand, J.B. swung up his Uzi with his left. He fired a 3-shot burst, aiming high so as not to damage the bike that Fate had conveniently provided.

J.B. didn't believe in Providence, but he took all freely offered gifts, regardless of the source. He saw the spurt from the woman's right shoulder, left bare by her sleeveless black top, indicating at least one bullet had struck home. The big Harley veered, then wallowed on its suspension as the full weight of Ryan and his heavy-laden backpack landed on the seat behind the driver. As the sled headed for the ditch he pitched the injured nomad off, then humped forward onto her seat.

Grabbing the handlebars, he easily got the bike con-trolled once more.

By the time J.B. had let his short but hefty machine pis-tol hang again and finished climbing down, Ryan had the long, low machine purring along beside him. A quick hop and J.B. was safely ensconced behind his friend.

The bike, as powerful as it was, was slowed perceptibly by the combined weight of the two men and their gear, but it still accelerated past the big rig, which the Stone Nation driver was smart enough not to crowd too fast on the un-certain pavement.

Ryan had the bike over to the margin of the blacktop as they cruised past the rig.

J.B. saw two blue eyes staring out of a crimson-painted raccoon mask on the pale face turned toward him. For just a moment. Then the face burst into an undifferentiated red mass as J.B. gave him a full charge of double-00 from his shotgun held up one-handed.

The biker's ruined head landed against the steering wheel. The tractor veered toward the eastern ditch as the motorcycle's engine roared and the overloaded bike surged away up the road.

As they separated, J.B. looked back over his shoulder just in time to see the big rig, now fully sideways to its original motion, tip over majestically to slam onto its side.

The rig wasn't traveling fast enough to keep rolling, but capsizing was enough to breach the tank. Fuel gushed as momentum kept the fallen vehicle and its tons of gasoline sliding forward along the road.

J.B.'s brows furrowed as sparks sprayed upward from friction points at the front and rear of the big tank. Results are all that matter, he reminded himself sternly.

He reached up to clamp his hat on his head against the wind of their progress.

Whooping, bikers converged on the fallen tanker even before it ground and squealed to a halt. The sparks stopped without lighting off the spilling gas.

The nomads began to halt their bikes and swarm up it. They completely ignored the wag that swung wide across the ditch and rolled past the wreck, jouncing wildly and kicking up dust. It was the chuck wag. J.B. felt a certain relief to see the distinct mop of black hair belonging to his young protégé flying in the breeze from the sandbag nest atop the box. He seemed to be alone now.

Also, it was only wag escaping the now distracted Stone Nation. So the cargo wag back there had been lost.

"Is it time?" Ryan called over his shoulder.

J.B. reached in a pocket of his jacket. "Just about," he said.

RYAN BRAKED the big bike. It pulled a little left. He used that to coast it into a full-on broadside turn and stopped.

More motorcycles converged on the fallen tanker. They were swarming down from the ridges that flanked the road now, too. With Speaker out of the fight—however temporarily—it seemed as if the nomad bikers had forgotten their vengeance quest. Their outlaw instincts were taking over.

In the face of such prime plunder, it was almost hard to blame them. But then, Ryan didn't much bother his mind with blame, either.

A single figure appeared on the side of the long, squashed-cylinder tank that was now its upper surface. It brandished two hatchets over its mostly shaved head. Sunlight, filtered by volcano smoke as well as high clouds, glinted off their steel heads.

"It's just a .32 ACP," J.B. said apologetically. He was speaking of the hideout blaster with which he'd belly-shot the Stone Nation warrior and subchief. "Probably just bounced off his body wall, slid around inside some without reaching his chitlins."

"Probably," Ryan said. "I'd say that means it's time."

J.B. took his hand from his pocket. He pointed the small flat object it held at the wreck and pressed a button.

During the first part of their flight, between escape and the inevitable ambush, the Armorer had set boobies in case the fuel wag got captured by their enemies. While Ryan had faith they'd work—for J.B. had a true master's touch with that sort of unpleasant surprise—the convoy's supplies didn't just contain some blocks of plastic explosive and blasting caps.

Bass Croom may not have managed to swing full-on radios for the convoy, not even talkies, but he *had* scrounged up a working remote radio detonator.

Seeing his fleeing prey halt, Raven held his hatchets straight up to the sky and gave them a threatening shake. He may have been caught up in the celebration, but he hadn't forgotten the real purpose of this chase, which for him, Ryan reckoned, included at least a few live captives to torture.

From the top rear of the wag Ryan saw a little white flash. In less than the time it took his eye to blink and fully reopen, a second flash occurred from near the same spot. Almost instantaneously it blossomed into a giant orange fireball, so bright Ryan had to narrow his eye. In a literal flash it enveloped not just the gloating Raven but dozens of bikes and riders.

As the roar of the explosion arrived, followed by a shock and blast of hot air, several figures staggered from the five-story bonfire. They were like moving statues of flame, and managed only a few paces before they fell to the pavement.

Ryan nodded in grim satisfaction.

Simply blowing up the tank would've probably accomplished little. On its own, gasoline burned like water. It was the fumes that caught fire. Or, under the right circumstances, exploded.

The first, smaller charge set off by J.B.'s thumb on the button had been a breaching charge, to crack open the fat tank, still more than half full of gas, and fill the air with fumes for the second, larger charge to set off in a full-scale detonation. It was a triple-huge version of the myriad tiny blasts in the cylinders that made the engine in their stolen motorcycle run. That created a classic two-stage explosion.

As it happened, of course, the tank was already breached by the crash; the first charge had been unneeded. But that was J.B. all over. He left as little as humanly possible to chance.

"You're an artist, J.B.," Ryan said, sparing a brief thought for the people killed by the blast.

The Armorer had put the command detonator back in his pocket. Now he took off his glasses and began to polish the round lenses with his hankie.

"Thanks," he said.

The chuck wag had driven well clear of the explosion. It had turned back across the ditch and was just climbing back when the blast went off. Surprised, the driver drove clear across the road and almost into the other ditch before correcting. But he did, and came barreling in pursuit of the rest of the convoy.

Ryan gunned the big bike's engine and looked back along the road. Even before stopping he'd confirmed that the wag with Krysty and Doc pulling sec up top was still alive and rolling, and that his friends were still functional. Now he set his ride in motion. Up the road, the Stones that had been attacking Croom's command wag and the other cargo wags came streaming back down both flanks of the road.

"Get ready," he called to J.B. He felt the man shift behind him as he unlimbered one of his blasters. The Uzi, Ryan reckoned.

But the Stone Nation bikers passed them without a sideways glance. Now they were totally focused on helping their brothers and sisters who had gathered by the fallen fuel wag.

J.B. grunted. "Looks like they've lost interest in us."

"For now," Ryan said. He leaned forward and opened

the throttle. The overloaded motorcycle roared and accelerated.

"They won't stop until they get what they want," he called over his shoulder, "until the last Stone's chilled. Or the last one of us."

"Well," J.B. said cheerfully, "we know which that'll be."

Chapter Thirty

Their pursuers brought the convoy to bay against the Upper Snake River.

The snow had already begun to melt up in the mountain heights. Spring runoff filled the grassy banks with churning, noisy water, red with silt. The road they had continued to follow led right up to it and stopped, in between pungent marshy meadows already filled with cattails and clouds of biting gnats. There was no bridge, nor sign one had ever been built across the river.

By that time the Stone Nation had been on their trail again for an hour, dozens of bikes, as if the losses the convoy had laid on them amounted to nothing more than a handful of flea bites.

Standing by the front of the Land Cruiser in its homemade armor plate, hearing the pinging of the long-abused engine cooling slowly beneath its dented hood, Ryan watched the nomad horde close in. The surviving wags, the chuck wag and two cargo wags, were parked in a sort of defensive semicircle in front and back of the command wag, with the rushing river as a backstop.

"Why do they have to draw it out like this?" Mildred muttered in disgust from behind him. Her face was puffed out of shape as if she'd gotten crosswise of a whole hive of bees, and the bruises on it had begun to turn a rainbow of fascinating color. Her right eye was hidden behind windings of bandage, as her brow had gotten split nearly to the skullbone when she got tossed from the blaster wag.

"Got no reason to hurry," J.B. said from her side.

"It's not like we're going anywhere."

"They want to draw out the moment as long as they can," Doc declared, as if he were teaching a class on the subject. "They have the innate love of pageantry and drama as such simple nomadic people often do."

He shrugged. "No doubt they will do their best to make our inevitable demises as protracted and…colorful as they can."

"Thank you, gentlemen, so much for comforting me," Mildred said.

The Stone Nation had particularly little reason for haste because the way west and east along the riverbanks was already blocked.

To the west, a quarter mile off, waited a mass of bikes interspersed with wags of various sorts, though running strongly to dune buggies and pick-'em-ups. They were garishly and imaginatively painted: some like peacock tails, others with rabid wolf eyes, or dancing skeletons. Their riders were no less colorfully bedizened, nor were their weapons.

"Absaroka," Ryan said, turning to look at them. "Sparrowhawk Nation."

He gave his head a single shake. "Remember them?" he said to J.B.

J.B. rubbed his jaw. "Too well," he said. "Not triple eager to renew our acquaintance."

"Coldhearts?" Sandra Watson asked.

The master merchant's mousy-looking chief assistant looked in better shape than her boss. For all that, her short nondescript-colored hair looked as if starlings had been plucking at it to make their nests. She stood at Bass Croom's elbow a few feet from Ryan's left.

Bass himself stayed silent. He slumped so hard it was a wonder he stayed upright. Ryan had never seen a man deflate like that.

"Not really," Ryan said, hitching a thumb under the sling of his Scout where it was commencing to chafe the front of his shoulder. "They're like the Stones. Little rough around the edges, but if you treat them with respect they shoot square."

"And if you get on their bad side?" asked García. The muscular, middle-size young man with the black mustache was the last remaining member of Dace Cable's original crew.

Throw in a couple of thoroughly dispirited drivers, huddled back in the largely illusory shelter of the wag half-circle, and you had all the survivors of Croom's outfit that had rolled out of the gates of Menaville what seemed like decades ago. Just them, the boss, his younger brother, and the companions.

And their mysterious passenger, Olympia, standing by herself in the grass out front of the other end of the armored car. She had her arms folded beneath her small breasts and her braid uncoiled and thrown over her left shoulder. Despite the bruise on her right cheek and the bandage on her left wrist, and the general blood and grime ground into her tan whipcord jacket and pants, she somehow managed to give the impression of remaining neat.

"I'll tell you," Ryan told the sec man. "See that volcano yonder?"

"Are you kidding?" García asked. "Hard to miss that bastard." He ended in a cough.

The stink of sulfur cut into the membranes of Ryan's nose and throat at every inhalation. That and the ash that collected on everything would have had them all griping up a storm if they hadn't had more immediate things to worry about.

The smoke from the volcano covered half the sky in black. The lowering sun was a red ghost occasionally glimpsed through it. The shifting red-and-orange glow cast on the underside of the smoke pall from the mountain's fiery throat was actually brighter.

"Get them mad," Ryan said, "and you'd be better off throwing yourself right into that crater than tangle with them."

"What about the bunch to the south?" Morty Croom demanded. His brother's gloom wasn't infecting him. Or maybe it was, making him shriller and angrier and more demanding than ever. "There're only a few dozen of them. Can't we break out that way? Can't we take 'em?"

"Maybe if we still had thirty-odd people with blasters to shoot our way through," Mildred said waspishly.

"I take it you never heard tell of the Road Weasels Motorcycle Club, son," J.B. said. "Your life was better before you did."

"Wouldn't think they'd be the types to line up with the Stones," Ryan said.

"No accounting for taste," J.B. said. "Didn't know they were riding in this part of Deathlands. Makes me glad we don't get up here much."

"Uh," Ricky Morales said hesitantly from behind Ryan. "They're, uh, they're getting close."

Ryan looked back. The kid cringed as if expecting him to bite his head off. Am I that big a bear? Ryan wondered. Then he reckoned now wasn't the time for such concerns.

"He knows," J.B. said. "But they'll come as far as they want whether we eyeball them or not."

"Isn't there anything we can do?" Morty asked.

"It doesn't look like it," Krysty said as she strode up to Ryan's left and slipped her arm through his.

Bass emitted a sigh, then moved with surprising energy to open the rear driver's door of his wag and rummage under the seat.

He came out with a mostly white handkerchief and an entrenching tool.

"What are you doing with those, Bass?" Sandra asked.

He frowned with concentration as he knotted a corner of the hankie through the enclosed grip of the short shovel.

"Only thing I can," he said, and his voice actually seemed to have some steel in it again, as did his spine. "What I should've done before."

He straightened and held up the shovel for inspection. The eye-searing wind made the hankie flutter like a flag.

"What I do," he said. "Talk."

"Talk about what?" Morty asked with a whipped-dog whine.

His brother looked at him for a long moment, then nodded toward the Stones.

The line of bikes had halted a hundred yards south down the road. It seemed to stretch endlessly left and right. Dead center of it Ryan saw a familiar figure, a tan face with big white teeth grinning out from the midst of a pyramidal mass of kinky black hair. The only thing different about Speaker from when they'd first laid eyes on him, the day before, was the sling that carried his disabled right arm.

The Stone Nation chieftain's eyes caught Ryan's gaze. "I'm not so easy to chill, One-Eye," he called. His giant shadow, Morning Glory, had her bike parked next to his right knee and stood astride it, gazing impassively as if she'd been carved from a log.

"I'm going to talk about what they want," Bass said to Morty.

"What they want? What's wrong with you? Are you a total idiot? They want to chill us all!"

"If they wanted that," J. B. Dix said, "what do you think they're waiting for?"

Jak appeared like a white apparition to Ryan's left, leaning against the rear left-passenger door of the command wag. Ryan gave him a brief nod. He felt comforted that all of his companions were standing together now.

Waving the white flag high over his head, Bass stepped out twenty feet toward the line of bikes. The Stone Nation had fallen silent now. They'd even switched off their bike engines. The only noises were birdsong, the sighing wind and a nasty protracted fart from the volcano.

"You don't need that rag," Speaker called. "We can hear you, you know."

"I'm asking you man to man, Speaker," Croom said. "What do you want?"

Speaker's handsome face took on a skull-like aspect.

"Vengeance," he said. "Justice, if you care to call it that. I told you what we wanted—the monster who raped and murdered our sister Little Feather. And that is all. Give him up, walk away free as air."

"But who?" Bass pleaded. "Is he even still alive?"

Ryan had stepped up to stand a little to his right. He saw a tear run down the furrowed skin of the master trader's cheek to vanish in his beard.

"He is," Speaker said.

Bass shook his head. "Why didn't you just tell us who you wanted at the outset, save us all this grief? There have been losses on both sides. Tragic losses."

"That much is true, Bass Croom. And we, at least, will mourn by our campfires tonight. And for many nights to come. But the fact is, we didn't say because you didn't ask."

Bass's head jerked back as if Speaker had punched him.

"It's not that simple, Speaker," Ryan called. "Don't play coy."

Morning Glory gave Ryan a hard look. Well, harder than she'd already been looking. He hadn't been sure her facial muscles were up to the task, truth to tell.

That she'd change expression less than that if she were being roasted on a spit, he took for granted. If it was him over the flames, and her hand doing the turning, *then* she might register more emotion.

But Speaker laughed. "You have balls, One-Eye," he said. He dipped his head toward his injured arm. "But I knew that. You've got brains, too. It's not that simple. The fact is, we didn't reckon your boss would give up the criminal. Not when he's no other than his precious younger brother!"

Bass's jaw dropped so hard Ryan was surprised it didn't dislocate. His weather-beaten face turned white beneath the grime and ash. He turned and marched without a word back to the half-circle of wags.

Ryan looked at Speaker and shrugged, then turned and walked back, too, hoping the Stone Nation boss didn't bear a grudge and shoot him in the back.

"That's it," Bass told the waiting people when Ryan walked up. "There's nothing we can do."

"What do you mean, there's nothing you can do, Bass?" Sandra asked.

"Surely you don't expect me to hand my brother over to them to be tortured to death?"

Morty laughed shrilly.

Sandra frowned. "I could say I don't want to watch you die, Bass," she said, "and that'd be true. I've worked for you for many years. I like you. I admire you. You're a strong man and a good one.

"But that would be cowardice on my part. The fact is, I don't want to die. Not for a rapist and woman-chiller!"

Bass gave her a look of sunk-eyed desperation, then turned furiously away.

García wouldn't meet his eye.

"But, Bert," Bass said. "Surely you're with me on this—"

"You took me in, too, boss," the dark-skinned sec man said. "Just like you did Dace. Like you did so many of us. I'll fight and die for you. That's what I signed on for. I'd be proud to join my bros and sisters who have already done just that. All of them."

He looked down at his scuffed sneakers a moment before he could go on.

"But not for this, man," he said. "You gotta give him up. He did wrong, and it's already chilled most of us."

"You can't listen to him, Bass," Morty said. "You won't give me up. You can't. You promised Mother!"

Bass looked at his brother and opened his mouth. No words came out.

"Bass!" Morty screamed. He looked frantically left and right, then gathered himself as if to bolt, but froze at a multiple metallic clicking from somewhere just behind his right ear.

"Just hold tight here, boy," Mildred said in a low dangerous voice. She held her ZKR .38 target revolver aimed at the younger Croom's head. "Given my druthers, I'd splatter your brains halfway back to the Columbia. Healer or not. But if the Stones want us to turn you over, I believe we'd better do that."

Bass turned to look at his drivers, still hanging back. They wouldn't even look at him.

He looked, at last, to Ryan. "I can't," he whispered.

"I can."

Ryan walked up to Morty. The young man ground his teeth and rolled his eyes like a panicked horse. He squirmed with the need to bolt, but he feared the rage he heard in the black woman's voice. And her blaster.

The one-eyed man punched him hard across the jaw. He went down. Shaking his hand slightly at the stinging in his knuckles, Ryan reached down and grabbed the young man's collar, hauling him bodily to his feet. He began marching the semiconscious Morty toward the waiting Stones.

"You have demanded we turn the murderer over to you," he called out. Morty began to wake up. Ryan transferred grip from left fist to right so he could twist Morty's left arm behind his back in a hammerlock.

"You've promised to let us go if we turn him over."

He was looking Speaker in the eye. The Stone Nation boss met his gaze, then nodded.

"I give my word, as Speaker for the Stone Nation," he said. "You have fought me, One-Eye. You know my honor."

I know no such triple-stupe thing, Ryan thought. But it's not like we've got a mess of options here.

"Then I'm turning him over to you," he called. "Come and get him."

He didn't hear Speaker utter a word or see him gesture, but he had to have, because four husky young warriors parked their bikes and hustled forward.

Ryan thrust Morty at them. They caught him neatly, turned him around and marched him back toward the other nomads.

Morty began to cry and plead.

With all eyes on the wretched captive, Ryan dropped his hand to the slender grip of his Scout. Dropping to one knee, he swung the weapon to his shoulder.

"Blaster!" a Stone Nation woman screamed, but it was too late.

Ryan got a flash picture over the iron battle sights. He let out half the breath he'd gulped down hard and squeezed the trigger.

The Steyr roared. The 174-grain boat-tailed hollowpoint slug punched directly through Morty Croom's spine at a level just before his shoulder blades, on its way to exploding his heart and punching a fist-size hole in his front ribs on its way out.

Ryan hadn't dropped for aim or stability, but for angle. Even if the hollowpoint deformed the bullet, it was likely to pass through a man's chest front and back with plenty of energy to chill a nomad waiting beyond. But at this angle it arced safely over the heads of the nomads.

They had pulled up in a single or double line to stop. If the bullet hit a straggler on its way back down, somewhere behind that line, Ryan reckoned it was their lookout.

The warriors froze, staring down at Morty's deadweight, pulling their arms inexorably toward the ground despite their youthful strength.

"You stupe bastard, you've chilled us all!" he heard one of the drivers shriek from behind.

By reflex he completed the motion he began automatically after riding the recoil, and rechambered a fresh round. Then he let the Scout drop on its sling and stood slowly. He held his open palms away from his sides.

The Stones were staring holes through him. Morning Glory's sled lay on its side; she had obviously dropped it to try to throw herself in front of Speaker when Ryan's blaster came up.

Speaker had just as obviously stopped her with a mere flopping-turning gesture of his right arm, since he couldn't raise it.

For a moment Speaker stared at Ryan, then he stepped off his bike, leaving it propped on its double kickstand.

The warriors let Morty fall on his face. At their leader's approach they quickly melted back to the sides.

Speaker strode forward to stand facing Ryan from six feet away. For a moment he simply gazed at the man's face.

Ryan gazed back. He reckoned he and his friends could make the Stones chill them all instead of taking them alive.

Speaker flung his arms wide and a vast grin split his face.

"You are a man, Ryan Cawdor!" he declared in a ringing voice. "The Stone Nation embraces you as a true bro!" He caught Ryan in a one-handed hug that was fervent and as awkward as Ryan felt.

The Stone Nation erupted into uproarious laughter, as if Ryan had just told them the greatest joke ever.

Releasing Ryan, Speaker turned and walked back to his people. He trod across Morty's body without hesitating or looking down. He remounted his bike and kicked its engine to life. A many-throated roar of engines echoed him down the line.

And then the Stone Nation, true to its word and ways, turned and rode away.

Chapter Thirty-One

"So there I was," Bass Croom said in a voice as hollow as the eyes that stared down into the low flames of the campfire. Krysty thought the yellow light gave a greenish cast to his underlit features.

"I was strapped," he went on. "Robbed of everything I had by Baron Doyle of Choad. Left to get by on the lint in my pockets."

The wind cried like lost children up the narrow mountain valley where they'd camped for what the master merchant told them was the very last night of their journey. The air smelled of smoke, cold and the ever-present reek of volcanic smoke and ash from the fire mountain, when the wind turned the right way. Krysty could see its evil glow lighting the smoke above the peaks to the south and west.

With the exception of Jak, who as usual was prowling restlessly in the darkness outside the little camp, the survivors were huddled in the lee of the parked wags. They numbered three, now, one of the cargo wags having busted an axle the morning after Morty's death and the withdrawal of the Stones and their allies.

By now they'd lost most of their food and meds, and burned up much of the ammo that hadn't gotten lost. Fortunately there were fewer demands on those resources now.

Sitting catty-corner across from Krysty, Ricky opened his mouth. Mildred, who sat beside him, clamped a warning hand on his jeans-clad thigh. His eyes got big but his mouth snapped shut.

Not that Croom would've likely noticed if the boy had blurted about the group's encounter with the nefarious baron of what was more recently called Doylesville. Even though it entailed vengeance of a sort for Bass's long-ago loss. The burly, bearded man seemed to be living far more in that moment twenty years ago than now.

The way Doc sometimes did.

"Now I'd spent the whole night listening to this drunk guy rave about how his daddy left him a map to someplace he called the Promised Land, where there was amazing scavvy just waiting for the taking. How his daddy had to keep moving, but always meant to go back—passed on the secret to him when he ran out of life instead."

He stopped and sighed. He'd been doing that a lot since the younger brother he'd loved and shielded for so long had died. Though to his credit, he had never spoken a word of reproach to Ryan, either for turning him over to the Stones, nor for chilling him.

Of course, he hadn't thanked Ryan, either, for saving everybody else's life as well as Bass's, or for saving Morty from death by torture. But Krysty knew her lover neither needed that nor expected it.

"So, I stole it. Stole the map from him."

Krysty looked around the circle: at Sandra, close to her boss's side, her face showing disbelief; at Bert García looking shocked yet also sympathetic; at J.B.'s mild expression of interest, with his eyes invisible behind eyeglass lenses turned by reflection to disks of orange fire, and Olympia, her face devoid of visible emotion and yet her eyes focused closely on the trader.

"It was wrong. I knew it was wrong even as I was doing it. But I was afraid to try giving it back. I was stuck without a washer to my name in a little crack in the Zarks not a whole lot different from this one, dead winter, at a gaudy where it was said those who caused trouble, or just couldn't pay, got dropped down an old mine shaft in the back. So I ran away.

"I set out to rebuild my life. I determined to devote my life to two things—living by utter honesty and building up to the day I could make my own journey to this Promised Land."

He covered his face with his hands. Krysty found the sight almost shocking. They were middle-aged hands, though obviously well used and not sheltered from hardship, but they seemed decades younger than the face they obscured.

"And now I've cost everyone so much. So many good people their lives. Morty—I—" His voice clotted like spilled blood. He had to stop for a moment and just breathe deeply.

"I know the wrong I did brought this on, but I've come too far. Tomorrow I'll press on. I'll find the Promised Land, if it's there, and I believe now as I have for every heartbeat of every day for the past twenty years that it is. And I will do my best to rebuild, and move on. Build a better life for myself and the rest of you.

"That includes all of you. Otherwise, feel free to take an equal share of whatever we got left and go your way, and all best to you."

Krysty looked at Ryan, who hunkered down beside her. As she did, she saw his features seem to harden, ever so slightly. She smiled. That meant they'd softened. Ryan was a man who always did what he thought necessary, as hard as he could. He could act as ruthless as any stoneheart. But his heart wasn't stone. That was why she loved him.

Croom had earned Ryan's respect. All his companions

respected and liked the trader. And while it was testimony to Bass Croom that those who knew him best, his assistant, his last sec man, even his two drivers, seemed shocked that he'd done a dishonest thing, well, nothing they'd seen or just heard of the man was anything they hadn't done or worse in the past year, truth to tell.

Bass sat there hunched over his misery. Ryan rose, stretched.

"I'm turning in," he said. "Got watch to stand later."

He looked down at Krysty. She smiled and stood.

As she did, she saw Olympia rise, as well. The young woman turned and walked away without farewell or explanation, as she usually did.

Surprisingly, Bass heaved to his feet and hurried after her.

Ricky jumped up. Even J.B. turned a questioning look on Ryan.

But Ryan shook his head once, then looked up and past the parked chuck wag. There in the darkness beyond the fading reach of the firelight Krysty glimpsed a white shadow, a ghost of Bass Croom's past, perhaps.

Or Jak, less aloof from the affairs of mere mortals than he liked to pretend, eavesdropping on their employer's confession.

This time Ryan nodded once. The hint of white became blackness.

The one-eyed man sighed softly, then hunkered down again.

"Reckon I'll sit by the fire a spell longer, after all," he said.

TALL AND SLIM, Olympia walked into a flat spot about twenty yards wide and thirty feet downhill from the wag circle. Springing lightly from rock to rock, Jak shadowed her, unseen in the dark—he thought, anyway. He had learned not to underestimate the strange young woman. Her wilderness and stealth skills were no match for his, but her senses were keen, and she knew how to use them.

Still, Jak was sure she'd never spotted him, ghosting her like this when she did her funny exercises. To protect her, he assured himself, as he usually did. After all, no matter how sharp she was, it was bad practice to go away from the others by herself in the dark like this. Ryan had said no one should do that right off, and Croom and Cable backed him. Even when the sec boss was carrying his hard-on for Ryan. But Olympia held to no law but her own, although she was as scrupulously clean and polite in camp as any could ask. Without saying so, though, she had somehow made clear that was because it was *her* way, not someone else's dictates.

Now, though, instead of standing with feet shoulder-width apart and slowly raising her hands in front of her face, she stopped, turned back and stood looking toward the glow of the campfire around the bulk of the parked chuck wag.

Jak heard the crunching of someone walking on dirt, without much skill at going quietly but not even trying for stealth. From the sound and pacing of the footfalls he knew who it was before the bearlike figure came out of the night.

Bass Croom's pace had changed, especially since the betrayal and escape at Raker's Rest. It had grown steadily slower and more tentative. Now it was at best the next thing to a stumble.

The master trader walked up to within six or seven feet of Olympia and stopped. His breathing was loud and ragged as if he'd run a mile. Even by the gleam of stars through high, scattered clouds chasing each other frantically across the sky Jak could see how deeply sunk his eyes were, how furrowed his face.

"Got something to tell you," Bass said huskily. "You alone."

She said nothing.

He stood a moment. Jak thought he was about to turn and run. But he licked his lips and went on.

"That story I told," he said. "It was true. Mostly. Up until…until I stole the map. But I left out the worst part."

Again he waited for her reply.

Again it was silence.

"I chilled him," he blurted, so loud Jak thought even the others had to have heard, a hundred feet away and upwind. "I—I couldn't help myself. Rage just got me in its teeth and wouldn't let me go till I beat him to death with a rock."

He covered his face and sobbed. "When I told the others that theft was the worst thing I ever did, well, it was true. Except for this thing. A thousand times worse."

Still Olympia stood unspeaking. Her eyes, though, focused on Bass's face as intently as an owl gliding silently in the night sky, watching the mouse it meant to swoop down and take for its supper.

He lowered his hands and stared at the palms. Even Jak, not given to such fancy flights, thought he had to be seeing them again covered with a chilled man's blood.

"I lived with it all these years," Bass said. "The guilt. The pain. The wish I could take it all back. I tried to lead as good a life as I could to atone. Told myself that when I found it—the Promised Land—I'd…I'd do something to pay the man back. But—"

He broke off and wept openly. Jak crouched and watched. Olympia stood and watched.

"When I had taken the map from around his neck," Bass said, his voice muffled by his hands, "I saw somebody

watching from the darkness, by a pail of old tailings between two shacks. Just a—just a slip of a girl. I could tell
that and no more. Then she ran away. So did I."

Slowly he lowered his hands and looked at the silent
young woman. Then he dropped to his knees. Jak was
surprised he managed not to fall forward on his face on
the clumpy grass or simply slump into a boneless sack.

"Forgive me," Bass said.

Olympia smiled.

"What makes you think I can forgive you?" she asked,
then turned and walked off into the darkness.

"His eyes," Bass said. "He had Asian eyes. Aren't you
his daughter?"

His only answer was her vanishment. He fell forward
on the cold, hard ground and cried like a baby.

In the early hours of the next day the convoy was halted
by a flock of sheep coming up the narrow streamside road
they were descending.

Ryan climbed down from his sandbag nest atop the
cargo wag and joined the others by Croom's command
wag. The rocky slopes were steep and close on both sides.
There was just room for the sheep to flow past on either
side. A group of small kids trotted along beside them,
chirping to them and calling out in some language Ryan
didn't recognize and switching lightly at them with sticks.
They seemed curious about the intruders but focused on
the woolly, bleating beasts.

An old man with a long staff and a bent back came last,
seeming in charge of the whole herd of sheep and kids.
He had a hat crammed onto his head, battered shapeless
and, beneath a coating of dust, stained to the point the
only color Ryan could think to call it was dark. He was
dressed in a baggy long-sleeved sweater with sleeves that

came down and bunched around his knobby wrists. They were made all of wool. Like the smocks and pants the kids wore, come to think of it.

He bobbed his head and grinned with a mouth that had about three teeth in it Ryan could see, twisted and well browned by tobacco.

"Hello," the old man said.

"Hello," Bass replied. He was riding in his wag alone. Except for ghosts, Ryan reckoned. As usual the master merchant tightened up when dealing with a new person, although all he could muster was a sort of ghastly parody of his early confident cheer. "I was wondering if you could give us some directions, please."

The old man smiled and nodded up a storm, then he shook his head. A torrent of words poured from his ruined old mouth, not a syllable of which made any more sense to Ryan than a dog barking.

There did seem to be an uncommon quantity of z's and k's. Ryan felt lucky to pick out that much.

"Wait."

It was Mildred, walking up from the chuck wag, last in line, which she was driving that morning. She wore a wool sweater of her own, if fortunately far less fragrant than the one the old man had on. She had her arms clamped firmly beneath her large, heavy breasts as if that would keep off the chill of the bright, mostly clear mountain morning.

"I caught the word Euska-something in there," she said. "I think these people are Basques. Like those people on the island."

The old man's face lit up like a wrinkled brown moon. He bobbed his head some more.

"We Basques!" he announced proudly.

"What are you doing here?" Ryan asked.

"Sheeps!" the old man said perkily. His rheumy old dark brown eyes lit right. "We tend sheeps!"

"Yeah," Ryan said as the last of the flock bleated its way past the parked vehicles. "I got that. Sheep. Yeah."

"The Basques are the best shepherds in the world," Mildred said. "So a few years back, uh, before my time, I mean, a bunch of sheep owners in Idaho and such places got the bright idea of importing a bunch of them."

"To herd sheep," Ryan said.

"Yes, yes!" the old man repeated. "Sheeps!"

"They seem very happy," Doc said. "Also the sheep."

For all the crises and disasters of the past few weeks—and the weeks preceding, of course—it had been a spell since Ryan had felt events slipping away from him at quite this dizzying a pace.

"Ace on the line," he said. "So these are Basques. Basques like sheep. Sheep like Basques. How does this load any magazines for us?"

"Can you tell us anything about a place that lies nearby?" Bass said. He spoke slowly and distinctly but didn't make the common English-speaker's mistake of shouting. "A beautiful valley? With a great treasure?"

"If he knows about treasure, Bass," Sandra said, "why wouldn't he and his people have claimed it for themselves?"

But the old man reacted in a way Ryan didn't expect. His mouth opened wide, revealing a stray tooth or two lurking hitherto unseen around the edges, and his eyes went round.

"No, no," he said. "Not go! Not go there!"

"Why not?" J.B. asked, taking off his fedora to scratch the top of his head.

"Cursed!" the old man yelped. "Bad, bad place. You go, you die, she die, everybody die!

"Die bad!"

Epilogue

"Well," Sandra said, "it is everything it's cracked up to be."

The mountains—foothills, now—had retreated farther and farther the last few miles. They had come into a wide, shallow valley that gave promise of the high plains Krysty could glimpse past the hills beyond.

But it was up and to the east that they were looking. Up a narrower valley perhaps a quarter-mile long and a little less than that wide. Its beauty took Krysty's breath away: the lush green perfection of the grass, so early in the year, that not even the crystal-clear waterfall breaking amid rainbowed spray, thin and pure down a sheer granite face that seemed to wall the upward end, could seemingly account for. A wonderland of wildflowers nodded to a gentle breeze, all gold and white and blue and magenta, as if bags of different jewels had been carelessly strewed around the meadow.

Off to the right of the narrow cascade, and the broad inviting pool at its base, Krysty glimpsed an oddly rectangular darkness in the dark rock. Though the sun was only just rising higher than the cliffs, she could still make out what looked like dull glints of metal masses at one edge.

"Redoubt," Jak breathed.

"This is the place!" Bass exclaimed, stabbing at the wrinkled map he held unfolded in his palm.

He raised his face, and instead of haggard misery, his

bearded features held a look of exaltation. As if, Krysty thought, he saw redemption there.

Jak had told them, privately, of the master merchant's midnight confession to Olympia. Ryan had shrugged it off, and Krysty understood.

It made little difference to them now.

"Hate to be the one to piss on everybody's parade," J.B. said, "and I don't hold with talk of curses, myself, but hasn't anybody else noticed all the rad-blasted skeletons?"

And skeletons there were. Some were almost completely overgrown, like the antlered skull with a spray of purple daisies spouting from one vacant eye socket. Some were half buried in the rich, ripe grass. Most were bleached white by the sun, but not all—like the sheep skeleton that lay not fifty feet in. As Krysty watched a raven perched on its side, bent, then flapped away with a dark strip of something clutched in its beak.

"I don't think we wanted to, J.B.," Mildred said in a tone of awe. "It's so beautiful the eye just wants to—edit them out."

Krysty nodded. None of the skeletons, she noted, was farther in than a hundred yards.

She turned to a crumpling sound. The map, which Bass had obviously cherished and cared for secretly for two decades, was wadded in one clenched hand.

"What are we waiting for!" he said. "It's here! The Promised Land! And as I told you, my friends, everyone shares and shares alike."

"I'll pass," Ryan said. "All I see get shared here is death. I don't believe in curses, either, but something's kept the Basques out all these years. And other people—there's a road runs right by here west that looks traveled regular. But nobody seems to have tried to settle here."

"And those who may have tried seem to have fared

poorly," Doc said, squinting beneath his palm. "Not all those skeletons are animal, my friends."

Bass looked at Ryan in disbelief and something like horror. Shaking his head as if in vast and unfathomable disappointment, he turned to his own people.

"Sandra?" he asked his quiet and devoted aide.

She shook her head.

"Bert?"

"No, boss." The young sec man looked stricken, but his head shake was firm. "It's like Ryan says. No treasure's worth it if you're chilled."

"But surely—Cherokee? Bit? You'll come with me, won't you?"

But the two drivers, the man Cherokee and the tiny brunette woman Bit, shook their heads.

Another person had come up to stand on the verge of the lush pasture, with its flowers and picked-over chills. As usual Olympia stood a bit apart from the others, calm and straight.

But her blue-jade eyes were fixed, not on the unbelievable, if lethal, beauty of the hidden valley, but on Bass Croom's bearded face.

He looked a plea at her.

She met his eyes levelly. Her lips didn't move, but it was as if something passed between them. Bass shook himself. As if accepting her unspoken judgment, he turned away. He dropped the map he had bought at such enormous price—to himself as well as others—on the bare ground by his boots, then strode forward into the valley.

After just a few yards, he began to run, then falter.

"Look!" Jak cried.

Krysty did. They all did.

Small, yellow-furred forms had begun to spring from

concealment in the grass. They stuck to him like cockle-burs, but they moved.

Bass Croom screamed, shrilly, like a man being burned alive.

Or eaten alive. A tiny creature with black-and-white stripes down its back and a stubby tail landed on the master merchant's shoulder. Blood fountained from his thick neck, shocking red in the sun.

"Bass!" Sandra cried. She started to run forward. J.B. caught her by the arm and held her back.

More and more of the furry shapes emerged to swarm over the doomed man. He fell to his knees, batting at them with his hands. It did him no more good than his increasingly shrill howls of intolerable pain. One hand came away spurting gore from the stub of a bitten-off forefinger. Bert García turned away and puked his breakfast of beans and hardtack onto the ground.

The blaster shot rang as loud as thunder from lightning striking a handful of feet away. Bass's head jerked. He stiffened, arching his back so violently some of his tiny tormentors were flung clear, wriggling and squeaking and shedding red drops.

Shot echoes chased each other up the walls of the treacherous paradise like mocking spirits. Bass pitched forward to lie half buried in the beauty of grass and flowers. Then he was covered over completely in yellow-furred horror.

"Now that," J.B. said, rubbing his jaw as Ryan lowered his P-226, "is something you don't see every day."

"Jesus!" Ricky breathed. He crossed himself. Mildred laid a comforting hand on his shoulder. Or maybe a hand to hold him up; his knees weren't looking steady to Krysty.

"Mutie piranha ground squirrels?" Mildred asked in disbelief. "You have *got* to be shitting me!"

"It would certainly appear so," Doc announced. He

spoke in his best scholarly tones, though he had gone dead white to the stained and rumpled collar of his mostly white shirt.

"I don't plan on finding out," Ryan said, "and that's a fact."

The sound of a door opening behind them made them all turn. Olympia was bending inside the rear of Bass's command wag. She backed out and straightened, settling her backpack over her shoulders. Without a word she began to walk down the road that led west into flatter, more arid land.

Ricky ran a few steps after her. "Wait!" he called out. "Where're you going? Why are you leaving?"

"Reckon you got a share coming," J.B. said, ever practical. "Of the swag from the wags, that is."

Olympia turned back. She smiled her enigmatic smile.

"It's yours," she said. "I paid for passage, and now I'm here."

She walked away.

The others stood staring after her as her form diminished down the dusty, rutted track. Wherever she was going, Krysty thought, she seemed confident about it. Then again, she had seemed confident about everything she did.

"Will somebody please tell me what in the name of glowing night shit that was all about?" Ryan demanded.

Doc turned to his companions with a light in his pale blue eyes and a strange half smile on his withered lips.

"Why, don't you know?" he said. "Nemesis, my friends."

* * * * *

TAKE 'EM FREE

2 action-packed novels
plus a mystery bonus

NO RISK

NO OBLIGATION
TO BUY

Reader Service.com

Manage your account online!
- Review your order history
- Manage your payments
- Update your address

We've designed the Harlequin® Reader Service website just for you.

Enjoy all the features!
- Reader excerpts from any series
- Respond to mailings and special monthly offers
- Discover new series available to you
- Browse the Bonus Bucks catalog
- Share your feedback

Visit us at:
ReaderService.com